"Do you ever wonder what might have happened with us?"

Tara couldn't stop herself from saying it. Her emotions were too stirred up to hold back. And she was with someone who truly knew her.

"All the time," Dylan said hoarsely.

And that was that. As if someone had shot a starting gun, they lunged for each other and kissed. Dylan's lips tasted smoky and sweet and like Dylan, the way he used to taste. He rose and so did she. Their chairs hit the tile with twin bangs and they slammed their bodies together, arms wrapped tight.

The kiss seemed to touch off a bonfire that roared through her. Everything faded except Dylan's mouth, his arms, his chest pressed against her breasts, his hips against hers, his hardness insistent against her stomach. She ached and ached, her body desperate for his.

Dear Reader,

Do we ever really grow up? Or are we always that wounded thirteen-year-old who feels unloved and unlovable inside? Can we forgive parents who let us down? Can we love them for who they are, not for who we wish they were?

These are heavy questions we all answer in our lives. My heroine Tara Wharton wrestles with them in this story, all while she's fighting to uncover the secrets that led to the accident that killed her father and put her sister—her real family—into a coma.

On top of that, she's face-to-face again with Dylan Ryland, the guy who broke her heart, the one person she trusted to love her truly, completely and unconditionally, who let her down when his father needed him more.

It takes Tara's return to show Dylan that he's sacrificed too much of his own dreams and desires for his father and the company they built together. Who better to hold up a mirror to us than the person we love? Tara shows him it's time he went for what he wants most—in his work and his life. And that means making room for the love of his life.

What does the song say? The first cut is the deepest? After the pain of their early heartbreak, it takes a leap of faith for these two to decide to trust each other—and themselves. They learn that first love *can* last a lifetime.

Writing this story made me vow to listen harder to my family, to hold them close, to appreciate every minute I have with them, to love and respect them as they are.

I hope this book will touch you the way it did me. I'd love to hear your stories. Contact me through my website at www.dawnatkins.com.

Best,

Dawn Atkins

Back Where She Belongs

DAWN ATKINS

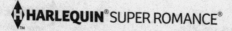

HARLEQUIN® SUPER ROMANCE®

Recycling programs
for this product may
not exist in your area.

ISBN-13: 978-0-373-71841-2

BACK WHERE SHE BELONGS

HHARLEQUIN®
™ www.Harlequin.com

Printed in U.S.A.

ABOUT THE AUTHOR

Award-winning author Dawn Atkins has written twenty-five novels for Harlequin Books. Known for her funny, poignant romance stories, she's won a Golden Quill Award and has been a several-times *RT Book Reviews* Reviewers' Choice Award finalist. Dawn lives in Arizona with her husband and son.

Books by Dawn Atkins

HARLEQUIN SUPERROMANCE

HARLEQUIN BLAZE

Other titles by this author available in ebook format.

To Sylvie, Amy and Maren,
for getting me through the story and reminding me
why it mattered

CHAPTER ONE

TARA WHARTON LIFTED her sister's hand from the hospital-bed mattress and rested it on her own palm. Faye's hand was pale and limp, the nails bluish, lined with dried blood and, worst of all, *cool* to the touch.

That alarmed Tara more than the tangle of IV tubes, the click and whir of the machines, or even Faye's face, with its purple bruises and bloody stitches.

Faye's hands were always *warm*—comforting as a hug to Tara as a child. Tara traced the beauty marks on the skin between Faye's thumb and forefinger that formed the shape of the Big Dipper. When she was six, Tara had joined the dots with a felt pen while Faye napped before her prom. Her sister hadn't noticed until the boy had handed Faye the wrist corsage. Faye had burst out laughing, which had thrilled Tara.

Once, when Tara had been unfairly sent to her room, Faye's hands had taught Tara the game cat's cradle. When Tara woke from nightmares, they'd traced words on her back until she drifted off against her sister's sleep-soft body.

When Tara needed stitches after a skateboard fall, Faye's hands had squeezed hers so tight Tara hadn't even felt the needle.

Years later, when Tara cried over Dylan, Faye's hands had dried her tears. Tara hated to cry. Crying was weak.

When Tara lowered Faye's hand to the sheet, she saw her sister's knuckles were wet. How…? She touched her own cheek and found that tears had escaped her eyes. Not good. Not with all she had to handle.

"You can't die, Faye," Tara said, her entire body tight with urgency. "The doctors have done all they can. Now it's up to you."

What a stupid thing to say: *Now it's up to you.* As if Faye weren't already trying with all her might to wake up. She'd had a second surgery to relieve the pressure on her brain from the accident.

Two measly brain surgeries wouldn't keep Faye Wharton down. Faye was indomitable. Faye was amazing. For Tara, who'd rarely seen or spoken to her parents since she left for college ten years ago, Faye was *family.*

"Please wake up, Faye. Please." The possibility that her sister might die poured through Tara like molten metal, dissolving her insides, making her want to collapse to the floor in wild despair. She didn't dare. She had to stay strong and alert. She had to watch and listen and analyze.

Because something was not right. She'd known when her brother-in-law, Joseph, had called her. *There's been a car accident,* he'd said in a near monotone. *Your father was killed. Faye's in the hospital. They don't know if she'll make it.*

Every word had raised more hairs on Tara's scalp. It wasn't his tone. Joseph Banes was Chief Financial Officer at Wharton Electronics, third in command after Tara's father and Faye. He preferred numbers to people, so he always sounded flat.

It wasn't even that he'd waited nearly two days to reach her at the Fairmont in San Francisco, where she'd been meeting with her newest, most important client.

It was more subtle—a hesitation, a breath held a microsecond too long, a shade too much tension in his voice—and it made her instincts flare.

Her ability to read people had been the key to her success as a corporate consultant, and had given her the nerve to break out on her own eighteen months ago.

Tara rubbed her eyes. The tears hadn't eased the gritty sensation. She was fuzzy with exhaustion after the 5:00-a.m. flight to Phoenix. She'd rented a car and driven to Tucson—the closest hospital to Wharton, Arizona, the town that had grown up around her family's electronics company—arriving midmorning.

Why had Joseph waited to call? He'd explained that they'd been *frantic*. Joseph Banes did not get frantic. Neither did Tara's mother, who prided herself on her calm dignity. She was what passed for royalty in Wharton, and took her role seriously.

Maybe he was being passive-aggressive. He had to know that Tara had tried to talk Faye out of marrying him three years ago, as it further shackled Faye to Wharton Electronics, ending forever her dream of studying art.

But why hadn't her mother called? That hurt more than Tara wanted to admit. Despite the strain between them, wouldn't her mother have reached out to her? If not for mutual comfort, at least because she knew how close Tara and Faye had been?

Where *were* Joseph and her mother? Tara had been here nearly two hours and neither one had appeared. *Withhold judgment. Assume good intentions.* Those were ground rules when she facilitated meetings between hostile employee groups. The least she could do was practice what she preached with her own family. They were suffering, too.

Being in Wharton would not be easy, she knew. It would bring back all the hurt she'd felt, bring her face-to-face with family she'd disappointed and hurt in return. She'd have to face the mistakes she'd made, the regrets.

Already, the last conversation she'd had with Faye filled her with remorse. It had been three weeks ago. Faye had mentioned she might want to hire Tara to consult with Wharton Electronics. The words had been casual, but Tara had picked up tension in her voice.

Instead of leaving silence for Faye to fill with her deeper intentions, Tara had been glib, joking that she'd be too pricey for penny-pinching Joseph to sign off on.

What had Faye said exactly? *We're going through a transition.* That was code for money troubles, Tara knew from experience with her corporate clients.

We fired the factory manager. I'm not sure that helped, but I'm too close to it. Your professional eye would help.

Tara would have been honored to work with Faye. Thrilled. Her father might have been an obstacle, but for Faye's sake, Tara would have cleared the air, done what needed to be done for the job.

After that, Faye had said, *I miss you. It's been too long,* which startled Tara, since Faye was as restrained as their parents.

Embarrassed by the rawness of her own feelings, Tara hadn't said what she felt—*I miss you, too. I need to visit.* Instead, over the lump in her throat, she'd said, *Get Joseph to write me a check and I'll be there in a heartbeat.*

I'll see what I can do, Faye had said, but her laugh had been hollow, her tone wistful. Why hadn't Tara really *listened?*

What if those were the last words Tara ever heard from her sister? Panic surged, but she fought it. She needed to stay calm and clearheaded. On top of that, she had the webinar tonight with the make-or-break client she'd had to abandon in San Francisco. The continued success of her new company depended on how she performed with Cameron Plastics. There had been opposition to hiring her—a general distrust of consultants—so her abrupt departure at the start of the meeting had put the job in jeopardy.

That had to wait. Faye was all that mattered right now.

She looked around. Faye's area, separated from the rest of the busy ICU by a beige curtain, seemed so desolate, the only furnishings medical equipment. Tara had had to leave the flowers she'd brought—peonies, Faye's favorite—at the nurses' station. Too many bacteria for the fragile patients in intensive care. Rita, one of the nurses, had said she could bring a photo and tape it up for Faye to look at when she woke. *If* she woke. The thought made Tara tremble so hard her teeth rattled.

The curtain rings sang as Rita breezed in. The sight of the trim black woman with kind eyes and a wide smile cheered Tara. She'd been in every fifteen minutes to check on Faye.

"How you doing?" she asked, glancing at Tara as she took Faye's temperature.

"I'm fine. How's Faye?"

"Let's just see." Rita performed the neuro check, running a flashlight across Faye's eyes, pressing her skin with the point of a safety pin, then gripping her hand. "Squeeze, baby," Rita said to Faye. "Do that for me now."

Tara held her breath, staring at her sister's pale hand in Rita's brown one, waiting for a twitch, a quiver, a flicker of life, but her sister was as still as the death that stalked her.

Rita put down Faye's hand, then turned to go.

"She could wake up any time, right?" Tara asked.

"She could." There was a hesitation in Rita's voice.

"Or…" Tara swallowed hard. "We could lose her."

Rita didn't answer.

"How does she compare to other patients with similar injuries?"

"I'm in ICU as a vacation fill-in, so I can't really say." The despair Tara felt must have shown on her face because Rita added, "She's made it this far. She's a fighter."

"She is." Tara's heart swelled with pride. Faye had always

been strong and brave. Surely that would save her. "What can I do to help? Bring in music? Read to her? Isn't that good for coma patients?"

"Once she makes it out of ICU," Rita said. "Long as it's good music," she added sternly, clearly joking to cheer Tara up. "She'll likely end up on my floor and I have my standards."

Tara went along with the joke. "I'm not sure what she's into now, but when she was a teenager, she liked the B-52s... Fine Young Cannibals...Madonna...U2. How's that sound?" As a little girl, Tara used to copy moves from MTV videos to practice with Faye, who'd been an uncoordinated teenager.

Rita made a face. "That's nasty. Better bring headphones."

Tara laughed, praying Faye would make it to a room, even if it were to torture Rita with bad music. She felt a rush of gratitude and lunged to her feet to give Rita a quick hug. "Thanks for taking such good care of her."

Rita's mocha coloring deepened. "No need to fuss over a person just doing her job, which I need to get on with right now." Rita hurried off and Tara turned back to Faye.

She looked so small, so still, so beat-up. Sadness built to a huge crashing wave Tara knew she wouldn't be able to hold back. She turned to go, to find the privacy of a bathroom, just as a man stepped in. *Dylan.*

"Tara?" He seemed to read her face, then opened his arms.

She went straight into them and burst into tears, muffling her sobs against his shirt, breathing in starched cotton, feeling the familiar comfort, the safety of Dylan's embrace. He rubbed her back, palms pressing hard, easing the muscle cramps she got when she was upset. He remembered.

If Faye was her family, then Dylan Ryland had been her home.

They'd been so close, so in love.

Until they weren't.

As the sadness ebbed, she realized how stupid this was. The first time she'd seen him in ten years and she bursts into tears in his arms? How clingy. How weak. She'd done the same thing years ago, when he'd told her he wasn't coming with her to college.

Ashamed, she broke away. "Sorry." Then she saw she'd left a wet blotch and streaks of mascara on his crisp blue oxford. "I ruined your shirt."

"Forget it." He whipped a tissue from the box on Faye's tray and held it out.

Tara took it and wiped his shirt, aware instantly that his chest was broader and more muscular than before.

He stopped her hand, his palm warm. "That was for you. My shirt's fine."

"Oh." She looked at him. He was as handsome as ever—maybe more so. His skin was the same golden-brown, his hair chestnut with glints of blond. He had the same ready smile and smoky gray-green eyes that used to make her catch her breath when they looked at her.

Her breath caught now. Startled, she stepped back, wiping her cheeks with the tissue, scrubbing under her eyes for the rest of the mascara, wishing he'd stop staring at her.

She felt a warm glow, that tight feeling down low, that ticking awareness of him as a man, of her as a woman. It jangled her nerves, already in turmoil from sadness, worry and the humiliation of sobbing in his arms.

"It's good to see you," he said softly.

The glow flared into a steady flame, warming her, softening her, tightening her, too. What was wrong with her? This was no way to feel. Not here. Not now. Not ever really.

It's good to see you, too. She couldn't deny that, but she didn't have to say it out loud.

Looking closer, she noticed changes—his cheekbones and jaw were more defined, his eyes more knowing. There were laugh lines outlining his strong mouth. He'd been more boy than man at eighteen. Now he was all man. *All* man.

The thought made the flame shoot through her like the adrenaline of sudden danger. She had to get control. "What are you doing here?" she asked more abruptly than she intended.

"I was in Tucson on business and I wanted to touch base with your mother." He glanced past Tara at the bed where Faye lay. "How is she?"

"The nurse says she's a fighter," Tara said, her voice cracking. "Sounds like the standard buck-up-the-family speech, doesn't it?"

"Faye's a strong person," he said firmly, as if that would be enough to save her. Tara hoped it would be. He studied Faye for a long quiet moment, as if sending her healing strength. It made Tara feel less scared.

"How are you holding up?" He looked at her the way he always had, searching, missing nothing, his gaze piercing but tender. He'd understood her without words. As a teenager in the throes of first-love, she'd been wild about that, basked in it, adored it.

Now it made her feel naked...vulnerable.

"Oh, I'm a fighter, too," she said, forcing a smile. She didn't want him to see how frightened and small and sad she felt.

"You are," he said. "I remember." There was tenderness in his gaze, and delight, and the same flare of attraction she felt. Ten years later. How strange.

"My mother's not here—"

The curtain rustled and her mother and Joseph stepped in. "So you came," her mother said archly to Tara, eyebrows lifted.

The insult stung, but a retort died on Tara's lips at her mother's appearance. Her eyes were puffy, her usually flawless skin blotched and her blond up-do was smashed on one side. Her cashmere sweater bore a coffee stain. Rachel Wharton didn't step onto her terrace for the paper unless she looked ready for the cover of *Town & Country*.

Pity surged through Tara. "I'm so sorry, Mom." She lurched forward and hugged her mother. The woman went rigid. This was not Wharton family protocol, but Tara didn't give a damn.

Her mother's body felt frail, as if her bones might snap under any pressure. Tara released her and smiled, trying to hide her alarm. Her mother's eyes were too shiny, her pupils too large. She'd taken something.

Her mother had always taken pills—pills to wake up, pills to go to sleep, pills to cheer her, calm her or distract her. Bubble wrap against emotion.

Tara used to raid her mom's medicine cabinet to give pills to her friends or to sell them for cigarette money. She wasn't proud of that. Being angry, lonely, sad and hurt didn't excuse her actions. Dylan had changed her. Sometimes it had felt like he'd saved her.

"They limit us to two visitors at a time," Joseph said to Dylan, no animosity in his tone. Joseph was gaunt, almost shrunken, his receding hairline prominent against his pale forehead, which was lined with worry.

"I'm leaving," Dylan said, not reacting to Joseph's brusque words. "I wanted to reassure you about the funeral, Rachel. I've arranged for the band students to be bussed to another high school."

"Thank you so much," Rachel said. "I'm sorry you had to intervene. Abbott spent three years on that school board. He should not have to beg to use the auditorium."

"It was no trouble. Part of the job."

"The job?" Tara blurted. What did Dylan have to do with the high school and her father's funeral?

"I'm the Wharton town manager," he said to her.

"You're kidding! You don't work for your dad anymore?"

"I work *with* him still, yes. But I'm also town manager."

"Wow," she said. "Wow." Twenty-eight seemed young for that kind of responsibility, but Dylan had been a student leader in high school—top grades, all-around good guy… her total opposite.

"For heaven's sake, don't sound so amazed," her mother said. "You've practically insulted the man. I apologize for my daughter's rudeness, Dylan. You do a great job…even part-time."

Annoyance flickered in Dylan's eyes, whether at Tara or her mother, she couldn't tell. "I'm sorry for your loss, Rachel," he said, then turned to Tara. "And yours. I'm sorry you lost your father." His words caught her short and her knees gave way. *She'd lost her father. He was dead…gone forever.* Tara had been so focused on Faye that fact hadn't sunk in.

"Thank you," she said. She could tell he'd caught the hitch in her step, though she'd shifted her weight to hide it. Dylan didn't miss much about her. That hadn't changed. With a last concerned look at Tara, he told them he'd confirm with the mortuary and left.

"Still blunt, I see," her mother said to her. Tara's directness had been her antidote to her mother's obsession with how things looked, with being proper and polite. That was partly the appeal of Tara's career, which demanded honesty and openness. The truth, no matter how painful, was always better than a lie.

"It was a simple question."

"You're too thin," her mother said. "And that hairstyle does not flatter your face."

That means she cares, Tara told herself. "It's good to see you, too." None of them would be at their best, she knew. She had to guard against dwelling on old pains or operating on old assumptions. She was better than that. She'd fought for ten years to rise above her past. This would be her test.

Her mother swayed, so Tara helped her into the chair, wondering if she'd taken too many pills.

"I need to get to work," Joseph said, looking at his watch. "Will you drive Rachel to the mortuary, then home?" he asked Tara.

"Happy to." She followed him out into the hall. He'd barely told her a thing about the accident. "I have a few questions—"

"Her car's at the mechanics, but she shouldn't be behind the wheel as shaky as she is. You'll likely have to take over with the funeral director. I did what I could."

"Thank you, Joseph. I appreciate your help. I'm sure things are chaotic at Wharton right now. That's a lot of weight to carry."

He softened abruptly at her tone. "Lucky for me I've got that home gym, I guess."

The joke made Tara wince, since she knew Faye had wanted the spare room for a baby. There had been some difficulty, though Faye hadn't said whether it was a physical problem or a disagreement about becoming parents, and Tara hadn't pried. Faye was a private person.

"If I can help out at Wharton, I'd like to," she said.

"Not unless you secretly got an engineering degree."

He knew full well what she did for a living, but she ignored the slight. "I did help a computer-chip company with the crisis plan that got them through a plant closure."

"I don't see how that fits," he said.

Crisis plans covered executive deaths and other contingencies, but Joseph was too harried and worried to hear that—or for her to mention that Faye had wanted to hire her. "How about if I stop in one day to talk about that?"

"No need," he snapped, then seemed to realize he'd been

rude. "If you'd like a tour, our HR person gives them to our bigger customers. Call ahead."

"I'd like that," she said, bristling at his dismissal, though she managed a smile. *Rise above. Be your better self.*

He turned toward the elevator, but she moved in front of him. "Before you go, can you tell me more about the accident? I really don't know much."

"There's not much to know." His eyes flitted to the side, avoiding her.

Zing. Her instincts flared. There was more here. She held her tongue, knowing Joseph would be compelled to fill the silence. It was human nature.

He licked his lips, shifted his weight, then blew out a breath. "Evidently Faye was driving your father back from his poker game when it happened."

"*Faye* was driving?"

"I know. Abbott was possessive about the Tesla."

"My father always drove." It was about control, she knew, not about any protectiveness about a particular car.

"But the Tesla was special. He traded in the Prius early." Her father was a frugal man who drove his cars forever, no matter how much her mother complained that it made him look cheap. He was never showy about his wealth. Tara had respected that about him.

She remembered something else he'd said that bothered her. "You said *evidently.* You didn't know what Faye was doing?"

"I'd gone back to the office. It's quiet after hours, so I get more done..." He was tense and stiff, which likely meant he was hiding something. Without knowing his baseline gestures, she couldn't say for sure. Reading micro-expressions was more art than science.

As good as she was at this—her clients sometimes asked if she was psychic—her exhaustion and distress were interfering with her instincts, not to mention how *off* she felt returning to Wharton.

"They found her car at Vito's," Joseph continued. "Perhaps she was eating there and ran into your father." The poker game took place upstairs from the Italian restaurant.

"But it was Monday night. That's Faye's TV night." Faye had told Tara about the guilty-pleasure drama she loved and had to watch real-time because she didn't know how to use the fancy DVR Joseph had bought.

"Then he called her. I don't know," Joseph said impatiently. "The point is she lost control on that bad curve where the hiking trail starts, went over the rail, down the embankment and into the trees."

She knew the spot. Her boyfriend Reed had crashed his motorcycle there the night Dylan had insisted she ride with him because Reed had had a couple beers. They'd found Reed limping along the shoulder. He'd cracked two ribs and broken his collarbone.

Now she pictured her father and Faye flying over the barrier, tumbling down the slope, landing with a crash.

No. Don't think of that. Focus on what's wrong. "Why would Dad ask Faye to drive him? Why not one of the poker guys? And why did he need a ride? Had he been drinking?"

"I told you all I know," Joseph said, barely hiding his frustration. "Ask Faye when she wakes up. *If* she wakes up." He took a sharp breath in reaction to his own words, revealing the pain he'd been holding back, then strode to the elevator, where he pounded the button repeatedly with the flat of his hand, face turned away from her.

"She's a fighter," she called to him. "Don't forget that."

Joseph didn't acknowledge her words. People so cut off from their emotions frustrated Tara. It was a hot button because, growing up, her parents had shut her out of their lives almost completely. They were all reserved, while she had big, big emotions. She'd trained herself to hold back, but it hadn't been easy.

She returned to Faye's room, where her mother sat with perfect posture, carefully avoiding the sight of her daughter's face. *Her poor mother.* If Tara could help her, she would. If Faye died, Tara would be all the family her mother had left. She was certain that if her mother had to choose a daughter to lose, it would be Tara, not Faye. There was no sting to that awareness anymore. In fact, it made her feel sorrier for her mother.

CHAPTER TWO

TARA PARKED HER rental car outside the Parthenon Mortuary, which bore a resemblance to the ancient Greek temple it was named for, and went to help her mother out of the passenger seat. Her mother had slept for most of the hour-long drive and seemed groggy, so Tara held out her hand.

Her mother waved her away and forged up the steps with her usual self assurance. They were met by Dimitri Mikanos, the funeral director, with twinkling blue eyes and a bright yellow suit. When Tara introduced herself, he clearly hadn't realized there was a second daughter, which pinched a little, but, truly, was what she should have expected. All her life, she'd longed to be invisible in Wharton.

The inside of the funeral home was painted bright blue with white trim, as cheerful as its director, which Tara appreciated, considering the gloom of their task. Her mother held it together until Dimitri ran down the list of decisions she had to make—casket color, style, upholstery, flowers, grave markers, clothing. Then she gasped and began fumbling in her purse for pills that spilled from the pillbox, trembling violently.

Dimitri helped her mother to a sofa in a small lounge, then Tara followed him into the casket room to make the selections. The organ music unsettled her, and the decisions were bewildering. Satin or plush, plain or tuck-and-roll, gold handles or bronze, casket spray or standing baskets, on and on.

Tara got through it, her emotions under control, until Dimitri brought out a clothing bag and took out three of her father's suits that Joseph had brought in. Tara had to choose the one they'd put on her father.

She tensed up, held her breath, but it was no use. It was the shoes that got her—specifically a pair of oxblood wingtips like the ones she remembered from her childhood. Custom-made in Italy, they'd been her father's favorites. *Buy a quality shoe and take good care of it*, he'd told her when she watched him polish them. She loved the smell of polish, the circular movements, how shiny the shoes got. She'd begged to go to the shoemaker's when he had new heels put on. Mr. Vanzetti had brought out a bowl of rock candy—a treat only for good children, he'd said. "Is she a good girl?" he'd asked Tara's father in his heavy Italian accent. Tara had held her breath waiting for her father's verdict. When he gave a solemn yes, Tara's heart had leaped in her chest. She chose a piece that looked like granite and tasted like a grape jellybean...and magic.

She could tell that Mr. Vanzetti had put new heels on the pair she now looked at, and the thought sent grief through Tara in a wave so deep she felt like she had to lift her chin to catch a breath. Her father was dead. She was choosing the clothes he'd take to his grave.

She would never get a grudging nod or even a disapproving glare from the man ever again. "Those." She pointed. "I'll get my mother," she blurted to hide her emotion, practically running down the hall to the small room, where her mother lay sleeping on a gold-embroidered white sofa.

Tara had the fleeting wish she could run into Dylan's arms again, but that made her feel foolish.

She sat near her mother's hip. She'd been surprised how devastated her mother seemed by her husband's death. Her parents had appeared to operate in separate spheres, hardly speaking to each other. Abbott's life was Wharton Electronics and her mother managed the social and charity functions that suited her role as the wife of the most important man in Wharton.

Growing up, dinners had been quiet affairs, her father an intimidating frown at the head of the table, where he ate in silence, reading the paper or a book, unless her mother was reporting one of Tara's crimes against the rules of comportment for the town's leading family. Then he would redden before tersely declaring Tara's punishment.

Looking at her mother's face, Tara saw lines that hadn't been there three years ago when she'd come for Faye's wedding. Her mother was nearly sixty, so her age had to show some. The veins in her hands were more pronounced, the skin crinkled like parchment.

One day she'll be gone and you don't even know her.

The thought startled Tara. Her visits home from college had been short—full of tense silences and brittle exchanges, with her parents lobbing thinly veiled insults about her classes, her major, her appearance and her ideas—so after she graduated, she'd never returned. Why put everyone through that misery? Faye visited Tara twice a year and they spoke often by phone.

Tara had lost the chance to connect with her father, but her mother was right here. Could they make peace? Become friends? That might be too much to ask. But, dammit, she was going to try. The idea filled her with tenderness, hope and a sense of purpose.

She could hear Dimitri speaking to someone in his office, so she sat with her mother for a few more minutes to settle her own emotions.

When Tara heard Dimitri's office door open, and what sounded like two people saying goodbye, she said, "Mom?"

"Huh?" Her mother jerked to a sit, her face blank, eyes dazed.

"It's all done. We can leave."

"Oh. Yes. Well." Her mother seemed to push past her confusion and gather herself, sitting taller. "I was a bit sleepy." She tugged her blazer straight, poked a strand of hair in place and arranged her smile. Tara averted her gaze, feeling like she'd accidentally seen behind the Wizard of Oz's curtain, and the Wizard preferred his privacy.

They went to Dimitri's door.

"You just missed Mr. Ryland," he said with a smile.

"We did?" Tara asked, her heart jumping a little.

"He arrived just after we finished."

She'd wished for Dylan to appear and he had. In high school, they'd believed they could sense each other from far away, draw each other closer by wishing very hard. It made her smile to remember how ridiculously romantic they'd been.

"So it's official. The auditorium is ours?" her mother asked.

"It is. Our Mr. Ryland gets things done," Dimitri said.

"I gathered that," Tara said, looking at her mother, who'd sung Dylan's praises in the hospital, if in a backhanded way.

Her mother hadn't minded when Tara started dating Dylan, probably because Tara stopped getting into trouble. Not that Tara and her mother had talked much. Mostly they glared and slammed doors in each other's faces.

That changed when Tara announced she would be going to Northern Arizona University, the state college Dylan had chosen because of the famous observatory there. Her mother went nuts, railing against Tara choosing a state school when she had more prestigious options, that it was childish to ruin her future over puppy love, which, of course, made Tara even more determined to go there.

Then Dylan changed his mind.

The funeral director held out a card and Tara realized she'd missed why she would need it.

"My email is there," he said. "To send what you want on the program."

"Oh. Right. Yes."

"Where is your mind, Tara?" her mother said.

Lost in the past, where it didn't belong. She'd better quit that. She needed a clear head and a calm heart to handle what lay ahead—helping her mother, watching over Faye and keeping her business afloat. She had no time or energy to relive lost loves or revisit broken hearts.

STANDING UNDER AN olive tree in the mortuary parking lot, Dylan looked up from his confirmation text to the bus company to see Tara help her mother into a car. Funny, he'd just been thinking about her.

They used to believe they were so tuned in they could sense each other from across a room…a football field…the whole town.

They'd been so young, so wrapped up in each other.

The embrace at the hospital had been automatic, and it was as if their bodies remembered. She'd melted into him and he'd closed himself around her. He'd felt the same lovesick jolt he used to get when they were reunited after being apart for a few hours.

He'd felt the same heat, the same bone-deep commitment to do whatever it took to soothe the tough, tenderhearted girl who let herself be weak only in his arms.

Seeing her so devastated had torn him up inside. He knew how much she hated breaking down. When was the last time he'd held her?

When he told her he couldn't go to NAU because his father was falling apart, bitter, broke and about to sink every penny he had into a pointless lawsuit against Abbott Wharton, her face had blanched, her eyes filled with tears. She'd trusted him and he'd betrayed her. That was a big deal, since the only other person she counted on was her sister. He'd hated letting her down.

It wasn't fair to make him choose between his father and her. They'd said ugly things to each other, stabbed at the most tender spots, hurt each other as only two people who'd been as close as they'd been could.

She'd cut all contact after that—ignored his emails and calls, shut him down completely. He'd been angry, but he should have known. With Tara you were in or out, friend or foe. He'd had this childlike belief that their love would outlast this trouble. He been so caught up in their love, so enmeshed with her, that the breakup had almost killed him.

He hadn't seen her since. He'd missed Faye's wedding, sending a gift in his stead. Tara had been a pretty girl. She was a beautiful woman. Her eyes were the same startling blue, even through her tears, but they had more power, more ability to assess and evaluate. She knew what she wanted now.

She was curvier, too, and he liked that. She wore her hair in a sleek style, not wildly spiked with color like in high school. She smelled like an expensive perfume, not patchouli and vanilla oil.

He was glad he'd fixed the funeral for her, though he hadn't appreciated Tara's amazement that he had the town job or her assumption that he was just his father's employee, not his second in command, the guy who'd practically put the place together, who'd set the company on the path that would lead to steady profits and a solid future.

Rachel's dig about him being part-time manager hit him wrong. It was true the town needed full-time leadership. Dylan planned to provide it. It was his dream. Within a year, he'd have completed his mission at Ryland Engineering and he could go for it. He intended to build up the town, bring in new business, more housing, boost tourism for the river area with its bird sanctuary. He'd pulled together a decent leadership team already. He needed to write some development grants, and do some outreach. All he needed was time.

And time was at a premium with the recent headaches over the Wharton Electronics deal. The contract had been the linchpin on his plan and now it was at risk.

He drove over to the Ryland Engineering plant. When he got out of his car, he paused, taking in the new sign he'd had done by a local graphic artist. The sleek sign, the dark brown gloss paint and the chrome accents gave the building a modern, streamlined look.

Inside, the redone reception area had white-leather furniture and apricot walls that subtly suggested Ryland's logo. It wasn't a showcase like the reception area at Wharton Electronics, but it was respectable.

Anticipating the increase in clients, he'd decided they'd needed a more polished public face. The sculpture he'd commissioned looked like an abstract fountain using Ryland circuit boards, curving up and out, wired so they seemed to float in the air.

His father had fought him on the renovation, but his father fought him a lot. It felt like he'd dragged his dad every step of the way to success.

Now that Dylan was near the finish line, he'd become weary of the struggle. He longed for the time when he could be friends with his father, when he could admire his brilliance and passion, instead of fighting to harness it.

"Your dad's asking for you," the receptionist called to him.

"Got it." He walked down the hall and entered his father's office.

His father looked up from some papers. "Where have you been?"

"Arranging to use the high school for Abbott's funeral."

"With all we've got going on here, you don't have time for that town-manager crap."

"I can handle it." He took pride in being a problem solver. He was good with difficult people—his father being a prime example.

"It's thankless work. You'll be begging for your job back in six months." His father thought his dream of becoming a town leader was foolish. "So did you get the funeral set?" His father held his frown, but he was clearly concerned. He'd been shaky and red-eyed since he heard that Abbott was dead. The two men had been fraternity brothers at MIT, then business associates for almost thirty years, with Ryland Engineering supplying parts to Wharton Electronics.

Then his father's business had failed. Abbott bought it, retooled the plant and turned it around, making a fortune. Believing Abbott had had insider information and had robbed him, his father sued, lost, then appealed.

The ten-year feud between the two men and their companies had ended six months ago, thanks to years of work on Dylan's part, when Ryland Engineering signed a contract to provide the drive circuitry assembly for the Wharton battery for electric and plug-in hybrid cars.

"I found town funds to pay for the buses, yeah."

"You tell Rachel?"

"Yes. I saw her at the hospital. Tara was there, too." His face felt hot. He hoped to hell it didn't glow red.

"I'm surprised that one even showed."

"Why would you say that?"

"She walked away from her family. Shook them off like water from a dog's back."

"She did what she had to do for herself."

"For *herself*. Exactly. I'm glad we raised you better. Though I blame that on her mother, who spoiled her rotten. That's what comes of thinking money makes you better." Dylan had felt the friction between his father and Tara's mother even as a kid when the families got together for picnics and card games. His father had always been sensitive about status and wealth.

Now, he turned a framed photo away from himself.

Dylan picked it up, recognizing it as the shot of his father and Abbott posing with a jet turbofan they'd first collaborated on. His father had designed the components and Wharton Electronics had assembled and sold it, back when the company engineered aeronautics equipment.

The photo usually sat high on a dusty shelf. His father had taken it down to reminisce, no doubt, though he would likely deny that to Dylan.

"Look at you two," Dylan said.

"We look like fools," his father said.

"It was the eighties. Everyone wore leisure suits." The men's expressions captured their personalities. Dylan's father looked dazed and humble. A scholarship student at MIT, he hadn't been able to believe his good fortune. Abbott looked relaxed and confident, knowing success was his birthright.

"Give me that." His father looked at the picture. "I was the real fool. I should have known he would cheat me blind."

"He saved you from bankruptcy."

"He took advantage of me." Dylan's father, a dreamer caught up in his ideas, had gone into debt on R&D, failing to boost production to cover costs. Abbott had bought Ryland Engineering at a fair price, not a generous one. Abbott Wharton was a businessman first.

"Abbott knew how to spot trends, Dad."

"Now you take his side?"

"I'm being realistic."

Growing up, his father had lectured Dylan, pride ringing

in his voice, about how he himself was proof that hard work and intelligence overcame wealth and privilege.

Abbott making a killing on his father's failed business had destroyed his father's belief, convinced him that wealth and class always ruled.

"Your mother wore the same blinders. I was a failure, while Abbott could do no wrong." Dylan's mother left—went back to her family in Iowa—because she couldn't live with his father's bitterness, though his father believed it was the shame of his failure.

His parents' breakup at Christmas his senior year had shaken Dylan to the core. Love was supposed to last. His parents hadn't even tried. They drew lines in the sand and folded their arms, stubbornly blaming each other.

They'd forced him to choose, too. He'd stayed with his father, the one who needed him most. His mother claimed to understand, but she'd been hurt.

"And, still, the man's trying to cheat me from the grave." His father stabbed a finger at the papers on his desk. "These specs are impossible."

"We knew there would be kinks to smooth." To reach this moment, Dylan had watched their profit margin like a hawk, held the line on R&D, no matter how hard his father pushed, and kept tabs on developments at Wharton.

When Abbott nailed the federal energy alternative grant to build the cheaper, lighter, more stable lithium battery his engineers had devised, Dylan made sure Ryland Engineering was positioned as the best provider of the crucial part.

"You know damn well they're scheming for a price cut," his father said.

"It's our bottom price. I made that clear." They'd gone with a razor-thin profit margin to seal the deal, buying components from a new plant in Tennessee with rock-bottom prices. Once the Wharton batteries hit the market, demand would skyrocket, and Ryland Engineering would be rolling in orders. He hoped to hire some of the workers Wharton had been forced to lay off two months before. Talk about coming full circle. His father wanted that, too, no matter how much he groused.

All along, Dylan's mission had been to redeem his father in his own eyes and, if possible, end the feud between the two men. They'd finally begun to warm to each other. Now Abbott was gone and his father was dredging up the old resentments to ease his grief and loss.

Dylan longed for the father he'd known growing up—a kind and patient teacher, a brilliant engineer with boundless curiosity and a total reverence for science. Dylan's best memories were the hours they'd spent in the workshop on projects—building a battery, a potato radio, a fighter kite, even a hovercraft, which took top honors at a science fair.

He hoped that once he had some distance from his father, he could go back to admiring the man, appreciating him for his good points.

His father looked up at him. "Any change with Faye?"

"She's still in ICU, still unconscious."

"That's got to be hard for a mother, though with Rachel, you'd never know she's suffering. She's prickly as a cactus."

"Maybe you could give her a call. Express your concern."

His father frowned, shaking his head. "It's on her to reach out. I'll pay respects at the funeral."

"Up to you." His father was as uncompromising with people as Tara had been. That wasn't Dylan's way. People were flawed. You accepted that and made the best of the good in them.

"It's a damn shame about Faye. She's the best of the bunch over there. Smart and fair and she works hard. Without her, the place just might fall apart. Her husband's useless."

"Joseph's good at what he does. They've got good people.

They'll bounce back." Dylan was concerned, though. A lot was riding on the success of the batteries for both companies. Deadlines were approaching. The too-tight specs were only part of the problem. For the past six weeks, Wharton had reported high test failures on the Ryland units. Dylan had to resolve the problem and quickly.

"And while we're on the subject, there's not a damn thing wrong with those units," his father said, glaring up at him. "You tell those Wharton thieves that in that meeting. I put one on my own car."

"I will. Don't worry. Did you look at the data Victor collected?" Victor was their factory operations manager, the man Dylan was grooming to take over for him.

"Haven't had time. I've been looking at the new circuitry they're working on in R&D. This could be big—a totally new direction for us."

"They're a long way from a prototype, Dad. Manufacturing is our bread and butter. You have to keep your eye on the target." Dylan worried that Victor wouldn't be able to keep his father on track once Dylan left. That might be the fly in the ointment of his plan.

"You'll pick me up for the funeral?"

"Yeah," Dylan said. He hoped to skip the reception, wanting to minimize his father's contact with the Wharton managers who'd be there. There was no telling how his father's grief and frustration would play out in a public setting. He'd be damn glad when he could stop managing the man.

He'd see Tara again at the funeral. His heart thumped at the prospect. Tara had been his port in the storm of his parents' breakup. He'd been so wrecked, he'd made his relationship with her seem better than it was, ignoring their differences, her all-or-nothing personality, the superhuman standards she set that he could never meet. If they'd stayed together, they'd have battled constantly. The hell of it was that holding her for that moment in the hospital, all he could remember was the wonder of love, of pure desire, the miracle of intimacy, and he'd wanted it, no matter how temporary, no matter how false, no matter the whiplash of pain that would follow.

Looked like his father wasn't the only one who should keep his exposure to the Whartons to a minimum. They should definitely skip the reception.

CHAPTER THREE

AS SHE TURNED onto the brick driveway that curved up the hill toward the Wharton house, Tara glanced at her mother, who'd been quiet on the drive home. She hadn't even grilled Tara about her choice of casket and flowers, which wasn't like her mother at all. "You okay?" Tara asked.

"Why wouldn't I be?" her mother said, jerking her gaze from the side window to the front, chin high.

So much for a tender moment of support. "No reason, I guess." Tara looked up at the huge colonial on the hill. Laughably out of place in the desert, it was still home, and she felt a rush of tenderness seeing it again.

She was ridiculously emotional.

As she pulled under the porte cochere, Judith Rand, the longtime housekeeper, came down the terrace steps to meet them.

"You came," Judith said to Tara in the same sarcastic tone her mother had used.

"How are you, Judith?" The woman had mirrored Tara's mother's attitudes toward Tara's rebellious ways, but she'd always done Tara secret kindnesses.

"Sheets are fresh on the bed," Judith said, helping Tara's mother out of the passenger seat. "Park in the garage. The Tesla's gone and the Mercedes is in the shop."

Her mother gasped and sagged, no doubt remembering what had happened to the Tesla. Judith caught her arm and glared at Tara, as if Tara were the one who'd brought it up.

She started up the steps with Rachel. "Breakfast is at seven," she said over her shoulder. "If you sleep in, you're on your own."

"I run at five, so I'll just grab some fruit," Tara called out. She assumed Judith was still making the hearty breakfasts Tara's father preferred—biscuits and gravy, steak and eggs or huge, cheesy omelets.

The gardener opened the garage and Tara parked, then rolled her bag along the path to the kitchen door.

The kitchen smelled of tomato soup, a Judith staple, which added to the homey effect of the buttercup walls, pale soapstone counters, stone fireplace and copper pots hanging over the dark-wood island.

Tara crossed the gleaming oak floors and lifted the suitcase's wheels onto the Persian rug in the sitting room, which was painted dove-gray with white molding.

Growing up, Tara found the antique furnishings, the elaborately carved staircase and mantel fussy and old-fashioned. Now it comforted her—especially the steady tick of the grandfather clock that had been in her father's family since the Civil War.

The grand piano gleamed in the light from the many-paned arched windows. As a girl, Faye had been an accomplished pianist, starring in every recital and playing for the high school jazz ensemble. Tara had taken lessons, but quit after three months. No one had objected. No one expected much from Tara. Faye had been the perfect daughter. That gave Tara the freedom to make her own way. It had been a gift, but a lonely one.

Moving closer to the window, she could just make out the hummingbird terrace tucked to one side of the property. She and Dylan had spent hours there, lost in each other arms. When she got a chance, she'd go out there for a break, to breathe easier, to watch the birds and listen to the fountain.

And remember Dylan?

What would be the point of that?

Reaching the wooden staircase, Tara rested her hand on the square newel post, as she'd done a million times bounding up or down the steps, her mother snapping at her to walk like a lady, not gallop like a horse.

The stairs creaked. She'd memorized which to avoid when sneaking in or out at night.

Her bedroom at the end of the hall was decorated like a luxury hotel room. As soon as Tara had left for college, her mother had thrown out Tara's band posters, social-issue bumper stickers, stuffed animals, crazy jewelry and the clothes she'd left. Her mother used to shudder over the vintage looks Tara created from the Lutheran church's used-clothes store. Tara had liked supporting the charity, being frugal like her father and, yes, irritating her mother.

She winced. She used to do things just to get a reaction. Born ten years after Faye, Tara had clearly been an accident her parents wanted to pretend hadn't happened at all. Faye had done her best to make up for her parents' neglect. She swore that they'd treated her just as absently, but Tara knew better. Even as a kid, she'd been good at reading people, and her parents plainly adored Faye.

Should she unpack? She didn't know how long she'd be here. It all depended on Faye. How soon she recovered. What if she…*died?*

That idea took Tara's breath away. *Don't die, Faye. Please don't die.* She got out her phone to call Rita. She'd convinced the nurse they should exchange numbers since Tara lived an hour from the hospital, and Joseph, the official family contact, wasn't big on sharing news.

Tara boosted herself up onto the high bed, sinking into the thick pillow-top, and waited for Rita to answer.

"This is Rita."

"How is Faye doing?" Tara asked.

"Holding her own." Was there a hesitation in Rita's voice?

"Should I come back out? Is she having problems? I've got a laptop. I can easily work there." Tara got to her feet.

"Stay where you are. Get some rest. Your sister's busy healing. She knows you're pulling for her."

Tara swallowed past the tightness in her throat caused by Rita's words. "I'll be there in the morning then, but if anything happens. *Any*thing—"

"I'll *call*. I promise. Now don't make me sorry I gave you my number."

"I won't. Thanks again."

Just as Tara clicked off, a text appeared on her display. It was from Jeff Cameron, the CEO of Cameron Plastics.

Natives restless re: webinar. Make this work.

He'd flown in his division managers to plan the company-wide conference Tara was to facilitate later in the year to improve manager–employee relations. Jeff was also president of the manufacturing trade association, so his praise could bring new clients. She was doing decently for a new company, but she had to keep building. Grow or die.

She reassured him as best she could, though live meetings were always more powerful. Eye contact drew people in, raised the energy level and built enthusiasm. In a webinar, people were easily distracted and she'd be unable to read body language.

A lively PowerPoint helped, so Tara would create that now. She managed to shut out her emotions and worries to make decent progress, though she dozed at the keyboard, waking up when Judith yelled that dinner was ready.

Her mother was eating in her room, Judith told her, so it was just Tara at the kitchen table. Besides soup, Judith had made fried chicken with gravy, corn on the cob, creamed spinach and homemade rolls. *Sunday dinner.* Judith had fussed, which touched Tara. She ate all she could knowing Judith would interpret any leftovers as not liking her cooking.

"I'm stuffed," she said finally, so full she feared she'd pop the zipper on her jeans.

"Good. You're skinnier than your mother."

Over Judith's head was a shelf loaded with cookbooks. Looked like Tara's mother had kept up the tradition of giving Judith a new one each Christmas—her mother's hint that Judith try something new.

"You ever use any of those cookbooks?"

Judith shrugged. "Your mother likes me to have things to dust."

She smiled. Tara liked Judith, despite her frostiness. The woman clearly loved Tara's parents, and was especially close to her mother.

Tara decided to hold the webinar in the sunroom her mother used as her office, so she lifted the roll top of the antique secretary and set up her laptop, plugging into the ethernet she found there.

This was her favorite room, cozy with soft furniture, an embroidered window seat and a half-dozen hanging plants. The heavy food made her sleepy again, plus her brain felt like it had been sandpapered, so she made herself a cup of espresso with her mother's expensive machine—and put the finishing touches on her presentation before the meeting was to start.

By the time she closed out the webinar at 10:00 p.m., Tara was wringing with sweat and totally wired on adrenaline and caffeine. Judging from the relaxed comments, the thoughtful questions and the absence of rustling, the meeting had gone well. Jeff had sounded pleased as he signed off.

She stood and stretched, thinking she'd make some tea or go for a walk to get rid of her nervous energy. The top of the secretary held photos—mostly formal black-and-white pictures in elaborate silver frames. There was one color shot in a contemporary frame. Tara picked it up. It was of Faye, Tara and their mother from the day trip to Sunset Crater they'd taken the day before Faye's wedding. Tara smiled. They all looked happy, and the light was beautiful. This would be the photo she taped to Faye's bed tray.

Tara headed to the kitchen to make tea and find a knife to lift up the frame tabs.

In the dim kitchen, she was startled to see her mother on a stool at the counter. Light from the full moon glimmered off ice in a highball glass beside a bottle of vodka.

"Is that a gimlet?" Tara asked. That was her mother's drink.

"Straight vodka. Gimlet's too…damn…com…plicated."

Tara went on full alert. Her mother never got drunk and she never used what she called *foul language,* including *damn* and *hell.* "I'm making chamomile tea. Would you like some?"

"I waited for you. We hafta do the pro…gram for the fun'ral. What was going on in there?"

"I was hosting a web meeting with one of my clients."

"Yes. You have *clients.*"

Was she being sarcastic?

"Faye says you're very…pro…fezzhional."

No. That sounded sincere.

"I try to be. I'm doing well, especially in this economy and—" She stopped, realizing her mother had bigger concerns. "What's up, Mom? What's going on?"

"You'll have to drive me to the hozzpital. Joseph's going too early and my car…my car…see…it's still—"

"At the mechanic's. I remember. No problem. I'm happy to drive."

Abruptly her mother grabbed Tara's forearm, her fingers digging in, her eyes fierce and desperate. "Is she suffering? I can't stand to think…that I… That my little girl…is in pain…"

"No, Mom. She's not suffering. Rita told me coma patients fidget when they're hurting. And Faye doesn't move at all." *She's as still as death.*

"You wouldn't lie to me?" Then her mother gave a small smile. "Not you. You're honest to a fault." That was a jab, but her mother's behavior was so troubling that Tara was relieved by the normalcy of the dig. Her mother noticed the photograph Tara held. "Wha's the pic…ture for?"

"To tape up for Faye to look at. What do you think?" She showed it to her mother, who blinked, as if to clear her vision, then studied it. "This was that trip we took before Faye got married."

"Yeah. Sunset Crater. We were talking about it and you said let's go so we did." It had been a rare instance of spontaneity from their mother, and Tara had loved it. As they set off, her mother had actually squeezed Tara's hand in excitement.

With so little reaction from her parents, Tara had learned to interpret the smallest gesture or postural shift. In a way, that had led to her skill with people. She knew well the way her mother's eyebrows lifted whenever Tara spoke, as if she expected Tara to be loud or wrong. She knew the sour lip twist when Tara's manners failed and the huffed breath when Tara bumped a chair, the relieved exhale when Tara left the room, the quick stiffening when she entered.

Her father had hardly seemed aware Tara existed. His neglect somehow hurt less, maybe because he neglected her mother, too, as far as Tara could see. When he was home, he was in his study or reading. His books, their places marked, were scattered throughout the house. Only Faye made him light up. Tara had been happy for Faye, but she'd also ached with envy.

"That was a fine trip." Her mother smiled, running her finger over the glass.

They'd parked on the lookout and asked a tourist to take their photo. They stood with the crater behind them, Tara and their mother on either side of Faye, who sat on the hood of their mother's sky-blue Mercedes, her heel braced in the heart-shaped dent in the fender their father had refused to fix. Her mother was notoriously bad at parking and her father had gotten fed up with all the bodywork charges.

"Faye looks so happy," Tara said. Her sister practically glowed with joy.

"Faye was always happy." *Unlike you.* Her mother claimed Tara had been a colicky baby, a cranky child and an impossible teenager.

"But this is more. You can see she's in love." At the time, Tara had dismissed that, insisting that Faye owed it to herself to go after her dream, to study art. *Love can wait,* she'd said.

Tara cringed at her nerve. The trouble was that Tara had never been in love. Not real, adult love. The thing with Dylan didn't qualify. She didn't understand love. Worse, in the back of her mind lurked the deep and painful truth that Dylan had blurted when they had that terrible fight:

You don't know how to love anyone, not even yourself.

Still, *still* that thought made her gasp as if from a stomach punch and left her feeling empty and aching inside.

Tara should have rejoiced that Faye had found love, that she was happy. Instead she'd harassed her about it, sounding eerily like her mother when Tara said she was going to NAU with Dylan. Her mother had said it was *puppy love.*

Tara had been just as thoughtless. It was the Wharton Effect—the feeling of being both lost and trapped because of growing up where everyone knew them and their family, and had opinions about everything they said or did.

Unlike Tara, Faye had shaved off her corners to fit Wharton's round hole, and Tara had thought she had to wake up Faye to what she'd sacrificed. Faye loved her life here. Tara knew that deep down. Faye loved Joseph. And she loved Wharton Electronics. Only Tara was the misfit.

"She shouldn't have been in that car," her mother wailed suddenly, turning the picture facedown on the counter, her face raw with pain. "Why would he do that to her?"

The prickling sensation came again. "You mean why did Dad ask Faye to drive? Is that it?"

Her mother just shook her head, looking down at the counter.

"Do you think Dad got drunk playing poker? Is that why Faye was driving?"

Her mother raised her gaze. "Abbott drinks iced tea in a highball glass...pretends iz whiz-key.... For a clear head... He hates to lose."

That made sense to Tara. Her father had always been competitive.

"But...that night..." her mother said. "Maybe...he did drink..." Her mother stared at Tara, urgent again. "Do you think if they were quick...er?" Her mother was really slurring now. "The E...M...Ts? Bill said it was quick. But if they were quicker, maybe she wouldn't be—"

"Who's Bill?"

"Bill Fallon."

"The police chief?" Tara had been in his office several times for lectures about how she was *killing her mother* by staging protests, drinking, driving too fast, or smoking pot. "So someone called 911 and he came? Wait, doesn't he play poker with Dad?"

"He missed poker. He wazz pazzing by." Her mother turned her glass with both hands, miserable. "Bill swore the helicopter was quick. He watches out for us, Bill does."

"He's a first responder, Mom. It's his *job* to help when

there's an accident." Goose bumps rose on her arms. Her mother seemed worried, too. Something was amiss. "What else, Mom?"

There was a long, long silence. Tara could hear the grandfather clock ticking. Her pulse seemed to thrum in time.

"We quarreled," her mother said so softly Tara almost didn't hear her. "Faye and I. I lost my temper. If I could take it all back, I would." She seemed to be pleading with Tara.

"What did you fight about?"

Her mother shook her head, not willing to say.

"People say things they don't mean out of anger. Faye knows that. Faye's a forgiving person," she said to make her mother feel better. Meanwhile, her mind raced. So the police chief had missed poker, but seen the crash somehow. That alone seemed strange. "Who else played poker that night?"

"I don't know. Jim Crowley, Mitch Bender, Paul Robins, Gary Hicks. Why?"

"Maybe they know why Faye was in the car."

"Oh, no." Her mother blinked at her. "Your father did not tell tales."

What the hell did that mean? Tara would find a way to talk to one of the men. Maybe at the funeral.

"If Faye dies…I can't go on," her mother said in a choked voice. Tara had never heard her mother sound so desperate.

"Mom…" Tara put a tentative hand on her mother's back.

Her mother tensed, then sat up straight, as if Tara's touch had been a warning. "I'm not myself. I apologize." She cleared her throat. "We'll discuss the program tomorrow. It must be perfect." Her mother's voice cracked. "Everyone loved your father."

She pushed up to her feet. She started away, then turned back and leveled her gaze at Tara. "Your father loved you. Don't forget that." With a sharp nod, her mother walked away, moving stiffly, the way people pretending not to be drunk walked.

Her mother was so formal, so strict. She wouldn't even allow herself a comforting pat. Tara hoped it wasn't that she couldn't allow herself a comforting pat from *Tara*.

No. Don't think like that. You're here to make peace. You can't look for ways to be hurt.

It might be easier if her mother gave any sign she wanted peace with Tara. She might be better off just leaving it alone, but she couldn't do it. She had to try to fix this, to make it right. Her whole career was about healing wounds between employees and managers. Shouldn't she be able to do that with her own mother?

Tara sat in the silent kitchen, feeling deflated and sad.

Your father loved you, her mother had said.

Yeah, right. That was her first reaction. She forced herself to be more positive. *He loved you in his own way.*

And what way was that exactly?

He'd let her come to the shoe shop that time. And once, when she was ten, she'd begged to go with him when he went to shoot skeet. He'd showed her how to shoot, but it hurt and it was loud and she'd cried, so he'd sent her to the shooting range office, disgusted with her for giving up so easily.

Later, Tara returned to the range for lessons, making the owner swear not to tell her father, determined to prove herself. By the time she got good enough, she no longer cared what her father thought of her.

Would sharing that have changed things between them?

It was too late to know.

Are you proud of me, Dad? Did you know how good I am? She'd sent him a packet, as CEO of Wharton Electronics, one of the dozens she sent to potential clients, but never heard a word. She didn't need his approval, of course, but the first hurts were the deepest.

You had to heal yourself. She knew that. But being here again brought up those old teenage feelings. The Wharton Effect all over again. Her job was to ignore it, rise above it, kick it to the curb until she could finally, safely, escape for good.

Then there was Dylan. What about Dylan? There'd been this lingering thing in her head since she'd seen him, like a singer holding a note until she was about to pass out.

She missed him. Still. She wanted him. Still.

And that was the most ridiculous thing of all.

SATURDAY AT NOON, Dimitri helped Tara out of the the limousine in front of the house for the reception. She was dying for air-conditioning. She'd forgotten that October in Arizona was too warm for the navy business suit she'd worn. The sun had beat down mercilessly during the graveside service.

Hang in there, she told herself. *Just a few more hours.*

Then she could peel off her clothes, go for a swim or a run, borrow one of her father's guns and shoot skeet until her shoulder throbbed, drive as fast as she could as far away as she wanted, or throw herself facedown on her bed and let the thick down pillows muffle her sobs.

Dimitri helped Tara's mother out of the car. She'd held her own since the night in the kitchen, handled the visitation and the funeral with dignity and grace, accepting hugs, pats and cheek kisses with a smile. Her friends, the women who sat on charity boards with her and planned food drives and hosted fund-raising balls, seemed to buoy her. Maybe she felt she had to put on a front for them. Whatever it was, it helped her hold it together. Tara would keep an eye out at the reception in case she started to crack. Her mother's dignity meant everything to her, so Tara would help preserve it.

The house was a cool relief, noisy with talk, smelling of rich food, flowers, wine and perfume. The dining room table groaned with food, waiters passed hot appetizers and the bartender was busy handing out drinks. Her father would have considered the full bar with top-shelf liquor too showy, but Tara wanted the best to honor him. She headed for the kitchen to be sure the caterers had everything they needed.

"Eat before you fall down." Judith thrust a plate at Tara with a hunk of beef covered in mustard and a piece of cherry pie—Tara's favorite as a kid. "You left that yogurt on the counter this morning."

"Thanks, Judith, for thinking of me. I ran out of time to eat."

"Can't have you passing out in front of company. I told the bartender to water your mother's gimlets. I'll keep an eye on her. You greet the guests."

She noticed Judith's eyes were red. "How are you doing?"

"How do you think I'm doing? Supervising these airhead caterers I should get overtime." She marched away in a huff, as private about her feelings as Tara's mother.

Tara started circulating. She noticed Chief Fallon leaning close to her mother to talk. He'd stayed awhile at the visitation, too, bringing her mother a glass of water. The big bouquet on the dining room table had come from him. What had her mother said? *Bill watches out for us.*

Yeah? Was there more to it than that? It gave her the creeps to even contemplate.

Tara greeted people, made sure everyone had food and liquor. It was exhausting to talk to people who knew her or thought they did—people who hated her or resented her, friends who wanted to rehash wild times, phonies who expressed sympathy with smug eyes. As the hours passed, she felt more and more suffocated. She wanted to yell, *you don't know me and you never did.* She'd put on an act in high school. She'd felt like she had no choice.

Since she'd arrived at the reception, she'd kept her eye open for Dylan. He might not come, considering the feud between their fathers. She'd spotted Dylan and his dad after the service speaking to her mother, but that was it.

For the three nights since she'd arrived, she'd had *dreams* about him. Steamy ones that lingered after she awoke, leaving her with a terrible longing for the real thing. Clearly they represented her need to escape her worries about Faye and her grief over her father.

Sex had been all-consuming back then—a desperate need, an undeniable force, a bonfire that *had* to be quenched or they'd die.

What would sex with Dylan be like now?

The instant the idea crossed her mind he walked through the door, his father behind him. She'd thought of him and he'd appeared. The old magic again. Afraid if he saw her, he might read her mind, she turned and nearly ran for the kitchen.

Stop this. Grow up.

It wasn't just the sex that was making her think of him. It was the relief of belonging, of being understood, of fitting in at last. That had meant so much to her back then. And now, her emotions were churned up. Who wouldn't want to escape into a time when all that mattered was being in the arms of the one person you loved above all else, who loved you the same?

But it wasn't true even then.

Let it go for good.

Here she was, hiding from him in the kitchen. Ridiculous. She decided to see how they were fixed for crab puffs.

CHAPTER FOUR

"QUIT STALKING HER and go talk to her."

Dylan's ex-wife's voice made him turn. He hoped his face didn't look as red as it felt. "I will when she's not busy." He *had* been tracking Tara since they'd arrived at the reception, catching sight of her as she raced for the kitchen on some urgent errand. The sight of her retreating back had been enough to set his heart pounding. He knew her shape from all sides. The way she moved—quick and graceful as a dancer—was a dead giveaway.

Since then he'd watched her slide from group to group, talking, fetching drinks, motioning waiters over with food. She was gracious and kind, with a smile for everyone, but he knew she was hurting. Even from a distance, he saw the same haunted look she'd had at the hospital.

"We do look a little alike," Candee mused. "Same hair color, same height, same build, but she's better proportioned."

"Don't do this." Candee had been convinced their short marriage had failed because Dylan had still had a thing for Tara.

"She's more...*striking*. That's it, isn't it? She has a celebrity aura. She totally rocks her clothes. That suit is tight, but not slutty, and those heels are quality. Expensive, but restrained."

"Now you sound like the stalker," he said, trying to joke her out of this comparison, which he feared would upset her, though they'd been divorced for eight years.

"Anyway, I get it," she said, a flash of hurt in her eyes. "I see why."

"You're beautiful and striking and you have an aura, too." Dylan hated how she underrated her own attractiveness.

"I do have bigger boobs," she said on a sigh. "You always liked my boobs."

"I did. I do. I mean…your boobs are great." These conversations never went well for him. Candee had moved to Wharton a year after Tara left for college and dragged Dylan out of his lonely cave with her energy and sense of fun. Things progressed quickly and they'd married. He'd been determined to make it work. He'd watched his parents' marriage fall apart. He wouldn't let that happen to him.

But it had. Candee became convinced he was still in love with Tara. *You built a shrine to her in your head. I can see the candles glowing in your eyes. I can't compete with a dream. She can't possibly be as great as you remember.*

He'd done his best to change her mind. He loved Candee. Tara was gone. Maybe he was still shell-shocked, still numb from the cascade of troubles—his parents' divorce, the breakup with Tara, the ongoing strain of helping his father get back on his feet.

To this day, he still regretted that he'd hurt Candee. He'd fought like hell to stay friends. Mutual loneliness had put them in bed together a few times. The last time she'd *dropped by to see Duster*—Candee code for wanting sex, since she barely looked at the dog, he'd gently declined and driven her home, making her swear to stop drinking beer and looking through the wedding album. At least not on an empty stomach.

"How's your dad doing?" Candee asked him.

"Not great. He's on his third whiskey." *Abbott always had the good stuff,* his father had said, downing the first glass of Pinch in one swallow, holding out the glass for a second while people behind him waited to be served. A few minutes later, he'd gone after the drink he now held. His father rarely drank, so this was proof of his deep distress at the loss of his friend.

"I wanted to skip the reception, but he insisted." *I'm not running off with my tail between my legs.* "I'm afraid he's going to get into it with somebody from Wharton." During the service, his father had fumed when the mayor mentioned Abbott's integrity and generosity. *Integrity, my ass,* he'd muttered. *He's a robber baron. And generous? He stole my company for a song.*

"He needs to eat something," Candee said. "I'll fix him a plate."

"That'd be great. He listens to you. See if you can talk him into leaving. His car's at Auto Angels."

"Will the shop be open?"

"Tony gave him a key, since he's always tinkering on something or other."

"I'll do my best."

"Thanks, Candee." He watched her head for the dining room.

When he turned back, he saw his father was talking to Joseph Banes, leaning in, intent. Joseph's face was bright red.

Dylan headed over, arriving just as his father said, "You don't know a thing about it, Joe," jabbing a finger at Joseph. People around them fell silent. Out of the corner of his eye he saw Rachel approach, Tara behind her.

"Don't expect us to hold to an unreasonable contract with a company about to fall apart," his father said.

"You are speaking out of turn," Joseph said. "In fact, you're in no condition to be speaking at all."

"That's enough." Rachel said in a low voice. "I will not have you squabbling like children at my husband's funeral."

Dylan's father looked stunned by the reprimand.

Candee lunged into the group with a loaded plate. "Wait until you taste the crab puffs, Sean." She thrust the food under his nose. Humbled by Rachel's sharp words, he took the plate. "Let's go sit and eat."

Dylan mouthed *thank you* to Candee as she led his father away. When he turned back, Rachel was gone and Tara was taking a crab puff from a waiter. "You need to control your father," Joseph snapped.

"Abbott's death has been difficult for him," Dylan said, wanting to ease the moment, but feeling protective of his father.

"That's no excuse for unprofessional conduct in a room full of my employees. As to the contract, rest assured we'll be taking another look."

"Excuse me?" *Was that a threat?*

He opened his mouth to say more, but Tara said, "She's right about the crab puffs. Yum. Here." She thrust one at Joseph and shot Dylan a look. *Chill.*

He chilled.

Joseph frowned, but her move had flummoxed him and he took the puff and ate it.

"Good, huh?" she said. "Judith made me a plate or I'd have passed out. Go fill one for yourself. You have to be starving. Your nerves must be shot." She half turned him and he walked toward the dining room, clearly not certain how that had happened.

"Thanks," Dylan said. "I was about to make it worse."

"He's been at the hospital every night late, so he's edgy."

"Understandable. Though the man's edgy period. I'm not sure how he stays upright with the size of the chip on his shoulder."

"He's got a home gym. That way he can carry the weight of the world, too."

He laughed, feeling the old rapport click in. "Good to know."

"What were they arguing about anyway? What contract?"

"Ryland Engineering makes the drive assembly for the new Wharton batteries."

"You're kidding! Our fathers made peace?"

"They were getting there. I wish they'd had more time."

A silence fell between them as she absorbed his meaning. The feud had troubled them both. For that moment, he and Tara were old friends sharing a sadness that went back years.

Abruptly her eyes widened at something over his shoulder. "Was that your ex-wife who kept your dad from slugging Joseph?"

"Yes. Her name's Candee." The topic change startled him.

"She wants you."

"Excuse me?" He jolted at Tara's conclusion.

"Behind you."

He turned to see Candee motioning toward the door where his father was already headed. She made her fingers walk, miming leaving. He nodded and mouthed his thanks.

"Nicely done," Tara said.

When he turned to her, he caught a glimpse of pure exhaustion before she slapped on her smile.

"You look worn out," he said.

"I feel that way. Too much smiling and nodding, too many back-in-the-day tales. I feel like I can't catch a breath. I need a hummingbird break." She put a hand to her mouth, realizing she'd used their code for making out on her back terrace where hummingbirds crowded the flower trellis. "I mean a real break, not a…" She blushed, which made her look more beautiful than ever.

"I know what you meant," he said, his body flooded with lust all the same.

Her lips parted and she took a quick breath, feeling it, too, he guessed.

"Just say the word," he said. "Need me to run interference?"

Tara looked around the room, her gaze pausing at her mother, standing with their housekeeper. "No. Mom's okay. The guests are content. I can duck out. Ask the bartender for the bottle of Patron Silver and meet me."

Tequila had been their drink—usually shots or over ice, once in a while in a margarita. Maybe it had been Tara's drink and he'd grown to love the bitter tang and kerosene burn because he loved her.

When he got to the terrace, Tara lay on a chaise lounge in just her blouse and skirt, the blouse open low, sleeves rolled, her arms folded behind her head.

"You look...comfortable." She looked sexy as hell. Her skirt ended mid-thigh, exposing long, tan legs and bare feet, toes painted as red as the flowers that lined the trellis before them. One tug on that slippery-looking shirt and it would slide right off her shoulders.

"I am." She gave him a lazy smile.

He made himself stop staring and sat at the table, setting the glasses, lime and tequila on the wrought-iron table.

"You always knew what I needed," she said, sitting sideways on the lounger to reach the table, her knees bumping his and staying there.

"This was your idea, not mine, remember?" he said, pouring tequila over the ice and lime, the smell alone taking him back.

"Yeah, but I was reading your mind." She grinned and picked up her drink.

"You think so?" He tapped her glass with his. If she *had* read his mind, she'd have slapped him or kissed him, he wasn't sure which.

Their eyes met over the drinks and he felt a flash of connection, like heat lightning slicing a summer monsoon sky. Just like that, ten years evaporated. They were together again.

They both dipped into their drinks and sipped. The sharp taste filled his mouth, his throat, burning a path to his stomach, bringing back the heady excitement of being with Tara, anticipating her naked body against his, the pleasure of knowing that she needed him, that he made her happy, the glory of sinking into a place that consisted of the two of them alone.

That was a lot to get from one sip of tequila, but those months with her had been branded into him, vivid as an acid etching in his head.

"Yum," she said, licking her lips in a way that almost stopped his heart.

"Yeah," he said. "I haven't had tequila in a while." *Ten years to be exact.* Too many associations. Stupidly sentimental of him, he realized, but he'd done it automatically.

"Me, either." Had she done the same thing? He doubted that. She'd cut all ties with him. That had to include the pleasant memories.

"It's nice out here," she said, looking out at the terrace. The marble fountain splashed peacefully, the arbor was thick with flowers—bloodred with dark green leaves, the stamens stabs of gold.

She settled her eyes on him. "You look good. More, I don't know, filled out, I guess." She dipped into her glass, as if embarrassed she'd noticed.

"You look the same. Still beautiful." He cleared his throat, hoping that hadn't been too sappy.

"The same? No way. It's been ten years."

"Your hairstyle is new. You seem more…mature." He wasn't about to mention her being curvier. No telling how she'd take that.

"Is that a polite way of saying *older?*"

"More confident. Like you know what you want…and how to get it."

"I do. I do know what I want." Her tone made his mind go straight to sex. He caught the flare of it in her eyes, too.

They watched each other. He remembered them together—the heat, the love, the hurt and loss. It flowed through him in a rush. He thought he saw something similar in her eyes.

A hummingbird suddenly darted between them, wings shivering, flashing metallic green and gold in the light.

"You think they remember us? The birds?" Tara asked. "How long do hummingbirds live?"

"No idea," he said, caught up in the pleasure of being with her again.

"I think I recognize that one. See that little fleck of black on his chest."

"Yeah?"

"He probably wonders why we're doing so much *talking,*" she said softly.

They'd spent hours making out on the chaise where she sat. One push and she'd be on her back and he'd be on top of her.

At her father's funeral? Really?

"I'd offer you a penny for your thoughts, but I think there's probably a couple dollars' worth in there," she said, sexual interest blurring the bright blue of her eyes.

"At least," he said.

The hummingbird zipped away, breaking the tension, and they both watched it go.

"I wanted to thank you for getting the auditorium for the funeral," she said. "I know you went to some trouble."

"I used the town's cultural exchange fund to bus the band competition to another school. We were supposed to bring in a Balinese dance troupe, but they canceled their tour. A band competition is cultural, right?"

"In this town, you bet." She glanced at him. "No offense."

"None taken." He knew she despised Wharton. *Small town, small minds,* she used to say. She likely despised him for staying, for settling. She'd said so when they broke up, calling him a coward, afraid of the world, using his father as an excuse to hide from life.

"You needed every seat in the auditorium," he said to change the subject.

"Of course. The funeral was mandatory attendance for Wharton employees, no doubt."

"That's pretty cynical."

"Old habits die hard." She grabbed her glass and gulped it down, blowing out a breath, clearly upset, her eyes wet— from emotion or the liquor, he couldn't tell. "It's confusing. My mom tells me everyone loved my father, but he wasn't exactly Mr. Warm and Fuzzy. He was respected, I'm sure. Maybe feared. He could be fierce. I remember that."

Dylan shrugged. He'd hated how coldly Tara's parents had treated her. Her father barely acknowledged her, her mother did nothing but criticize, and that was long before she started raising hell.

Growing up like that, it was no surprise she was hypersensitive to rejection. At least he'd known his parents loved him.

"I couldn't believe the mayor saying all that about the hundreds of turkeys he donated and the pancake breakfasts on New Year's Day and all the charity crap. It sounded like a campaign speech."

"It was all true. Your father funded the day care at Wharton. He's been on the school board. He paid for the playground in the park. Both your parents have done a lot for the town. Your mother's a tireless fund-raiser for—"

"Please." She raised her hand. "Don't hype my parents to

me. Don't." Her eyes brimmed with tears. "Don't you dare tell a soul I broke down," she said.

He hated to see her in pain like this. He put his hand over hers. "It's okay, Tara. It's me." His voice was rough with emotion.

The tears slid down her cheeks and her face crumpled. "I didn't expect to miss him so much, you know."

"He was your father, for all his flaws."

She nodded. "I guess I had this fantasy that one day we'd have a real heart-to-heart and he would tell me that he was proud of me, that he knew all along that I would be a success."

His heart went out to her. She'd left Wharton to prove herself to her parents, the town and, most of all, herself.

"Too late now," she said. She grabbed the tequila bottle, crashing it into her glass in her hurry to pour.

"Tequila's got a slow fuse, remember?"

"You're right." She set the bottle down. "I don't drink much anymore. Not like high school, for sure. You used to look out for me."

"I did."

"What an uptight pain in the ass you were." But she was smiling. She would pretend to resent his concern, but there'd been relief in her eyes. He cared about her. That was the point. Even now he felt the urge to protect her, look after her.

She pushed the glass of tequila away, watching the birds dip and flit. "I'm sure Abbott was proud of you," he said to be kind.

She shot him a look. "Please. I doubt he knew what I do for a living."

Wouldn't surprise me. "Human resources, right? You opened your own consulting firm?"

"Corporate culture. Heard of it?"

"Of course."

"Really?"

"You don't believe me?" She was talking down to him, as she had in the hospital, amazed that he worked for the town, as if he were an ignorant hick. "I have a business degree, Tara. I did an accelerated online program for working professionals. At Ryland Engineering, I'm the business manager. Second in command."

"Sorry. I didn't know."

She seemed honestly sorry, so he gave her an out. "That stands to reason. You haven't been back in...years."

"I have a life and a business," she snapped.

"I know that. I didn't mean to say—"

"That I'm a selfish brat who abandoned her family?"

"Right. And I'm sure you weren't implying that I'm a clueless rube whose world ends at the town limits." Joe Banes had nothing on them when it came to edgy.

"Sorry. I guess I'm sensitive about that."

"I guess I am, too."

"So you manage your father *and* Wharton. That's a tall order. Your father's impossible and my family owns the town."

"I wouldn't put it that way," he said, irritated that she was still mocking him.

"I'm sorry. I don't know why I said that. We chose different paths, but we both got what we wanted, right?"

"Right." He could see in her eyes she didn't quite buy it. Her views about Wharton were entrenched, as burned into her soul as their time together was in his. She would never see his life—or the town—the way he did. He wasn't about to tell her his development plan. She'd never stop mocking him.

The silence hung, tension humming in the air between them like the wings of the birds zipping from flower to flower before them.

Finally Tara sighed. When she spoke, her tone was conciliatory. "The contract between the two companies, our fathers making peace... You did that, didn't you? I don't see either of them backing down."

"Yes, I did."

"How'd you manage it?" She looked straight at him, blue eyes digging in. She really wanted to know.

"To start with, when the lawsuit failed, I convinced Dad to reopen Ryland Engineering. That got him moving forward. I tracked what Wharton was up to through engineers who used to work for us and made sure we moved in a direction that dovetailed with Wharton's ventures. We had parts Wharton needed at the right price, so it all came together."

"It wasn't that simple. Not with our fathers' attitudes."

"They both wanted to make peace. I just gave them a way that made business sense and let them keep their pride."

"You're being modest. I know what you faced. The hardest part of working out conflicts between employee groups is restoring trust. You did an amazing thing." Her gaze held respect.

"It was important to me to repair the rift between them. I knew it would restore my father's faith in himself." It felt good to have his achievement recognized by the one person who truly knew the people involved. He'd love to talk about his next steps—leaving the company, building up the town—but it wasn't worth the risk. Deep wounds stayed tender and he didn't trust her not to jab at him again.

"So that's me," he said. "What about you? How's your business going?"

"Reasonably well for eighteen months on my own. In this economy, corporations see consultants as a luxury, so I have to prove that what I do impacts the bottom line."

"I'm sure you're convincing."

"I have to be. My survival depends on it." He liked the

fire in her eyes, the determination in her voice. He'd bet she was a formidable force on the job.

"This is nice," she said, smiling softly. "Talking to you. I feel almost normal." She inhaled deeply, then blew it out. "I can even breathe again. I suppose that means I should get back inside," she added reluctantly, standing.

He stood with her.

She looked at him, her gaze appreciative. "You always were a good listener. You never tried to fix me. You just let me talk it out."

"You always knew the answer. You needed to convince yourself." They stood too close together, but he didn't want to step away. Not yet.

She smiled and leaned past him for her jacket, brushed against him, her breast against his arm. She wobbled and he caught her. Their eyes met and a current passed between them, making the air seem to crackle. He'd forgotten the power of their physical connection, the way it took down all his walls, pushed past any caution, any sense.

He was so close he could see the flecks of navy blue in the sky-blue of her eyes, the dots of perspiration on her sculpted lips, the way the lace of her bra pushed at the silk of her shirt as her ribs expanded with quick breaths. Her hair trembled against her cheek.

Or maybe he was the one trembling, wanting to kiss her, to see if she tasted the same, felt the same, if she let out the same sighs. His sensible thoughts had zipped away like that nosy hummingbird.

No. Stop this. Like with that hug in the hospital, they were on automatic pilot. This wasn't real. It was a pointless response to their past, some misguided nostalgia.

He didn't want to feel that wild again, that crazy in love. He knew the pain that followed, and he was done with the roller-coaster ride.

The buzz of a cell phone made them both jump. It was like a smoke alarm, alerting them to a fire in the making.

He handed her the jacket—the source of the buzz. She pulled out her phone and looked at the display. "It's Faye's nurse!" She shot him a panicked look, then put the phone to her ear. "Rita? Did something happen?" Her eyes were wild with fear. "Oh…okay…whew."

Relief filled her face. She listened a bit. "Got it," she said with a nod. "Thanks for everything, Rita. I hope we'll see you." She put her phone away.

"What happened?"

"Rita's going back to her regular floor, so she won't be Faye's ICU nurse anymore. She wanted to let me know so I'd stop calling her."

"You call her?"

"I talked her into giving me her number since I'm so far from the hospital." She blew out a breath. "That was scary. I thought Faye might be failing." She locked gazes with him. Sudden tears shivered in her eyes. "If Faye dies…I don't know what I'll do."

He leaned forward to hug her, comfort her, but she held up her hands.

"No. I'm not staining another of your shirts." She managed a smile. "But I will take a curiously strong mint if that's what's making the bulge in your pocket." She grinned. "Your *shirt* pocket."

"You got it," he said, opening the tin so they could both take mints.

She put on her jacket, then rubbed a finger under each eye. "Can you tell I've been crying?"

"Not at all," he lied, because the effect only intensified her beauty, made her eyes shinier, her cheeks pinker, her lips brighter. "You get to be sad, you know, Tara. You don't have to tough it out."

"I have to try, Dylan. You know that."

"I do. I thought it was worth a shot." He watched her gather herself, straighten her spine, shake out her hair and jut her chin, ready for battle. He admired her strength in the face of adversity. She was an amazing person and always had been.

"I don't know how long you'll be in town, but if there's anything I can do…any way to help…" He took out his wallet and handed her a card. "Contact information's on both sides."

She turned over the card, which had his Ryland Engineering numbers on one side, the town manager's on the other. Her brows lifted in surprise.

"Even hicks need business cards."

"Hey, now, I didn't say that."

"But you were thinking it."

She smiled, then got serious. "I may call you. I have some questions about the accident and if I get stalled, you'll probably be able to help. You're town manager, right?"

"Right. What kind of questions?"

"Some details. Why my sister was driving my dad's car, who called the police chief, stuff like that. Some things don't add up."

"I'm here if you need me," he said, wondering if he'd live to regret those words.

He was still wondering that as he headed home. She'd needed him in high school, for sure, just as he'd needed her. They'd been inseparable. She'd brightened his life. He'd steadied hers. In a way, they'd saved each other.

Until he'd disappointed her. He'd had no idea her love for him balanced on a razor's edge. He hadn't wanted to give up college, all their plans, but he'd had no choice. He couldn't let his father sink any lower, but she refused to accept that.

It's only a delay. I'll be there in a year. He's my family. He needs me.

I need you. You're my family.

I can't walk away. He needs help to get back on his feet. I'm the only one he'll listen to. When you love someone, you have to be there for them, even when it's inconvenient.

Then it got ugly. She'd called him a coward, afraid of life, hiding behind his father. And he'd said the worst thing he could have said to her. He'd told her she didn't love anyone, not even herself.

He'd backtracked, explained it wasn't her fault, it was the way she was raised, but the damage had been done. He'd grabbed her by the throat with her deepest fear and that was that.

Eventually he realized she was right to cut him off. If her love for him was so fragile that it couldn't bear a delay, couldn't forgive harsh words said in anger, then it wasn't the kind of love that would last—the kind of love he wanted. Love sacrificed, love forgave, love was sturdy, not brittle, not contingent or conditional. Tara had never felt that kind of love, so how could she give it?

Pulling into his driveway, however, Dylan noticed he was still wound up, playing back the way she'd smelled, the sound of her laugh, the glint in her eyes, her lips. Oh, her lips. His body seemed to have a mind of its own.

He didn't need this in his life. Not ever again.

What he wanted was a solid, resilient, steady love. A love that could last a lifetime. And he would go after that once he finished at Ryland and got things rolling for the town. Seeing Tara was helpful, really. She reminded him of exactly what he *didn't* want.

CHAPTER FIVE

BY THE TIME TARA returned from her hummingbird break, the house had nearly emptied out. She felt guilty for abandoning her host duties, but talking to Dylan had helped. She felt calmer and less exhausted by the hours of accepting condolences, reporting about Faye, smiling the frozen smile that made her cheeks ache. Dylan had rescued her.

He'd always done that for her. Too much, she'd realized later. She'd let herself depend on him, leaning back like a trust exercise, except he'd let her drop to the dirt, rattling her to her core.

It had been a hard lesson, but an important one that had served her well: stand on your own two feet, count on yourself more than anyone else. She'd dated, had boyfriends, but she stayed self-sufficient.

Standing there with him, when he'd caught her arm, she'd been so tempted to kiss him. She'd felt the same rush to be with him, to shut out everything but him, to be safe in his arms, to be home. But that was stupid. He belonged in Wharton and she belonged anywhere but.

She had the uneasy awareness that part of the reason she'd never gotten close to a man was that she'd been waiting for the heart-stopping rush of rightness she'd felt with Dylan.

But that was first-love lunacy, right? And look how that had turned out. That horrible fight, when he'd confirmed her worst fear—that she wasn't capable of love—proved how wrong she'd been to get so close to him. She never wanted to go through that again. Like an addictive drug, the high wasn't worth the hangover.

She noticed her face still felt hot. From Dylan? Maybe the tequila. She wasn't much of a drinker, after all.

She'd been stunned by how much she'd wanted him to kiss her, to kiss him back. Of course, it made sense. She was upset, sad and scared. It would be natural to want to escape, to get caught up in something intensely physical.

She'd done that after the breakup. The first week of college, she'd slept with a guy just to stop missing Dylan, to block the pain for a little while, to have someone's arms around her. It had been a mistake. She'd never felt more empty in her life. Cold to her bones and lonelier than ever.

Sex with Dylan would stay a fantasy. That would be best. She was glad that he seemed happy. He'd made the best of getting stuck here, managed a degree, done remarkable work with his father—and hers. But then, he was brilliant, so he'd do well anywhere. What might he have done if he'd escaped like she had?

Not fair. The Wharton Effect again. Like she'd told him, there were other paths. She'd better get that through her head.

She pushed away thoughts of Dylan and focused on the remaining guests, speaking to each one, noticing again the way conversations broke off when she approached. Were they gossiping about her, her family or Wharton Electronics? Maybe all three.

"Señorita Wharton." She turned to face a short Latina, probably early thirties, who held out her hand. "So sad to lose Señor Wharton."

"Thank you," she said, shaking the woman's warm palm.

"I'm Sonya Manos." The woman searched her face. "Mr. Wharton give me a chance I never have before. On the job, I learn." Her *j* had that soft *y* Spanish lent English. "I supervise now. Nine people."

"That's good to hear."

"Mr. Wharton…he can be *duro*…*hard*. But he see in your heart, what you can do with only a chance." She pressed her palm into her chest. "He save my family."

"I'm sure he felt lucky to have you working for him."

"Always I am grateful," she said, then walked away, leaving Tara choked up all over again. The funeral speeches hadn't all been PR. Her father had done good things. She wished more than ever that she'd cleared the air with him.

On her way to the kitchen to finalize things with the caterer, she ran into Faye's secretary, Carol Conway, filling a trash bag with plates and plastic glasses.

"You don't need to do that, Carol. The caterers will handle it."

"I have to do something," she said, shaking the sack. "I'm so mad."

"What happened?"

"It's the gossip." She leaned in and lowered her voice. "That's a terrible curve. Anyone could have missed it. Faye would never drink and drive. She—"

"Wait. People are saying Faye was drunk?" Tara was stunned.

"It's an ugly rumor. In the first place, she wasn't even drinking her one glass of merlot a night anymore. She'd gone low-carb. And what was she doing at Vito's? Pasta is totally off her diet. Walking by and smelling tomato sauce was too tempting, she told me."

Chills raced along Tara's nerves. Here was another person with doubts about the wreck. "Do you know who started the rumor?"

"No. And when I find out, he's getting a piece of my mind. Or she."

"I'm puzzled that Faye was driving my father's car…" she said, leaving a gap she hoped Carol would fill.

"I know. Especially since they weren't getting along."

"Really?"

Carol's eyes went wide. "You didn't know? I'm sorry. I hope I'm not speaking out of turn."

"You're not. Not at all. Do you know what caused them to disagree?"

"Not exactly. Mr. Banes and Faye were arguing, too. It might have been about the quarterlies. Mr. Banes had asked for an extension."

So Faye had quarreled with her mother, her father *and* her husband in the days before the accident. Did it have to do with the "transition" Faye had mentioned? Was the company in financial trouble and the management team at odds about how to handle it?

Maybe Faye had gone to Vito's to confront her father. Or make peace. Or maybe she was sick of depriving herself and dropped in to carb load. It could be a million things. All Tara knew for sure was that the prickling sensation she'd first felt had become a cold chill.

And what was this about Faye driving drunk? She could not allow that to stand unchallenged. On Monday, she would talk to Chief Fallon, who'd been first on the scene…and whispering in her mother's ear at the funeral.

"I love Faye," Carol said, her voice breaking. "She's the best boss ever. She was training me to become a project manager. She paid for extra computer training. Now…I don't know what will happen to me."

"You'll be needed, Carol. You know that."

She shook her head. "Joseph doesn't like me. He doesn't like that Faye includes me in meetings or lets me handle personnel memos."

"Is that so?"

"They argued about you, too."

"They did?"

"Yes. Faye wanted to hire you and Joseph threw a fit. He said they didn't need a clueless consultant nosing around their business."

"A clueless consultant? Really?"

"He didn't mean it in a personal way. Just consultants in general. He blurts crap like that when he's upset. Plus, you're expensive. Faye defended you. She told him to read your website about your clients and all you've achieved."

Her sister's confidence in her warmed Tara's heart and made her more determined than ever to help out at Wharton. Joseph didn't want anyone *nosing around*. When managers got secretive, that usually meant it was time to shine a klieg light on their doings.

She'd have to approach the situation carefully. Carol could be an ally, especially since Faye had trusted her. "Faye did ask me to help out. She called a few weeks ago. I'd like to do that, but I know Mr. Banes will take some convincing."

"That's for sure."

"What I'd like to do first is look over Faye's files and emails, just to get a sense of what she was working on, but without upsetting Joseph. Is there a time I could do that when he's out of the office?"

"Monday mornings the managers meet upstairs in the conference room. Our floor is quiet with just us worker bees. Joseph will have to run the meetings with Faye gone, so it'll probably go all day."

"Perfect," Tara said, thinking it through. "Joseph offered me a tour. I could check Faye's office, then pop in to meet the managers and ask about the tour. That'll be perfect."

"I'll help however I can. With Mr. Wharton gone and Faye so sick, we're all scared about the future."

"How about before the accident? Were people afraid then?"

"Some were. There was talk about another layoff. It was

kind of upsetting when they fired Mr. Pescatore—he was the factory manager. It was because production got behind, but people said it was because he talked about Wharton closing down or outsourcing the factory to some plant in Kentucky. Some engineers left because of the rumors—took jobs in other states."

"That would be alarming."

"Yeah, plus Mr. Pescatore was so mad he ran a forklift with a palette of batteries right off the loading dock. He wasn't on it and no one got hurt or anything. He kept yelling that he would sue Wharton, that he'd make them regret this. Everyone was pretty flipped out."

"I'll bet."

"Mr. Goodman is calmer. He took Mr. Pescatore's place. Some think he's too calm, that he won't push production. I try not to think about it and just do my job."

So Faye hadn't been kidding about tensions being high. What the company needed now was strong, stable leadership, and a clear communications plan to reassure employees, clarify the company's status and counter false rumors. That would be a daunting job for anyone, let alone a man more comfortable with numbers than people, who was worried about his wife.

Joseph would need help—anyone would—and Tara could provide it. When emotions ran high, a neutral professional could be invaluable when it came to setting priorities and making crucial decisions.

"Will you confirm the meeting for me?" she said to Carol. Monday would be busy, if she intended to meet with the police chief, too, but it was a relief to have more to do than worry and wait at her sister's bedside.

"Absolutely. Faye would be glad you're here."

"I hope so. I hope I can make a difference." As they exchanged numbers, a terrible thought occurred to Tara. What if the car wreck wasn't an accident? What if it was related to the troubles at Wharton?

The livelihoods of a lot of people depended on Wharton's continued success. If her father and sister were seen as failing the company, would someone take action against them? What about Joseph? He'd been acting strangely. Could he have run the car off the road in a rage?

No way. Joseph was not a rash or violent person. What about the man they'd fired? Pescatore. He'd threatened a lawsuit and vandalized company property. He'd wanted them to regret firing him. Would he have forced her father into an accident?

It seemed far-fetched, but she would be careful about sharing her doubts with people. Every person she talked to raised her suspicions. She would find out what happened that night and do what she could to help her family's company. She couldn't imagine a better use for her talent and training.

THE NEXT MORNING, Tara woke exhausted. She'd had a restless night full of worries and plans. She dragged herself out of bed to run, ate the freshly sliced peach and yogurt Judith had set out for her, then took her laptop to the hospital to work on new client proposals between visits with Faye. She missed Rita's warmth, though the other ICU nurses seemed efficient and caring.

Joseph brought her mother in the afternoon for a short stay. The control her mother had marshaled for the funeral seemed to have drained her. She seemed shaky and small, the circles under her eyes darker than ever, her face gray and drawn. Joseph seemed equally exhausted. She knew he faced a huge challenge the next day at Wharton. The meeting would likely involve dividing up Faye's and her father's duties among the managers.

When Tara returned home late that afternoon, Judith was

accepting delivery of a huge basket of food and wine. "From Bill Fallon," she said to Tara, rolling her eyes. "Again."

Tara jolted. Was the police chief hitting on her mother? Had her mother encouraged him? Tara couldn't imagine that. Her parents had never seemed close, but she'd believed them to be faithful to each other. "What's he up to?" Tara asked.

"He's always been a kiss-up," Judith said. Judith didn't seem to be suspicious, which relieved Tara a bit.

Uneasily she realized that her questions might uncover secrets about her family she'd rather not know. That couldn't stop her. She had to know the truth, good or bad.

Early Monday morning at the hospital, Tara found Joseph asleep, slumped against the back of one of the waiting-room chairs, his briefcase on his lap, legs sprawled, wearing one black sock and one blue one. *The poor guy.* Tara tapped his shoulder and held out the to-go cup of coffee she'd grabbed in the cafeteria.

"Wh… What is it?" he said, rubbing his face.

"Drink. You need this more than I do."

"Thanks." He clutched it in both hands and sipped as if his life depended on it. "Did you bring your mother?"

"Judith's driving her later. Mom's car is back, but she doesn't seem steady enough to drive."

Joseph nodded, drinking more coffee.

"How's Faye doing?" she asked, wishing she could ask him about the office quarrels, but knowing it was too soon and too abrupt.

"They're moving her to a regular room." He took another sip. "This coffee's good. You get it downstairs? Was there cream or just powdered crap?"

"Wait! What? She's getting out of the ICU? She's better? Why didn't you call us?"

"She's far from better. This just means she's stable."

"That's big, Joseph. It's great news. We have to tell Mom. It's a first step."

But her enthusiasm had no effect on Joseph who maintained his grim expression. "Don't know when they'll move her. Could be anytime...or hours from now. I've got to take off. Lots going on at work."

"Absolutely." Like the meeting she hoped to drop in on later in the morning.

A half hour later, two orderlies arrived to move Faye. Tara peeled the Sunset Crater photo from the bed tray, and accepted the plastic bag with Faye's personal belongings from one of the techs. She tucked the bag under her arm and walked beside the bed as they rolled it toward the elevator.

On the second floor, they headed down a hall. Tara spotted Rita backing out of a supply closet and stopped to talk to her, watching as the techs entered the last room on the left. "Rita?" she said.

The nurse jumped, dropping two boxes, the beads in her hair clicking wildly. "Damn, girl, you took a year off my life."

Tara bent to pick up the boxes of latex gloves, handing them back. "Sorry, but Faye's moving onto your floor. Last room on the left." She pointed.

"And here I thought I'd ditched you." She grinned. "Don't forget headphones when you bring in that foul music."

"I won't." She realized Rita might be able to help her with a crucial question. "You can look at my sister's chart, right?"

"Why?" Rita's eyes narrowed.

"I need to know if she had alcohol in her bloodstream when they brought her in. Could you check for me?"

"Sorry. Your brother-in-law is the family contact. He would have to ask one of her doctors to do that. Talk to him."

"I can't, Rita. He'll take it wrong. It's a long story, but, trust me, it wouldn't go well." She didn't want to make Joseph more guarded around her. "People are saying she was driving drunk. It's her reputation on the line." She threw in a guess. "Plus, it could mess with our insurance coverage."

"No can do. And don't give me those sad-girl eyes. People lose their jobs for violating patient privacy."

"What about her regular M.D.? Could he see her chart?" Their longtime family physician Dr. McAlister had been at the funeral.

"Depends on what releases got signed, whether or not he's got privileges at this hospital."

"I'll ask him, I guess. They brought my father here, too. He died in the accident. He'd have a chart, right?"

"And his next of kin would be the one to request the information."

"That would be my mom, I guess, but—"

"You know what I'm going to say."

"Patient privacy, right. But if you happen to glance at the chart…"

"The favor shop is closed," Rita said. "Now leave me be." She set off with her armload of boxes.

Tara sighed. Asking her mother did not sound like a promising option. She headed for Faye's room. The orderlies were gone and the room was eerily quiet compared to the ICU, where a nurse was always popping in to change an IV bag, get blood or check vital signs. This room was utterly still. It almost echoed. It was like they'd given up on her.

In a way, they had. Medically, they'd done all they could. *Hurry up and heal, Faye,* Tara silently commanded, looking down at her sister. She seemed to barely raise a bump in the sheets, as if she were wasting away. Tara attached the photo to the new bed tray. Faye's smile in the picture was a heartbreaking contrast with how she looked now. The bruises had begun to fade, but she was so pale, so lifeless.

"What you need is a makeover," she said cheerfully.

"That'll be fun." Tara would bring in makeup, nail polish, a flatiron and comb for Faye's frizzy hair. Faye hated when it got bushy like it was now.

The room could use livening up, too, she thought, looking around. Yeah. She'd make the place so homey that life would be far more welcoming than death. At the very least, it would make Tara feel like she was *doing* something.

Her phone buzzed with a text from Carol. Meeting postponed until Wednesday. Joseph must not have felt ready. That wasn't a good sign for the company, Tara knew, but that cleared Tara's day for a visit to Chief Fallon.

She still held the sack with Faye's belongings, so she carried it to the cupboard. What was inside anyway? Bloody clothes? Probably. She twisted the top of the sack, not wanting to see any of that. Then she noticed it felt boxy at the bottom. And heavy. Faye's purse probably. And it might have her phone. It felt heavy enough to have an iPad. Both might contain clues about that night.

Tara braced herself to look inside. The first thing she saw was a shoe. It had splashes of dried mud…or was that blood? Her stomach lurched and she averted her gaze, checking the contents by feel. She found Faye's purse—leather, messenger-bag style—and pulled it out by its strap. It was merely dusty, thank God.

Inside was the usual purse debris—lipstick, mirror, wallet with cash and credit cards, tissues, gum, pen, keys—and an iPad. No phone.

The iPad would have contacts and a calendar, if Faye was as organized as Tara knew she would be. At the very least, she could get Dr. McAlister's number. Her heart racing, Tara clicked the on button and located Faye's calendar. The only thing written for the day of the accident was a grocery list: *Crowley's—low-carb ketchup, salad stuff, prescriptions.*

What medicine had Faye been on? Tara would pick up

the pills when she got to town. Sure enough, Dr. McAlister's name and number were listed. Tara left a message for the doctor on the machine, which informed her he would return calls at the end of the day.

That was that. Tara shoved the sack into the cupboard and shut the door, unwilling to examine its contents further. She'd felt only one shoe, she realized. Where was the other one? She didn't want to think about that.

"I'll find out what happened," she said, bending down to kiss her sister's cool forehead. "Just wake up, okay?"

She was so preoccupied driving back to Wharton that she missed the business loop exit. As the highway curved and began to climb the mountain, she realized she was about to pass the accident site.

Her stomach bottomed out. She stared straight ahead, trying not to see, but her peripheral vision caught orange warning cones in front of the crushed guardrail and the flutter of a torn strip of yellow caution tape tied around a eucalyptus tree.

Her mind conjured up the accident again, this time with more detail—her sister's shriek as she wrestled with the wheel and slammed the brakes, her father's bellow, the crunch of metal, the snap of breaking branches, smashing glass…the car rolling and rolling, finally stopping with a sickening thud.

Panic surged inside Tara. Her vision grayed and her stomach heaved. Scared she might wreck, she gripped the wheel, slowed down and pulled to the shoulder to compose herself. When she finally felt normal, she looked out the windshield. Across the highway she saw more caution tape tied to a railing. On the highway below were bright black tire marks in parallel snakes. Was this where the accident had begun? This far back from the rail? Had her sister swerved to avoid hitting another car or an animal? There were deer in the hills, coyotes and javelina. It could have been a dog.

She got out of her car and surveyed the distance between the swerve marks and the rail. Not another mark on the highway. Surely slamming on the brakes would have left more rubber. In fact, she realized the car had to have been going pretty fast to hit the barrier hard enough to go over.

This did not make sense. Had the brakes failed? Should she go down the embankment and check the crash site? She didn't have the nerve.

Tara took several slow breaths, forcing her stomach to settle, digging her nails into her palms to distract herself from the woozy sensation. When she felt safe to drive, she went into town.

Her first stop was Crowley's for Faye's pills. She pasted a smile on her face, then marched straight to the back of the store, where the pharmacy was, relieved not to hear her name called by any shoppers, thankful she didn't recognize the pharmacist, either.

"I'm picking up for Faye Wharton. I'm her sister."

The pharmacist's eyebrows lifted, clearly knowing about Faye, but she hesitated for only a moment before she said, "Certainly," and went to get the orders. There were two pills—one for anxiety and one for depression.

Tara carried them out to the car, troubled to learn her sister was so emotionally upset. How long had she been struggling? At least a month, since the orders were refills. Faye had always been even-tempered and optimistic. Happy, as her mother had pointed out. What had shaken her so much she'd sought medical help? The prescribing doctor was Eli Finch, not McAlister, so probably a psychiatrist. Locating the number among Faye's contacts, she called it. Pretending that she wanted to cancel an upcoming appointment for her sister, Tara chatted with the receptionist, learning that Faye had seen Dr. Finch in Tucson five times, starting not long before the call she'd made to Tara. No doubt Faye would have shared a little of her troubles if Tara hadn't been so damned oblivious, busy showing off instead of listening.

Then she had another thought: What if the medication had affected Faye's driving? Made her sleepy or inattentive or slow to respond? That would be horrible. And when Faye woke up and learned her condition had caused the accident, she would be devastated.

Setting aside that worry, Tara drove the few blocks to the town complex and headed inside the seventies-era building. She was still reeling from seeing the accident site, but she was determined to find out what she could from Fallon.

Tara entered the complex. The police department was to the right, the utilities department and post office to the left. Down the center was a wing of glassed-in offices. She was startled to see Dylan through the glass of the second office. He was town manager, so of course that made sense. Just the sight of him cheered her, she found, eased a little of her distress.

As if he felt her eyes on him, he looked up. Tara felt that swirl of excitement and relief…that twist and sink of her stomach that she used to feel when they spotted each other. Had he sensed her presence?

He smiled, then started out of his office, but was intercepted by a woman with a file. Tara nodded and waved her hand, telling him to stick with his work. She would stop by when she'd finished with Fallon.

She headed for the police receptionist, who was flipping through a magazine. *Cosmopolitan,* Tara saw when she got close enough.

"I'd like to talk with Chief Fallon, if I may," she said.

"Do you have an appointment?" The receptionist lifted her eyes reluctantly from *Sixty Tricks to Unman Your Man.*

Really? Was the guy that busy? Tara took a deep breath. She had to be patient. Small towns weren't known for their efficiency.

When the receptionist saw Tara, she grinned. "Tara Wharton! Hi! Robin Walker. Reed's little sister? Remember?"

Oh, yeah. Robin had been a chunky thirteen-year-old with braces and acne, miserable in the way only girls who'd just walked into puberty could be. "Sure."

"You gave me this expensive makeup you said you didn't need and made Reed apologize when he said I looked like a slut wearing it."

"That's right." Tara had emptied out her cosmetics bag for the girl, who had to cope with four older brothers, including Reed, the guy who'd dumped his motorcycle the night Dylan acted as her white knight.

"I still use that brand. It's the best zit cover-up *ever*." She turned her face side to side to demonstrate.

"You look great, Robin." She smiled. "So how about—?"

"Chief Fallon, right. He hates drop-ins. Hates them." She studied Tara. "Tell you what. He's pretending to prepare for a town council meeting, but he's actually playing online poker. If I catch him, he'll get flustered and say yes to whatever I ask."

"I really appreciate your help."

"It's the least I could do. Pay it forward I always say." She jumped up and went to tap on Fallon's door before she entered. When she came out, she gave Tara a thumbs-up. "The chief will see you now," she said in an official tone.

It was ridiculous to have to play games to talk to an officer of the law, but she hadn't really expected better. She was glad to learn she'd helped Robin. Thinking about it, she realized the girl would likely tell her brother that Tara had come in to talk to the police. Word would spread and soon the whole town would know. She hadn't thought about that. She'd always hated living in the fishbowl of Wharton.

Chief Fallon came around his desk and clasped her hand in both of his. "So sorry for your loss," he said, holding her gaze too long, as if to impress her with the enormity of his sympathy. He was a big man with a barrel chest, gray hair in a military cut and a florid face. "How's your mother holding up?"

"She's doing fine," Tara said, knowing that was the image her mother wanted to present, though Tara was worried about how much she'd been sleeping. "I know she appreciates everything you sent her. That was above and beyond the call of duty."

She watched his face. Sure enough, the red in his face deepened to magenta. Something was up with him and her mother. She prayed it was just a harmless flirtation.

"It's the least I could do." He cleared his throat. "Please have a seat." He motioned toward a chair, then sat behind his desk, sizing her up like a suspect.

"So, this has to feel strange, huh? You being in my office and not in trouble." He gave her a self-satisfied smile. "Glad to see you cleaned up your act. Maybe those little talks we had did you some good."

She had the urge to grab the World's Best Cop mug on his desk and chuck it at his head, but she only smiled.

"I know your mother used to worry herself sick over you." How long had he had a thing for her mother? Now that she thought about it, he had always patted her mother's arm and consoled her over Tara's screw-ups. Ick. "So what can I do for you? One of my guys give you a speeding ticket you need fixed?"

"No. No tickets."

"You haven't been in town long, though, have you?" He chuckled.

She supposed she deserved the dig, considering all the mischief she'd gotten into, but did he have to be such a patronizing jerk about it?

"Actually, Chief Fallon, I hoped you'd tell me a little more about what happened that night…about the accident. The sequence of events…how you came to find them—" She stopped before she said *at suspiciously the right moment*. She didn't dare push too hard.

"I know what you're after," he said solemnly, leaning across the desk. For a second, she thought he might help her. Then he rested his elbows on the desk, hands clasped as if in prayer, a gesture that often meant, *I'm holding back what you want because I know best.* "You want peace of mind. But this won't give you that." He smiled a knowing smile. "Go home, comfort your mother, let time do its duty. That's what you need. Believe me. I've seen this many, many times."

Stay calm. Be easy. "I appreciate your concern, but I'm prepared for whatever you can tell me." She hoped she was. She'd been afraid to look down the embankment or peek at her sister's clothes. If the details were gruesome…

She braced herself. *Be strong. This is for Faye and Dad.*

He stared at her, irritated, but trying to hide it.

"If you'd prefer, I could simply read the accident report," she threw in.

"That's not possible." The way his eyes slid side to side suggested he was dodging the truth. "The report's still in process."

"So you're still investigating the accident?" Her heart skipped a beat. Maybe he was handling it, after all.

"You know…cops and paperwork. These things take time. Hunt and peck even on the computer." His smile invited sympathy. "We want to get the *i*'s dotted and the *t*'s all crossed. With everyone so lawsuit-happy these days, we have to be awfully careful, don't we? In the meantime, your insurance agent took my statement, so that's all cleared up. Your law-yer should get you a nice fat settlement, no problems."

She took a deep breath, fighting frustration, and took a new tack. "We owe you our thanks for responding so quickly. If Faye has any hope of recovery, it's because she got im-mediate treatment."

"We all just hope she recovers," he said, trying to sound humble, but clearly proud of himself for his heroic efforts.

She had to step carefully here. "It was lucky you were passing by, since my mother said you usually play poker with my father."

"Wife was under the weather, so I missed the game. I was on my way into town to grab flu medicine and noticed the downed rail." He'd put his hand to his face, scrubbing at his jaw, another sign of discomfort, possibly lying. He'd looked up and to the left, too, which typically meant the person was drawing on the right brain, the creative side, making up a tale. People remembering something looked right and down, engaging the left brain, where memories resided.

"The timing was a miracle," she said, leading him to say more.

"Cop instincts. We're always on duty. When you've been on the job as long as I have, you know what to look for." He shifted in his seat. He seemed wary by nature, so the cues she was picking up could have been simply tension over being put on the spot.

"As I said, we feel so fortunate." She attempted a smile, but felt her lips crack. Her mouth had gone dry as dust, an-ticipating the tougher questions to come. "When I drove by, I noticed the caution tape near some swerving tire marks. I'm no expert, but it looked like the driver tried to avoid something. The odd thing was how far away from the crash site the marks were. Nothing near the rail. The car had to be going fast to knock it down, right?"

He leaned back, as if to escape. "Like you said, you're no expert. We'd need an accident reconstruction engineer to answer that question and those fellows are plenty pricey. Big police departments have them. Insurance companies hire them. Luckily we don't need an expert to tell us they went over the rail and crashed."

"What about the car? I imagine its condition and position would indicate if there'd been a collision, say, with another car or a large animal."

"My concern was only for your injured family, not their car."

"But you took pictures, right? That's required, I believe. And don't you have to sketch out the accident, describe what happened? For example, if the car was struck from behind, you'd need to look for the hit-and-run driver, right?"

He breathed harshly through his nose, clearly riled. "I'm not sure what you're getting at here, but, out of respect to your family, let me lay out the facts. We don't live in *CSI* land. We don't use crash dummies to reenact wrecks. We don't have fancy labs and if we did we wouldn't use them on a cut-and-dried one-car accident on a dangerous curve."

Dammit. He wasn't going to help her. The emotions she'd struggled with over the past two hours balled up in her chest. "Except it's not cut-and-dried, is it? People are saying that Faye was driving drunk."

His hands shot up in twin stop signs. "You don't need to worry about that. I told you we were clear with your insurance company. You'll want to leave that alone for everyone's sake."

What was he saying? "Was my sister drunk? You were there. You checked them." Or had her pills thrown off her reflexes? What could possibly have prevented Faye from slamming on her brakes?

"I look out for your family and I always have," he said in a low voice, sounding eerily like her mother.

"What does that mean?"

"I'm saying leave it alone," he snapped.

"I have a right to know what happened." Her voice broke. Dammit, she would not cry in front of this Daddy-knows-best asshole. "Tell me what you saw, please."

He glared at her for a long moment. "All right. I'll spell it out. Was there a strong smell of whiskey in that car? Yes. Did I say that to the insurance adjuster? No, I did not. Will that appear in my report? No. Maybe it was gasoline fumes. Maybe I was mistaken. I could not say. And I refuse to guess. That's how much respect I have for your family."

"I can't believe Faye would drink and drive. It could have been my father, right? And that's why she was driving. He'd been drinking."

He stared at her again, hatred simmering in his eyes now. When he spoke, his voice held a threat. "You never did know when to quit, did you?" He blew out a breath. "Okay. We're not exactly sure who was driving. Don't make me draw you a picture you won't want to see."

"How could you not know who was behind the wheel?"

He huffed out a breath. "They were together on the ground—one of them thrown from the vehicle, the other walked or crawled over to check."

She swallowed hard, horrified, but fighting not to show it.

"Strange things happen in car accidents, freakish things. Pens sticking out of necks, arms twisted in bad ways, people in the backseat who started out in the front, you don't want to know—"

"So you're saying it might have been my *father* driving? Was *he* drunk? The blood tests would show that, right?"

He gave her a calculating look. "When they set up an IV, EMTs use an anticlotting agent that screws with any alcohol reading. Even if your insurance company lawyers sub-poenaed the lab work, they'd get shit-all, if you'll excuse my language. This is good for you, since that way they can't re-fuse to cover your family's vehicles in the future. It's all been taken care of, *as I've told you more than once*."

"So, what, you lied to the insurance company? You're falsifying your report to protect my father—or my sister—from a drunk-driving charge? Is that what you're implying?"

"I suggest you stop right there."

"I don't think so. Not until I find out the truth. If I have to subpoena the hospital records, I will. I want to see your report, Chief Fallon, false or not. Accident reports are pub-lic record. Certainly I'd like to see the photos of the accident scene and the car, since you don't seem to remember what it looked like. Where is the car, by the way?" Shaking, she pulled out a notepad to write down his answer.

"It's wherever your insurance company had it towed," he said with a smirk.

"You must know where it went."

"No idea whatsoever." He snapped his jaw closed and folded his arms. "Better call your insurance guy. See how far you get with him with this nasty, demanding attitude you've got."

"So you refuse to help me? Even though you have all this *respect* for my family?" Sarcasm was a mistake, but she couldn't stop herself.

When he spoke, his voice was nearly a growl. "You're in grief, I know, and half hysterical, so I'm not going to take offense at your insults to my competence and integrity." Both hands on his desk, he pushed to his feet, leaning for-ward, as if to loom over her. She stood, not stepping back, not intimidated one bit. "I accept your apology," he snapped. "Now please leave."

"My apology?" She'd lost her temper, she knew, but she

refused to be put at the mercy of this self-righteous small-town tyrant. Before she could say more, the door opened. Dylan stepped in. "Everything okay in here?"

"No," Tara said. "Everything's not okay. This man, who is a public servant, refuses to show me the accident report I'm entitled to see as a citizen and a relative of the victims."

"Miss Wharton seems to think there's some conspiracy going on," Fallon said. "She thinks I've got secret evidence I'm keeping from her. Could you tell her there is no mystery here, no TV drama? Could you tell her to go on home and help her poor mother and be done with it?"

Tara was so furious, she was afraid she might slap the guy. This rinky-dink cop wasn't going to keep the truth from her. She would contact the state police or the sheriff's office and ask them to investigate. She would hire an attorney. She would file a suit. Whatever she needed to do she would do. "This is not over, Chief Fallon. Count on it." She turned for the door, shaking with rage, catching Dylan's stunned look as she left.

CHAPTER SIX

UNEASY ABOUT HOW Bill Fallon might respond to Tara's questions, Dylan had headed over to the police chief's office just to take the temperature of the room. He'd arrived in time for the mercury to spike.

"Can you believe that?" Fallon seethed. "She rolls into town and starts throwing her weight around. Typical Wharton."

"I'm sure she's trying to make sense of what happened."

"You don't think I know that, *boss?* You forget I was doing this job when your mom was still cutting your meat for you."

Fallon resented having to answer to a man young enough to be his son. It hadn't helped that Dylan had questioned the padding in Fallon's recent budget request. "I tried to reason with her, but she had a tantrum." He gave Dylan a wily smile. "But then I guess you know all about her tantrums."

Tara was right about one downside to small towns—people knew your history. Normally that didn't faze him, but he'd always been sensitive about Tara, and Bill Fallon could be an ass. Dylan thought the lead officer in the department, Russell Gibbs, would make a great police chief. Bill was close to retirement and talked a lot about moving to Sun City when he did.

"Why not give her the report, Bill?"

"She doesn't want my report. She wants someone to blame. She's asking me what I saw, did I take pictures, was there a hit-and-run."

"A hit-and-run?" Where had that come from?

"What she needs is someone to hand her tissues and say *there, there, you poor, poor thing*. That's not my job. I'm the peacekeeper. I smooth the waters, keep the ship afloat. That's what you pay me for." He tapped his skull. "If people knew half the stuff I keep in here for their own good…"

Dylan fought the urge to roll his eyes. Fallon bent the rules when he saw fit. He'd likely traded a screaming deal on his own pool for tipping off the contractor to the other bids for the town swimming pool. By the same token, he had patrols drive Mrs. Johnson's neighborhood whenever her husband was out of town, ran a Scared Straight program for the high school and coached Little League, all on his own time.

The I'll-scratch-yours-if-you'll-scratch-mine stuff bothered Dylan at times, but it was human nature to want favors. It happened everywhere—big city or small town. That didn't mean he had to engage in it. Once he was working for the town full-time he'd do some housecleaning and make sure everything was aboveboard. People expected no less from him.

"She won't let this go, Bill. I promise you that, and this town can't afford a lawsuit. Figure out what you *can* give her—your notes, photos, the report, something. In the meantime I'll talk to her."

"You do that. Go hold her hand, or whatever else you want to do with her." He smirked.

It took everything in Dylan to keep from cold-cocking the guy, but he knew that would only fuel the man's speculation about Dylan's involvement with Tara. Besides that, no one— least of all Tara—would benefit from a fistfight in town hall.

Still fuming, Dylan left and drove toward the Wharton place. As he rounded the highway curve, he noticed a white sedan parked at a sharp angle on the shoulder, as if the driver had stopped abruptly. He recognized it as Tara's rental car, but she wasn't inside. Where the hell was she?

Then he noticed the orange cones and dangling caution tape. This was the accident site. She must have gone down the embankment. That would be like her. If she couldn't get Fallon to tell her what she wanted to know, she'd find it out herself, by God.

With a sigh, he parked and jogged across the highway to the caved-in guardrail. Looking down the slope, he caught a flash of Tara's red shirt, so he stepped over the barrier and headed after her, passing crushed bushes, broken branches of mesquite and palo verde, and gouged trunks—damage the tow truck had likely contributed to.

"Tara? It's Dylan," he called so he wouldn't startle her. She got up from the boulder she'd been sitting on, and turned to him. She was breathing hard and chewing on her lip, trying not to cry. She looked small, beaten down and sad. Beyond her, a tree had been nearly snapped in half. Had to be where the car ended its fall.

What a terrible thing for her to see.

He started closer, but she stepped back, as if afraid he might hold her and she might lose control. He saw she gripped a cell phone in both hands.

She swallowed hard. "Look at all this." She motioned at the ground, covered with glittering pieces of safety glass, chunks of plastic, twisted strips of metal, broken bulbs, torn padding and wires. "This is all *evidence*. It should have been collected."

"This is a lot to take in, Tara," he started, wanting to get her away from this horror.

She held up one of the phones. "This has to be my father's. It's the old flip style. He held on to things forever. Faye had an iPhone, I think, but I can't find it. This one's mine," she said, lifting the phone in her other hand. "I've been taking pictures with it." She swallowed hard.

"So where is Faye's?"

"I've been looking." She walked forward, staring at the ground.

"Maybe you've seen enough for now," he said, joining her.

She stopped dead and sucked in a breath, staring at the ground, where there was a large rust-colored spot—blood—and a woman's pump on its side. "Faye's other shoe," she said. "And all that blood." She shot him a look of pure horror, then lurched away to throw up in the weeds.

He went to steady her, an arm at her waist, then offered his shirttail to wipe her mouth.

Gasping, she shook her head. "Not another of your shirts."

It gave him a pang that she'd joked as a way to get herself back in control. She went to sit on the boulder. Setting the two phones on the ground, she used the hem of her silk top on her face. He sat beside her, resting his hand lightly on her back.

An old habit. It made him a little sad to remember all the tender touches they'd shared, their bodies in tune, their moods in sync. She leaned into his hand, and he was glad.

"Fallon said they were found together on the ground," she said shakily. "He couldn't tell who was driving. He said he smelled alcohol. I'd bet anything he was the one who started the rumor that Faye was drunk."

"Faye was drunk?" This was the first he'd heard of that.

"Faye's assistant, Carol, said there was a rumor, but it could have been Dad, for all I know. And that was why Faye was driving. I tried to get the nurse to find out from Faye's chart, but no luck." She shook her head. "Fallon's lying, but I don't know how much. He's just a patronizing ass."

"Why would he lie?"

Tara jerked her gaze to him. "Excuse me? Are you siding with him?"

"Hang on," he said softly. "I'm asking a question. That doesn't make me your enemy." She'd always been that way. If you disagreed with her, she assumed you were against her. She had to reject you first. The defense mechanism reminded him of his father and he was pretty tired of handling his father's defensiveness.

She blew out a breath. "Okay. Sorry. Fallon made it sound like he was going to falsify his report to protect my family's name. Would he do that?"

"He considers himself the town's guardian, that's for sure."

"I don't want his protection. I want the truth." She grabbed one of the phones from the ground. "Look at this picture." Clicking a button, she extended the display to him. "It's blurry, but see the swerve marks? They're way back from the crash spot. The brakes must have failed or someone plowed into the car from behind."

That seemed an extreme conclusion to him.

"He won't even say where the car is now so we can check the brakes. He was the first on the scene. What a coincidence. He missed poker that night…supposedly he was going for flu medicine for his sick wife when his cop instincts kicked in and he saw the bent rail. Do you believe that?"

Her eyes were frantic, her words spilling out. "Plus, he's been hitting on my mom, sending her gift baskets. She's *grateful* to him, like he's her hero. It's so creepy. I can't believe she would cheat on my dad. But Fallon's hanging around, whispering in her ear."

She stiffened suddenly, shifted to look at him full-on. "Maybe Fallon hit the car! No wonder he's covering up."

"Hang on, Tara. Let's back up some."

"Back up? You don't believe me?"

"You just accused the chief of police of a hit-and-run or, hell, murder. You don't think that's extreme?"

She opened her mouth to argue, but then she seemed to pull herself together. "You think this sounds crazy, huh? Maybe it does."

He was impressed that she'd backed off, thought it through. That was new.

"I need to tell you everything, I guess." She held out a palm. "Mint, please?"

He pulled out the tin and shook three onto her palm.

"*Three?* I have three-mint breath?" She smiled faintly and sucked on the candies, her lips and tongue moving in a way that distracted him. He looked away.

"So, here's what I know so far…"

She told him about Joseph Banes, his odd reactions to the accident, the arguments the man had had with Faye and Abbott, the dispute between Faye and her father, possible financial troubles at Wharton, the violent actions of the former factory manager, as well as why it had been strange for Faye to be at Vito's and driving her father's car. She finished with a blow-by-blow of her conversation with Fallon, including a quickie lecture on the theory of microexpressions.

"Something's not right," she said finally. "Can you see that?"

"There are odd aspects to this, yes. But just because you don't know the explanation doesn't mean there isn't one. What is it doctors say about diagnosis? *When you hear hoofbeats, think horses, not zebras.* Mostly what you're telling me is that it *feels* wrong to you."

"For your information, I get paid a lot of money for my *feelings*. My instincts are what my clients value most."

"I don't doubt that, Tara. I know you want to make sense of this tragedy, but—"

"You think I'm wrong. You're placating me. Tell me this.

If Bill Fallon is so innocent, why isn't he asking the questions I am? Why isn't he doing his job? That's required, isn't it, even in this corrupt little town?"

The insult irked him. "Bill Fallon is lazy and he's got a big ego, but I doubt calling him incompetent, corrupt and a liar did much to advance your cause."

She winced. "No. That was bad. I lost my temper. But Wharton P.D. is not the only law enforcement agency that can look into this. If he won't do his job, I'll contact the state police or the county sheriff's office."

"And they'll likely defer to Fallon. Law enforcement entities are territorial. They have to coexist with each other."

"So I have to find proof that he bungled the case. That means I need to do some preliminary work myself. Take pictures, gather the broken car parts, find out where the car is, get a mechanic to test the brakes and look over the engine." Her eyes still gleamed with emotion, but her voice steadied as she outlined her plan.

"Tara, I don't know if—"

"I'm not done," she said. "Fallon mentioned accident reconstruction engineers. If I have to, I'll pay for one of them to look at the crash. I'll do whatever it takes to get the truth. You know I mean that."

"I do." Hearing her talk, feeling her pain and frustration, he knew he couldn't let her fight this fight alone. "So, how can I help?"

She stared at him, clearly surprised. "You'll help me?"

"Before you call out the cavalry or spend a fortune on experts, let's see what you and I can find on our own."

"Yeah?"

"I told Bill to cooperate with you. I *am* his boss. He won't bend over backward, but he'll give you something—his notes, his report, answers to your questions. When you locate the car, I can ask my mechanic to examine the engine for you if you'd like."

"Will he know what to look for?"

"He should. Tony Carmichael is the best in town for hybrids and electrics. Auto Angels is his shop. The place just past the skating rink? I think he works on your dad's vehicles, too."

"That'd be great, Dylan. Really." She sighed. "It means a lot to have some help." Relief softened her features and erased some of her despair, and he realized he'd do all he could to help her. Her pain was his pain. Still.

"So will you do me a favor?" Dylan asked. "Next time, bring me in before you start swinging?"

She winced. "I know. I shouldn't have blown up at him. Being back in Wharton is not good for me. I slide back into how I was…my old habits."

"I think I know what you mean," he said, thinking that she'd had something like that effect on him.

"You're doing it, too? Sliding back?"

He nodded.

"Yeah. We do go back, don't we?" She smiled, a flicker of the heat from that moment on the terrace. "We have history."

Again he had the urge to put his arms around her, pull her close, breathe her in and go from there. But that wouldn't help either of them. "*Ancient* history," he said. The best they could manage would be to be friends. He and Candee had managed that, after all.

"Yeah," she said, but he thought she looked sad about that.

"You have all you need here?"

"For now. I'll come back with a camera and a tape measure to record the distance from the swerve and how far the car traveled."

"How about I do that?" He wanted to save her another

visit to this terrible place. "I'll get Bill to send someone out to collect the broken car parts that seem relevant, as well."

"That would be great," Tara said. "Ask to see the photos he took. They'd be better because they'd be before the tow truck tore up the scene."

"I'll ask." Did Dylan think anything would come of this? Probably not, but Tara had a point about small-town short-cuts. Fallon had clearly been lax. He doubted there were photos. One of Fallon's budget requests had been for a new camera.

He followed her up the slope to the highway and they stood together, catching their breath from the climb.

"Can I buy you lunch?" she said. "We could go to Ruby's." They'd spent a lot of time at the bar and grill when they were in high school.

"I can't today. Town council meets over lunch."

"Oh. Sure." She looked so disappointed, he had to offer an alternative.

"How about you come to my place tomorrow night for supper? Say seven? I've got a recipe for beer-butt chicken I want to try."

"Beer...*butt?* Sounds gross." She scrunched her nose, but he could tell the invitation had pleased her.

"It's not. You prop a chicken over an open can of beer on the grill. Comes out savory and moist, I promise." Candee had served it to him and given him the recipe the last time they'd *slipped.*

"Sounds fun. I'd love to come," she said, her smile wide and open. "Thanks again." She lurched forward, as if to hug him, then thought better of it and gave him an awkward wave before turning to her car.

They seemed to have agreed to leave the past in the past. That was good. Mature. Sensible. Still, watching her walk to her car, he realized he looked forward to having her in his house, just the two of them, at night.

What the hell was he up to?

Maybe he hadn't grown up much, after all.

CHAPTER SEVEN

TARA DROVE HOME, shaken by what she'd seen at the crash site—the smashed and torn trees, the scattered car parts, the dried pool of blood, her poor sister's shoe. Her throat still burned from bile, despite the soothing mints Dylan had given her. Her head throbbed and her eyes stung.

Think about Dylan.

Dylan was on her side. Thank God. The idea sent relief pouring through her like massage oil over sore muscles. There would be dinner tomorrow night, too. The thought gave her a little thrill.

What are you doing? Teasing yourself? Teasing him?

There was no point resurrecting the past, and they both knew it. She associated Dylan with suffocating in Wharton. She'd done all she could to escape. She wasn't about to be dragged back. Dylan was helping her with the investigation. As a friend. Period.

Something he said stuck with her: *Asking a question doesn't make me your enemy.* Was he right? Did she expect him to oppose her?

Probably. He was part of the town, after all. He'd chosen to *manage* it, for God's sake. He loved the place she hated. Wharton *was* her enemy. All her training in accepting many viewpoints and interpretations didn't seem to be able to overcome her feelings about this place and her past here.

At home, she climbed into a scalding bath in the whirlpool tub and thought about the case. Being in Wharton had dampened her instincts, but Dylan was wrong about the zebras. People were lying, hiding things and evading her questions. What she needed was solid evidence. Prickling neck hairs wouldn't convince Dylan *or* the authorities.

Her only hope of success would be to treat the investigation like a job. She would gather data, ask questions and listen carefully to the answers, then analyze the results for clusters, divergence, patterns and repetitions. She would be neutral and professional.

She would do the same with Dylan. She sighed, ducking under the water, letting the bubbles roar in her ears.

The sexual attraction was a problem. But she was mature enough to handle that. There was that pesky feeling of being safe and cared about and understood.

You're lonely. That's all.

Busy with her career, Tara had set aside her social life. She'd handle that when she got back to Phoenix. Lonely people took rash actions, like jumping into bed with a memory.

Now she knew. Now she would be prepared. Whew.

She made a mental list of what she had to do: locate the Tesla, check her father's phone for messages or calls that night, figure out a way to talk to his poker buddies, go to Vito's to see if anyone saw or spoke with Faye that night.

When she pushed to the surface, her phone was buzzing. She got out of the tub, grabbed a towel and picked up the phone from the hamper lid. "Hello?"

"Harold McAlister, Tara. I'm so sorry for your loss."

"Thank you, Dr. McAlister. I appreciate that. You've taken care of all of us over the years." Even her father, now that she thought about it.

He assured her that Faye was getting the best of care and that her neurologist was top-notch. Tara thanked him, then eased into her real questions. "Faye was taking medicine for anxiety and depression." She named the pills. "Could they have had any effect on her driving?"

The doctor was silent for a few seconds. "I'm not the prescribing physician, Tara. I couldn't—"

"Hypothetically. How about that?"

More silence. "If used as prescribed, they shouldn't interfere with normal activities, but there could be other factors—"

"Like if she'd been drinking?" Tara threw in. "You're not supposed to mix those meds with alcohol, I know. It's important to be sure she hadn't been drinking that night. Don't you agree?"

The doctor didn't speak, so she rushed on. "You could look at her hospital chart, right, and check that?"

When he finally spoke, the words seemed to be dragged from him. "Even if I could arrange to see her records, I couldn't discuss it with you because of—"

"Patient privacy laws. I know. But there are rumors that she was drunk, Dr. McAlister. I can't let that stand."

He blew out a breath. "I can't help you. I'm sorry. The law is quite strict. However, a family as prominent as yours surely has endured gossip over the years. You know your sister. She is a smart, responsible woman. Trust what you know about her and ignore the rest. That's my advice."

Her heart sank. He'd say the same thing about her father's chart, she knew, so she thanked him and hung up, no better off than before.

Tara dressed and made a few client calls. She'd asked her old boss to be her backup with current clients while she was in Wharton, so that would relieve some of the pressure, though she would have to scramble to make up for lost income when she returned. That was a worry for down the line.

Next, she needed to call the insurance agent. Her mother was napping so she couldn't ask her for the name and number. Tara decided to look through her father's files, since he handled all the bills anyway. Plus, his phone cord would likely be in his study.

Stepping into her father's sanctuary, Tara caught her breath at the familiar scent—her father's pungent aftershave and the hot-metal smell of the factory floor. It was like he'd just left the room.

She braced against the stomach punch of sadness, closing her eyes until it passed. When she opened them, she saw first the floor-to-ceiling shelves full of her father's books on history, philosophy, science and technology.

She pictured the shelves in the sleek new condo she'd purchased five months ago. Her books were the one personal element. She had tons of nonfiction like her father, though she preferred biography, sociology and psychology to his hard science choices. Also, she liked fiction—especially stories of transformation and redemption.

Behind her father's massive antique desk was an impressive shelf of ships in bottles. Faye had helped him build them, Tara remembered. As a little girl, Tara had memories of playing on the floor with LEGO while her father and Faye worked with tweezers and string and glue, talking softly, heads close.

Feeling left out, Tara had once tried to help, but she'd messed up the sails using too much glue and her father had snapped at her, sending her to her room.

Faye came later to console her. She promised their father would forgive Tara, though it would take time. *When you love someone you forgive them,* she'd said, as if it were as automatic as breathing. It was to Faye. Whatever capacity Tara did have for love had come from her sister.

Her father's study was a man's room, for sure, painted hunter green, dark wood everywhere, a wet bar, guns in a display case.

She went to sit in the leather chair, which squeaked in

complaint. Like the desk, and the Tiffany lamp she clicked on, it had been passed down from his grandfather, who'd had it shipped from Ohio when he'd founded Wharton Electronics in 1950.

The new Mac computer looked incongruous, surrounded by so many antiques. Her grandfather's fountain pen lay beside the sleek mouse.

On the wall to her left was a sepia-toned photo of the Wharton foundry in Ohio, the source of the family's wealth. Beside it was a large oil portrait of three generations of Wharton men. Where were the women? In the background, of course, managing the households, hosting gatherings, leading charity drives, all in service to the powerful men they'd married.

Her mother had a college degree, though she'd never used it in the workplace. She'd met Abbott at the college bar where she worked to support herself at the state college. She'd come from a working-class family of seven children, which seemed to shame her, since she rarely spoke of them and never visited.

Tara couldn't imagine living in a man's shadow like her mother did, glorying in the role. Had her parents ever been in love? Maybe in the early years. Tara hoped so. A loveless marriage seemed so bleak. Would Tara ever marry? It seemed impossible at times. Marriage required faith and trust. The whole idea of love made her uneasy. She didn't understand it. She might not be capable of it. That thought made her ache, like ice on a sensitive tooth.

There were two books on the desk—probably the last two books he'd read. *The Selfish Gene,* by Richard Dawkins, and a more scientific-looking book about genetics. Shifting them to one side, she noticed a photo under the glass that protected the desk's surface. It was her favorite picture of her father. He and Sean Ryland grinned at each other over the Wharton assembly line, where they held up the jet engine part they'd built together. They looked so young, so excited, like the future before them would be forever bright.

It hadn't turned out that way for Dylan's father when his business failed. Had her father exploited him, paid too little for his company? She didn't want to believe that. He'd bailed out a friend, risked money that could have gone down the drain. Besides, the feud was over, thanks to Dylan. No matter what Dylan might have done in the larger world, that was a remarkable feat. He'd healed a decade-long wound between two old friends. And he'd managed it before her father was killed.

Tara reached for the file drawer, where she expected to find insurance papers, then saw deep gouges around the lock. The drawer had been pried open. She pulled it open quickly. It was empty inside save for some loose paper clips, a restaurant receipt, a blank message slip and a business card for Randall Scott, ESQ. Where were the files? Had her mother taken them out? Why? Very odd.

Stymied, she checked the drawers for a Rolodex or datebook that might have the insurance agency information. She found nothing but unopened office supplies. She turned on the computer, but it was password protected.

Beneath the desk, she saw a phone charger plugged into a power strip. At least there was that. She attached the cord to her father's flip phone and activated it.

On the screen was a text message from Faye the day of the accident.

Nothing changes. Let it go.

Tara's heart raced. Here was a clue. What had her father been doing that Faye wanted him to stop? Or had she been discouraged that he'd failed to make a change? She had no idea. Her father had not replied to the text. She checked his voice mail. There were no messages, new or old.

She *really* needed to check Faye's phone. Where was it? In her office? She'd look when she went to Wharton on Wednesday. It might have fallen out in the car during the crash. When they located the car, she'd check.

First, she find the number of the insurance adjuster. She'd have to ask her mother when she woke up. Rachel had been sleeping a lot—drugging herself to escape her grief and worry about Faye. Tara would try to talk to her mother more, share the sadness somehow. That had to help, didn't it?

"You into his liquor again?" Judith leaned against the doorjamb, her arms folded, a half smile on her face. "Stay away from the guns this time."

Tara winced. Judith was referring to a party Tara had held when her parents were out of town. She'd been fourteen. Her friends had wasted two bottles of pricey brandy, ignorantly mixing it with Hawaiian Punch. The worst thing was that a guy had opened the gun cabinet and taken out her great-grandfather's custom-made shotgun—her father's prized possession, which he never used. *The parts are irreplaceable,* he'd told her once, when she asked why he never took it skeet shooting.

The guy hadn't put it back and her father, upon returning, had found the gun lying around. He'd gone white with rage. She'd been scared he would hit her. She'd always been a little afraid of the man.

"No guns, I swear," she said now. "And I haven't touched the Pinch." Judith leaned against the doorjamb. She rarely stood still long enough for a conversation. "If you want a drink, I'll fix it for you."

"No, thanks. What are you doing in here anyway?"

"Looking for the insurance agent's number, but the files are missing. Looks like the drawer's been pried open. You know how that happened?"

"Don't look at me. I only dust and vacuum. This was

your father's kingdom. He might have mislaid the key and cracked it open himself. He was not patient with household objects. He snapped off the nozzle on the first espresso machine your mother bought."

"It's odd the files are gone."

"He probably took them to the office. He never really worked here. Whenever I looked in, he was reading."

Tara supposed that was possible, considering the unopened office supplies.

"Your mother asked Joseph to make all those calls—to the lawyer about the will and the insurance people. She was too shook up herself."

Interesting. "Was Joseph in here? Would he have taken the files?"

"Don't know. He came and got some clothes. It's possible."

She would ask him for the agent's number and mention the files—see how he reacted. Maybe this was why he'd acted so fidgety. He'd nosed through the files. Why would he take them? To hide something he thought was there?

Judith started to leave.

"How do you think Mom is holding up?" Tara asked.

"She's doing her best."

"She seems so brittle."

"It takes a lot out of her to put on a face for you."

"Why would she do that?"

"She thinks she has to be strong for you."

"She doesn't. I'll talk to her."

"Don't you dare say a word. Leave her her pride. She'd have my head if she knew I said anything."

"I want to help. What can I do?"

"Then lend a hand on this big charity dinner she's trying to set up. It's a lot of work and she's trying to do it all. Doesn't want her friends to think she's suffering."

"I'll do that. Great. Thanks for the tip."

"I think she dreads Thursday at the lawyer's."

"Going over the will? Is she worried about money?"

"It's not that. Your father's a good provider. It'll be real then. That he's gone forever. That's what I think anyway."

"You're a good friend to her," Tara said, risking Judith's displeasure over her mushy remark.

"When you run a person's house, you have to be civil." She sniffed.

"You mean a lot to my mother, Judith," she said. "And I'm grateful to you for that. And for all you do for us."

Judith had bought fruit and yogurt for Tara's breakfast, even though she'd claimed that no decent person would call that a meal. She'd made Tara's bed when she forgot. She'd even bought the jasmine incense Tara used to burn as a teenager to hide the smell of cigarettes.

"That's just sickening," Judith said. "You act like I've dying or about to quit. I'm not, so stop."

"Sorry. Can't help myself."

"You never could. And it got you in a lot of hot water." She sighed. "I remember."

Judith considered her for a moment. "For all the misery you caused, I have to say I wish my girl had some of your gumption."

"Ruthie?" Tara hadn't known Judith's daughter, since she was closer to Faye's age than Tara's.

"Yeah. She's a great cook. She's over at Ruby's. Some friends asked her to go in on a food truck in Tucson. She's got no money to invest. Her share would be as cook. She turned them down. Afraid to leave home."

"I'm sorry to hear that."

"I pushed her, but she won't listen. I'm just a mom. What do I know?"

"It's hard to see someone waste their talent. I know that."

In Wharton, it happened all the time. People shrank to fit the smallness of the place.

"When you go to Ruby's, order her goat and nopalitos empanadas. You'll see God."

"Definitely. Thanks. I won't be here for supper, by the way." She was headed to Vito's to ask about her sister.

"You sure? It's fried chicken livers and twice-baked potatoes."

Her stomach churned at the prospect. "Thanks anyway."

"More for me," she said with a sniff, then seemed to think better of her tone. "I'll save you a plate."

An hour later, after she'd talked to the manager, bartender and two waitresses at Vito's, Tara looked over the menu, still nowhere. No one had noticed Faye, so she must have met her father in the parking lot or slipped upstairs unnoticed.

When the birthday song rang out from a nearby table, she looked over. There were balloons floating above a girl's chair, a pile of gift bags beside her.

Tara smiled, remembering a birthday party she'd had here when she was young. You got a free entrée and dessert on your birthday.

When the song ended, a man stood. She recognized him as Jim Crowley, who owned the grocery store and was one of her father's poker buddies.

He headed for the restrooms. Here was her chance to talk to him. She made her way to the hallway and pretended to talk on her cell phone until he stepped out. "Mr. Crowley?" she said breathlessly.

"Tara." He went instantly on alert. "How are you?"

"I'm fine." She shifted so she subtly blocked his path. "I was just wondering, since you were at the poker game with my father, was he acting, I don't know, unusual in any way?"

"It was a regular poker night. That's all I can tell you."

He looked past her into the dining room, clearly wanting to leave.

"Was he drinking? Did he seem upset?"

"Your father was himself. The game was the game. I'm sorry for your loss." His mouth was a tight line, closed against her. Why was he so guarded? "I'm here for my niece's birthday, so if you'll excuse me."

Then it dawned on her. "Bill Fallon called you, didn't he?"

He paused, considered that, then leveled his gaze at her. "Bill Fallon does a good job for the citizens of this town. He doesn't owe you one more word. Your father would not want you upsetting your mother with wild accusations." Anger flared in his eyes. "But then I guess other people's feelings don't mean much to you, do they?" He meant the grocery store protest she'd organized over unfair wages and hours. She'd been inspired by a unit on labor unions in her history class and organized a march with picket signs.

"Now, if you'll excuse me. *I* have a family I care about."

That stung. "I care about my family. I care that lies are being told about them. My father was your friend."

"Yes, he was. And he would not want this. For once in your life, respect his wishes." He walked past her.

She stood there, her cheeks hot, stinging as if he'd slapped her. *This town. These people*. So smug, so judgmental, so closed off, so infuriating.

She walked back to her table, aware that eyes followed her. When she glanced at Crowley's table, Mrs. Crowley was glaring at her.

Perfect. Yeah, she'd interrupted a birthday celebration, which was impolite, perhaps, but there was no reason to be hateful.

For once in your life, respect his wishes. Did that mean her father had complained about her to his friends? The idea made her cheeks flame.

So blowing up at Bill Fallon had gotten her shut out of the entire poker group. He'd likely called all the guys to warn them she was on the warpath. Hell, the whole town would likely close rank on her. What if word got back to her mother?

It made her feel ill. *Small towns. Small minds.*

Except she should have known better. She should have controlled herself in the first place.

Talk to me before you come out swinging. She'd promised Dylan she would. Instead she'd confronted Jim Crowley at a birthday party.

She was dying to leave. Her appetite had fled, but she refused to give the gawkers the satisfaction of seeing her run. When the waiter arrived, she calmly ordered a glass of merlot and pasta marinara, her head high, her face serene.

Jim Crowley was wrong about one thing. Her father would want the truth. And she was going to get it. As long as she had Dylan on her side. She had to make sure he stayed there.

CHAPTER EIGHT

THE NEXT NIGHT, Tara parked in front of Dylan's adobe-style ranch house situated on a huge expanse of manicured cactus and desert plants, and climbed the steps to his porch. Tile mosaics of hummingbirds decorated the twin posts at the top. Was it just coincidence or had he had the mosaics made in honor of the hours they'd spent on Tara's terrace?

Surely he wasn't that sentimental.

If he was, it was sweet. Or sad.

Maybe both, which was how she felt about their past.

She shifted the tequila bottle to the other hand, since her palm was so sweaty. She'd taken forever to decide what to wear. Since when had she dithered about clothes? She'd tried a silk top with spaghetti straps and a white denim skirt, but decided the shirt was too clingy, the skirt too short. She didn't want Dylan to think she was trying to look sexy.

She'd settled on purple silk slacks and a modest white linen blouse—business casual after she'd removed the gold hoop earrings, throwing on an amethyst pendant that didn't look datelike.

Sheesh. Get a grip. It's a chicken dinner, for God's sake. A chicken with beer up its butt, no less. To talk about the investigation.

She'd gathered all the clues to share with him, including the conversation she'd had with Joseph that morning at the hospital when she'd asked for the insurance agent's number, so she had a serious reason to get together with Dylan. Right?

Ignoring the pounding of her heart and the squeak of the tequila bottle against her clammy hands, she rang the bell.

In a few seconds, Dylan opened the door. The sight of his face lifted her heart. His eyes held hers, sexual interest flaring, warming her everywhere, despite her determination to keep the meeting focused on business.

"Come in please."

She stepped into the entry area, taking in his home—roomy, friendly, neat and full of personal touches. Nails clicked on the sand-colored tile floor and she looked down the hall to see a dog lumbering toward her.

"Oh, my God, is that…Duster?"

"It is."

Tara had adored the golden retriever. She thought they'd had a special rapport. "He has to be so old now…"

"Fourteen. Yeah."

"Damn." Tara dropped to eye level with the dog. He'd put on weight, his muzzle was gray and his eyes cloudy, but it was unmistakably Duster. He rose on his back legs, put his front paws on her shoulder and dipped his nose to touch one of her cheeks, then the other, as she'd taught him. "He remembered *European greeting*." She swallowed the lump in her throat.

"He's deaf and almost blind, but he'd never forget you," Dylan said softly, his expression full of tenderness.

"Good dog, Duster," she said, scrubbing his ears the way he used to like, giving herself time to recover, breathing in the familiar doggy smell, while his tail thumped heavily against the floor.

She got to her feet. Being here with Dylan and his dog stirred up old feelings, like dust, making it hard to breathe or even see. It was ridiculous. They'd been teenagers, for God's sake. You didn't find your soul mate at seventeen, though she'd been *so sure* at the time. She'd been so sure about everything back then.

"I'm afraid to ask what you're thinking," Dylan said.

"You should be. The upshot is I thought I was smarter at seventeen than I think I am now."

"Ah, but now you're wiser. Wise beats smart every time."

"I hope you're right." She didn't feel very wise at the moment. She felt happy to be near him. She'd been back in Wharton for a week and, if anything, her reactions to him had grown stronger.

"You look sexy as hell. Damn." He ran his gaze down her figure, making her feel nearly naked, business casual be damned. His compliments had always been sincere, never knee-jerk. He'd made her feel so attractive.

"You, too." He wore dark jeans and a black-and-gray silk bowling shirt, and looked meltingly hot. This wasn't a date, but she felt the same thrill—the delicious chance to be alone with him, anticipating brushes and touches and intense looks and maybe more. She held out the bottle of tequila. "For old times' sake."

He laughed. "Actually, I bought Mountain Dew and Grey Goose."

"God. Dew-V-Dews! I forgot about them."

"Remember Halloween when we had the water balloon fight on Hangman's Hill?"

"Yeah. I wanted to sneak up on the couples hooking up in cars and you wouldn't let me."

"We would have scared the crap out of them. It was Halloween. They'd think they were being attacked by real zombies."

"I know. That was the point at the time. It was mean of me." She'd been too angry at everyone. Dylan's love had softened her. She'd be forever grateful for that.

"So what's your pleasure?" he asked.

You. Being here with you. "Let's do the Dew-Vs."

"You got it. Make yourself at home." He left for the kitchen. Tara put the tequila bottle on the table and looked around. The great room was done in contemporary Southwest style, one wall painted coffee-brown, another mustard-yellow. The art on the wall included two stylized desert landscapes in vivid earth tones and a large whimsical abstract painting.

Dylan returned with ice-filled crystal tumblers, the yellow drink glowing golden in the warmly lit room. They took sips, watching each other, the ice tinkling merrily. She couldn't stop grinning. The vodka warmed her stomach, Dylan's gaze the rest of her.

"Your home is lovely," she finally said, turning to survey the room again. Are those paintings originals?"

"Yes. Done by local artists."

"Supporting the community, huh? Being town manager and all?"

"Wherever I can, sure." He glanced at her, hesitated, then spoke. "Actually I have my eye on a state grant to establish a co-op gallery, complete with studios. We've got quite a few talented artists in town."

"You're taking the job seriously, that's obvious," she said. "So did you decorate the house or did, uh, your ex-wife?" She felt a nasty twinge. *Jealousy*, of all things.

She'd felt it back then, too, and it had been horrible. Secretly she'd hoped he would come to NAU sophomore year as he'd promised. Instead he'd gotten *engaged*. Within a year he'd replaced her with someone he wanted to spend his *life* with, not just college.

"Me. I bought this place three years ago. Candee and I divorced way back. Eight years." He glanced away.

"Sore subject?" She shouldn't be prying, but she couldn't stop herself.

"Not really. We managed to stay friends."

"Looked that way at the funeral." In fact, she thought she'd caught a flash of longing in Candee's eyes when they'd mouthed their goodbyes. "Friends with benefits?" she teased. *What is wrong with you?*

Dylan colored.

"Look how red you are. You *do* sleep with her." She did *not* want to know that. Thinking of him making love to Candee, looking at her the way he'd looked at Tara, as if she were the most important thing in his life.

"Not in a while. It's not a good idea." He shook his head, clearly embarrassed.

"Maybe not." Why not? Did one of them want to get back together? Probably Candee. None of her business. If she asked more questions she'd sound as gossipy as the worst Whartonite.

"Anyway, what about you?" he asked, clearly wanting to change the subject. "I would have heard if you'd gotten married. Did you ever come close?"

"Not yet, no. Building a business is tough on the social life. I travel a lot, so there's that…" That sounded lame. "I've dated, had boyfriends. Nothing too heavy. When the time is right…" *And when would that be?*

"That makes sense." He looked down at his feet. Did he feel sorry for her? God, no. "I bought a condo," she blurted, as if that were a substitute for true love and marriage.

"Yeah?"

"In Scottsdale. Great view. It's the top floor."

"A penthouse…wow."

"It was a killer deal from a client. I put in an extra month after they ran through their budget for my services. We were so close to this amazing employee-management agreement that I had to see it through. They were selling the condo they used for visiting execs, so they gave it to me for a great price."

"Very cool."

"Yeah. That project was the cover story of my professional association's magazine, and got included in a feature in *Business Week* on innovative management. The publicity brought me customers."

"Plus, you got a penthouse out of it. What's it like?"

"It's a showplace really. High ceilings, huge windows, warm wood floors, tons of built-ins, a chef-worthy kitchen."

"You cook?"

She laughed. "I should learn, huh? I haven't really settled in, I guess." She paused, thinking that through. "It's funny, but I've been there five months and I still feel like I'm in a pricey hotel, not my home, you know?"

"It's probably all the travel." He honed in on her, waiting for her to say more, letting her sort her thoughts.

"Maybe." The truth was that no place she'd lived had ever felt like home. She used to blame it on the fact she'd always rented and never for long. "Now, here, your place, this feels like home. It feels…cared for, personal."

"I like it. I don't spend much time here, though. Juggling the two jobs has me keeping crazy hours."

"I'll bet."

He looked at her for a few seconds, as if he wanted to say something, but wasn't sure he should.

"What?" she said. "Tell me what you're holding back."

"It's just that I plan to change that. The juggling."

"Yeah?"

"Once the Wharton batteries hit the market and the demand increases, we'll be in great shape. My plan is to quit the company and work for the town full-time."

"Full-time? Wow. Can they pay you?"

"Not at first, no. But I plan to write development grants

to increase our infrastructure. I want to bring in new businesses, more housing and tourism for the river area. It has
untapped potential. It'll take time and work, but I've got
good people on the council and serving on commissions. A
lot can be done and I plan to do it."

New energy had come into his face, and his gestures were
big; his whole body seemed lighter.

"I'm impressed. You really want this." He looked the way
he used to when he talked about college. It made her chest
tight to think that he'd waited ten years to do what he really
wanted with his life.

"I do. I figure within a year, I'll be safe to leave Ryland
Engineering."

"How will your dad handle that?"

He shot her a look. "He'll be fine. The company will be
on solid ground. Victor Lansing, our factory manager, will
take over for me. I've been briefing him.

"And your dad knows?"

"Of course," he said, frowning, irritated, she could tell,
that she kept bringing up his father, who she could imagine
would be damned hard to convince of anything he didn't
want. "I've let a few key people know. The guy I want as my
deputy director. Troy Waller. He's vice mayor now. A couple
of town council people."

"Sounds like you're prepared. You were into student government, I remember. You headed the social service club.
You've always been a leader."

"It's what I want to do. It's important. I like working for
people. I'm good at solving problems, working out com-
promises. I'd like to see Wharton be more than it is." He
looked almost boyish with pride. Her heart squeezed with
tenderness.

"They're lucky to have you, Dylan." She fought the feeling that he was wasting himself, that he could do so much more in a city, hell, in state government, maybe Congress.

"Who knows? In a few years, this place might be big and sophisticated enough you might actually like it."

"Yeah, right." She assumed he was joking. Then she caught the light in his smoky eyes, the quirk of his lips. *He wanted her here.* In Wharton. It was sweet, actually. Impossible, but sweet. "Anyway, I hope it all works out the way you want it to."

"Thanks. I appreciate your good wishes, Tara. It means a lot."

She felt a rush of affection for him and lurched forward to hug him. It wasn't easy with the drink in one hand. She lifted her face to give him a quick kiss on the cheek before she backed away. Totally friendly and supportive. But his fingers pressed into her back, his chest against her breasts. He took a ragged breath. Her own pulse pounded in her ears. She backed away, unsteady on her feet. Her pulse pounded in her head. It felt so good to be in his arms, to touch him.

The glass in her hand sloshed some of her drink onto the tile. "Whoops. Sorry."

"It's fine," he said, looking at her, his eyes a little hazy.

She couldn't keep staring at him, so she jerked her gaze to the left and noticed a sculpture on a stand beside the slate fireplace. "Wait…is that what I think it is?" She walked closer.

"The battle bot, yeah," he said, clearly relieved by the shift in focus. "I had it repaired and painted afterward."

"How cool." It had been the night of Reed and the motorcycle, the night Dylan and Tara first got together. Dylan had staged a battle with a science club friend as part of the kegger in the desert. "I won fifty dollars that night," she said. They'd all placed bets, turning it into a drinking game, which was how Reed got plastered.

"You never said you bet on me."

"All the girls did. You were hot for a geek. Why would I give you the satisfaction of telling you? I was pissed. You had to jump in like Captain America and save the girl. Reed wasn't that drunk."

"He dropped his bike."

"If I'd been on it he'd have driven more slowly. You embarrassed the hell out of me." Her friends had stared wide-eyed when she let Dylan drive her home. Nobody told Tara Wharton what to do.

"Why did you go with me?"

"I'm still not sure." But it had been the way he looked at her, like he was concerned and he didn't care who knew, that he'd do anything to keep her from getting hurt, even risk her rage. No one had looked at her like that before—or since, for that matter. She'd never let anyone that close.

"The whole way home you yelled at me, said I was a macho asshole, a self-righteous jerk, a—"

"Stop!" She cringed. "I was awful to you. Why did you ask me out?"

"I knew you were showing off for your friends. We used to play Parcheesi when our parents had card parties, remember?"

"I do. And I used to cheat."

"I remember."

"I couldn't stand to lose. What a brat I was."

"I didn't care. You made me laugh. You viewed the world so quirky. It was like you tickled my brain."

"I tickled your *brain*. I think there were more parts involved than that."

"That goes without saying."

Zing. It hit again. That low, swooping charge through her body, zooming to the spot between her legs. When her knees gave way, she said, "Let's sit down." She barely made it to the overstuffed brown leather sofa. Dylan sat close to her, his knees turned toward hers, eyes on her face. They both set their drinks on the table.

"So that was why? You asked me out because I tickled your brain?"

"Also I'm a masochist."

She gave him a playful slap, though she knew she hadn't been easy to be with, restless, always pushing for more, testing his love, his patience. She'd been a pure mess.

"The truth is I asked you out because Reed Walker was an ass," he said in a low, serious voice. "He didn't get you. You were wasting your spark on him."

"Oh." She felt hot all over. "What a nice thing to say."

"It's true."

"You were good to me, Dylan. I know I was…intense."

"We were good to each other." He paused. "When my parents were ripping into each other every night, you made me feel better."

"You steadied me." He still did. Since she'd returned, he'd had that effect on her. He'd cheered her, comforted her, made her feel like she belonged…at least for now and at least with him.

"We really had something," he said.

"It was something, all right."

"I keep thinking about us." He smiled wistfully.

"Me, too. The good parts anyway."

"The sex?" He grinned that wicked grin she'd always loved.

"Oh, yeah. The sex was great." Why admit it? What was she doing?

"Yeah, it was." His words sent a charge zooming along her nerves, lighting everything up like a pinball machine.

Tara could smell him. His cologne, laundry soap and that sweet tease that was just his skin. Sometimes, just smelling him would make her feel so light-headed she thought she might faint.

She remembered being in his arms, swept away by a passion so hot that nothing else in the world mattered. That had been mind-blowing. How had she forgotten passion?

Duster gave out a groan, as if he felt the tension between them. He lay below them like he used to when they would make out in Dylan's living room. Their knees touched, pressed together. Dylan's arm was across the back of the sofa, his fingers just brushing her shoulder, feeling natural. All she had to do was turn toward him, lean in and they would slide right into it.

It? What is it? Kissing? First base? All the way? Stop acting like you're seventeen.

"But you can't go home again," she said, scooting a few inches away.

"Nope," he said, leaning into the corner of the couch. "Nothing stays the same, even when you stay."

They both looked away at the same time, then back, smiling sheepishly at each other, as if they'd gotten caught with their hands in the cookie jar.

"And now I have my own company and you saved your father's," she said on a big breath in a bright voice. "Does he realize what you did for him, what you sacrificed?" She sounded harsher than she intended, still reacting to the earlier temptation. It was true, though. Dylan's father had taken advantage of his son's loyalty.

Anger flared in Dylan's eyes, which surprised her. She'd clearly hit a sore spot. "Staying was my decision, not my father's, and I have no regrets."

That hurt a little. Her teenage self lurked inside, she guessed. She had needed more than anything to be first in his heart. It had killed her to learn she wasn't. He'd chosen his father over her. "Really?" she said. "No regrets about giving up NAU? Astronomy? You missed out on all that. It seems sad to me."

"People change. They grow up. You did." There was an edge to his voice. "You work for big business now. What happened to the pyramid of exploitation, the evils of corporate greed, all your ideals?"

"Wow," she said, falling back against the sofa. "You jabbed back. I'm impressed. You always used to fold when we argued."

"You were a bad loser. It was rarely worth the fight. I figured you could take it now." His eyes twinkled with mischief, the friction gone.

She laughed. It just burst out of her. "You called me a sell-out, a sore loser and a baby and I'm laughing. Only you could pull that off." She shook her head.

"I did regret hurting you, Tara," he said, touching her knee. "I regretted that a lot. I still do." He looked closely at her, telling her he meant it. His words helped, but didn't touch the deeper ache—that he thought she was incapable of love.

"I hurt you, too," she said.

"You did that." Pain flickered in his eyes, remembering.

"I'm sorry, Dylan."

"Me, too." They held each other's gaze letting the feeling settle and fade.

"That was then and this is now, and we're friends, right?" she said brightly, determined to get past this. "Like you and Candee?"

"Like me and Candee."

"But without the benefits." She winked and tapped his glass with hers, proud of her jaunty tone, though she felt heavy inside, weighted down, as if she were saying goodbye to something she didn't want to lose.

"I need to check the chicken," Dylan said, pushing to his feet.

She followed him through the kitchen—cranberry-red with dark granite countertops, fancy pots and pans hanging over an island—and out to the patio, where a table was set with colorful pottery plates and cloth napkins rolled around flatware.

Dylan opened the grill to baste an upright chicken, its skin just browning. The aroma was mesquite smoke and dark beer. "Mmm, smells like Ruby's minus the cigarette smoke," she said.

He laughed. "Ruby's doesn't smell like cigarettes anymore. No smoking in restaurants, remember?"

"Right. Probably ruins the food."

"You'll see. I'll take you there—" He stopped abruptly, probably realizing he'd sounded like they were a couple, making dinner plans. "Anyway, looks like another fifteen minutes. The rest is ready inside."

He sat at the table. She sat across from him. "You must be a great cook. You've got all that gourmet cookware."

He laughed. "I got talked into buying all that. Long story."

"Judging from your face, it was a woman, right?"

"Yeah. Candee. She does these home sales parties—candles, jewelry, handbags. She'd been hounding me to come to one and I figured cookware was about as masculine as they were going to get."

"How sweet. You help out your ex-wife." Candee was lucky to have such a generous and kind guy in her life. Tara envied her.

"There were no benefits involved, okay?" he said firmly.

"I didn't say anything."

"But you were thinking it. I know you."

"You do. You do know me." Better than anyone ever had. It had been ten years. The thought made her stomach drop. She finished her drink in one swallow. Dylan did the same.

Beyond his pool on a concrete rise, she noticed a telescope on a stand. "You still do astronomy?"

"Yep. That's computer guided. You can really see a lot."

"I took an astronomy class, you know," she said. "Freshman year."

"You're kidding."

"After all you raved about Lowell Observatory, I had to. I mean, I hated the snow, so I had to get something out of being there."

"Sorry about that." He winced. NAU had been his choice, not hers.

"It's fine. I got what I wanted. I escaped Wharton and didn't let my parents buy my way into an Ivy League school." She shrugged, remembering that time. "I was lost at first. I knew who I *didn't* want to be—Abbott and Rachel Wharton's screwed-up daughter—not who I *wanted* to be."

"We all have to figure that out, whether or not we have a town named after us."

"True." There was more she wanted to say, more questions she wanted to ask, and she could feel that Dylan felt the same, but she knew they were tender around each other and always would be. They'd crossed lines not meant to be crossed, gotten too close, hurt each other too deeply. You truly couldn't go home again.

"How'd you end up in the business you're in?" he asked, clearly changing the subject.

"I took a sociology class, and there was an expert on corporate culture. He walked us through a few of his case studies and it just set me on fire."

"Yeah?" He leaned in, eyes focused on her face, eager to hear whatever she had to say. He'd always been a good listener.

"What we do is fix employee-manager dynamics in the workplace. Managers become more humane. Employees feel empowered. People over profits, you know? See? I still have my ideals."

"I never doubted that."

"It's about relationships. Building trust. Open and honest communication. Shared values."

"Sounds like marriage counseling."

"It's like that. Companies are families, really. There are issues, conflicts, personality clashes. Our job is to develop better ways to be together." She hadn't needed a shrink to tell her that her own terrible family played no small part in her passion for her field. "I talked the guy into an internship, ended up working for him until I opened my own company a year and a half ago."

"I'm glad you're happy."

"I feel the same about you." They were wrapping it all up and tying it with a bow. They'd been in love, they'd broken up, they'd made happy lives for themselves, so long forever. Something in her resisted that. She didn't want to slap on a friendship bracelet and call it a day, dammit. There was more here. Lots more.

Tara took in the gorgeous sunset, the orange light making the telescope glow. "I used to love sitting out in the chill, taking turns looking into the eyepiece."

"Tonight's a good night for stargazing," he said. "If you'd like that." His tone said they were talking about more than a telescope. Tonight was a good night for stargazing and getting naked and tangling in the sheets, and not leaving the bed for hours, days, weeks....

"I would like that." She felt herself being pulled into this moment, like the tug of stars on their planets, steady and sure. Irresistible. She saw that same tug in Dylan's smoky gray eyes.

They were daring each other to go for it, to kiss, to make love. She tingled with the thrill of it, the burn and ache of it. It was like the time they'd challenged each other to jump from higher and higher ledges into the river. They got to the highest spot, dripping, breathing hard, looked down, then at each other and burst out laughing, chickening out at the same time.

"I'll make more drinks," she said, jumping up, her heart racing, her cheeks on fire. Despite their earnest, wish-you-well speeches, she wanted something to happen. She thought he did, too. Her hands shook as she dropped in ice, added a splash of vodka and poured in Mountain Dew.

At the last minute, she dumped in more vodka. *What the hell, let's try the high jump.*

"To us," Tara said, lifting her glass.

"To us," Dylan repeated. The fading sun turned the drinks into liquid gold in their hands, some magic elixir that would put a spell on them both. Tara's eyes held that familiar mischievous light that made him want to skip the drinks, the food, the talk and just haul her into his arms.

Despite what they'd said about not going home again, here she was, and he felt it all again, just as big, just as all-consuming.

It didn't help that she looked so good. She'd become softer and tougher at the same time. Sexier, too, because she was more certain of her appeal, more secure in herself, more sure of what she wanted.

And what did she want right now? Sex?

Damn, he hoped so.

He took a gulp of the drink and had to cough. "This is straight vodka."

"Pretty close," she said, coughing, too. "How 'bout we get hammered. For old times' sake. Escape all this." She made a circular motion over her head.

That would work. Vodka would fuzz their brains and

drown whatever inhibitions remained. It would distract Tara from her troubles and him from his mixed feelings about helping her out.

Go for broke. That was Tara for sure. She took things too far, ready to ride the raft straight over the falls, heedless of the danger. His job had been to stab the oar down to bedrock, anchor them in place before they tumbled to their deaths below.

Yeah, they could get drunk and have sex. It would feel good in a blurry way. But they would be sorry later. He didn't want to see regret in Tara's eyes or feel it in his heart, or hear them mumble that they'd been too wasted, that they barely remembered what happened.

He didn't want that. He doubted she did, either. He knew what she did want—to find out all she could about the car accident—and he had information she would appreciate.

"I talked to Fallon," he said, putting down his glass.

"You did?" She set hers down, too, and honed in on him, the dare forgotten, as he'd hoped. "What did he say?"

"He'll write you a report, but it won't give you more than he already told you. If any pictures got taken they've been deleted from what he claims is a, quote, lame-ass camera with next-to-no memory, unquote. The insurance adjuster took the photos he needed and that was all that mattered, according to him. I asked him to send out a detective to photograph the scene and bag the debris."

"Will he do it?"

"Oh, yeah. If he wants those two new cruisers."

"You blackmailed him for me?" She grinned.

"Negotiated, I believe, is the proper term."

"Negotiated, then. You did that for me?"

"I did." He cleared his throat. "The irritating thing is that he thinks I'm doing this to get back together with you."

"What an ass."

"You don't know the half of it." What he'd said was *get in her pants,* though the look on Dylan's face had scared the guy enough that he'd mumbled an apology and promised to get a detective out there.

"Thanks for doing that, Dylan."

"I said I would help, didn't I?"

"I know, but…" But he'd let her down before and she wasn't convinced he truly had her back. That was Tara.

"Anyway, thanks. It's more than I would ever get from him. In fact, I kind of blew it again." She winced.

"What happened?"

"I went to Vito's to see if any of the waitstaff saw Faye that night, and ran into Jim Crowley, who was there for his niece's birthday dinner."

"Not the best setting for an interrogation."

"I didn't grill him. I was polite. But he gave me this speech about what a good man Bill Fallon was and that my father wouldn't want me upsetting my mother by asking questions."

"Interesting."

"Interesting? Don't you get it? Fallon got to him. He probably called all the poker guys and told them I'm on a rampage and not to tell me anything. Crowley still hates me over the grocery store protest."

"I forgot about that. It was about unfair wages, right?"

"Yeah. He was making part-time workers work full-time and not paying them or giving them benefits."

"It made the paper, I remember."

"After I broke Fallon's headlight to get him to arrest me. It was worth it. Those people got paid so little they qualified for food stamps. They had to leave their kids alone late at night to work double shifts. And Crowley cleaned up his act, too, so he wouldn't get busted for breaking labor laws."

"Mission accomplished."

"Exactly. Anyway, now that I blew it with the poker guys,

I need you to talk to them—find out what really went on with my father that night. Can you ask Crowley? Or one of the other guys?" She listed the names.

"What reason would I have?"

"Curiosity? Checking out what Fallon said? Because you're the town manager. They'll tell you. You're one of them."

He bristled at the built-in insult she'd delivered. "The *poker guys* and I are all individuals with separate motivations, beliefs and attitudes, Tara. We're not all part of some small-town hive mind."

"I get it, okay? Don't be so sensitive."

"If it makes sense to talk to one of them, I will."

"Good," she said, as if he'd agreed to do it. "We should talk over the rest of the case."

"It's a case now?"

"What would you call it? I put all the clues on a spreadsheet on my iPad so you won't think I'm a paranoid nut job."

"No. I'll think you're an organized paranoid nut job."

She went to give him a playful slap, but bumped her drink. Trying to catch it, Dylan splashed Tara's shirt.

She gasped from the jolt of cold.

"Sorry," he said. He grabbed a cloth napkin, sending flatware rattling to the table, and brushed at her chest, aware of her body beneath his fingers, the softness of her breasts. She closed her eyes, caught by the contact.

They were on dangerous ground, so he stopped. "I hope that won't leave a stain."

"No big deal. This makes us even. One ruined shirt apiece."

"You're too much," he said. He couldn't take his eyes off her. The minute he decided sex was a bad idea it was all he could think about. He was about to take her hand and pull her toward him when mesquite smoke billowed out in a cloud, accompanied by a roaring sizzle.

"Time to eat," he said on a sigh, saved by the grill.

He cut up the chicken, brought out the rolls, a pasta salad and some marinated peppers, and they dug in.

"Mmm," Tara said, swallowing a bite. "Heaven. Moist. Savory. Beerlike. Perfect." She did everything with such relish. When she licked her fingers he had to look away and think about baseball. "Where'd you get the recipe?"

"Uh, Candee. She made it for me once." He felt himself blush, remembering the circumstances.

"I thought you said the cookware didn't include benefits."

"Just forget it, okay?"

"You two," she said, shaking her head in amusement.

When they finished eating, she wiped her hands on the napkin. "I'll go get my iPad so we can go over the clues."

She started to rise, but he caught her hand. "Wait."

Tara sat, looking at his hand on hers, then at his face, her eyes gleaming, pupils large. "Yes?" she asked breathlessly. She couldn't possibly think he was going to yank her into his arms and kiss her, could she? Though the idea sounded damn good to him.

But he'd had a point to make. What was it? Oh. "How about you just talk me through it?" He released her hand.

"Sure," she said, taking a sharp breath. "Yeah. Okay. Let's see. Where to start?" She tapped her lip. "How about this? Someone broke into my dad's desk and stole all his files. I think it might be Joseph."

"Why?"

"I had to ask him for the car insurance agent's number and he got defensive about it. He warned me not to do anything that might delay the settlement our attorney will be working out with the insurance company. Bodily injury, lost earnings, pain and suffering. It'll be millions. He got this gleam in his eye about the money. That made me wonder more about the finances at Wharton."

"What does that have to do with him stealing the files?" Her thought process seemed convoluted to him.

"He's been handling things for Mom—insurance, our estate attorney, even the clothes for the funeral—so maybe he was afraid something incriminating was in the files."

"You didn't accuse him of any of that, did you?"

"No. I'm not an idiot. Well, despite picking a fight with Fallon and harassing Jim Crowley at a birthday party." She smiled ruefully. "I simply asked if he'd seen them and he got excessively defensive."

"You're not thinking Joseph had something to do with the accident, are you?" That would be way over the top.

"No. But something's up with him, for sure. I'll see what I can find out when I'm at Wharton."

"What are you going to do at Wharton?"

"Investigate a little, but mostly help out." She pushed her plate forward and back, frowning, thinking hard, abruptly upset. She lifted her gaze to his. "Faye wanted to hire me. She called a few weeks ago and said she'd like my perspective on the transition Wharton's going through."

"Yeah?"

"Yeah." She steadied her gaze on him, regret clouding the clear blue of her eyes. "But I didn't take her seriously. I joked about Joseph being too cheap to pay my fees. I totally blew it. I should have dropped everything and come out. Maybe if I had…"

"What? You think you could have prevented the accident?"

Tara shrugged. "Faye started seeing a shrink around the time she called me. She was taking pills for depression and anxiety. She was worried, Dylan. Really worried. But I didn't pick up on that. I let her down."

He stayed quiet, knowing there was more she had to get out.

"Faye was always there for me. Always." She swallowed. "And what did I do? I harassed her for trying to please our father instead of going to art school. I told her marrying Joseph was a mistake. Who does that to someone they love?" She looked so anguished he had to intervene.

"Someone with strong opinions and big feelings."

"You mean a spoiled brat? Don't you dare pity me. You're supposed to give me hell." She gave a twisted smile. "I can't stop thinking that the last talk I had with Faye was her begging for my help and me blowing her off. Why didn't I *listen?* That's one of my strengths with clients. Faye is the dearest person in my life and I barely paid attention."

"She wouldn't see it that way."

"That's because she's too kind." Tara grimaced, then grabbed her neck, so he knew her muscles had gone tight.

"You're knotting up." He moved his chair beside her and motioned for her to turn so he could rub her shoulders. He gripped the muscles at the base of her neck. They twisted like snarled rope under his fingers.

"You haven't lost your touch," she breathed, relaxing under his hands.

He focused on easing the knots, not how right it felt to be touching her again, how much he wished he weren't so damn adult, that he would just give up and go to bed with her. His gaze landed on the sweating drinks, both nearly full. Maybe Tara was right. Maybe vodka wasn't such a bad idea after all.

CHAPTER NINE

THIS FEELS SO GOOD. Tara all but melted under Dylan's skilled hands. She'd forgotten how good he was at this. Revealing her guilt over Faye, then this amazing massage, was making her distress slip away.

Such a relief. Her stomach let go of its clinch, her shoulders loosened, her headache faded. She noticed how silky and cool the night air felt on her skin. The lights tucked into the landscaping began to wink and glow, turning his yard into a wonderland.

This was way better than getting drunk. *Good call, Dylan.* He'd always been sensible.

She found herself doing what she used to do when he rubbed her shoulders. She turned into his arms for more comfort, rested her cheek against his collarbone, felt the steady bump of his heartbeat, breathed in the sweet, sweet smell of his skin. Mmm.

Dylan's breathing hitched in surprise at her move, then he shifted his upper body so their curves fit just right. His massage slowed, as if he, too, were remembering this experience.

The best massages were in bed in his room, when they lay skin to skin, free to take the touching further. She would feel relaxed and aroused at the same time, anticipating the moment when Dylan's hands would slide from her back to her butt and pull her tight against him, and they'd be lost in each other's bodies for hours.

It was happening again, she noticed—the neural pathways lighting up as if they'd never gone dark. It would be so natural to go to bed together, so easy. Why was it a bad idea again?

Dylan froze, as if he'd had the same thought, and answered her question by patting her back. "Hope that helps." He pushed his chair back hard, the scrape loud against the tile.

"It did," she said, turning to look at him, to see if it had been tough to stop. Embers glowed beneath the smoky color of his eyes and he was breathing hard. Good. She wasn't alone in the struggle.

If he could resist, so could she. She was bigger than her urges, bigger than her past. She had to focus on *now*. Now, they were friends. They were investigating the accident together. The past was the past. They'd even apologized to each other. Done and done.

Sex would only complicate things.

Right. Good. Check.

There was another reason…simmering below the surface.

What if the sex was amazing? What if it felt too good? What if it made her want more?

That would be bad. Wanting more meant wanting Dylan and Dylan was all about Wharton, now and forever. His dream was to fix the town the way he'd fixed his father's company. He belonged in Wharton. He fit here.

She didn't. She'd worked too hard to break free of the town and who she'd been here. If she stayed, she'd lose all the gains she'd fought for—her independence, her confidence, her pride. She'd fall back into her old ways, turn into the same lost, sad failure she'd been.

The problem that was eating at her now, the reason she was so tempted was that she was *lonely*. She had to correct that—make friends she trusted enough to confide in. Get a boyfriend for the physical part. Talking about it with Dylan she realized she was not only a guest in her condo, she was a guest in her life.

So that was the lesson of seeing Dylan again.

"I missed you," he said. "A lot."

Zing. His words flipped a switch inside, lighting her up all over again, reversing every sensible thought she'd just had. "I missed you, too. I was miserable that first year. It was all I could do to make it to class. I had had all these plans for us, how we'd study together, go on hikes, learn to snowboard and, hell, look at stars. I felt like I'd lost a limb."

Dylan looked surprised. "I had no idea. You cut me off cold. I figured that was that for you."

"I cut you off because it hurt too much to hope." Her entire body felt electrified by the words they were sharing. Truths she'd never spoken aloud, not even to Faye. "Even then, I hoped you'd come sophomore year like you said. Instead you got *married.*"

He stared at her for a long moment. "Yeah. I did. And it was a mistake. And, the truth is, seeing you again, I realize Candee was right. I wasn't over you."

"That's what happened?" she asked, shocked, but also reassured that she hadn't been alone in her own misery.

"I thought I was over you. I wanted to be and I fought like hell to prove it to her, but once she got that idea in her head, she wouldn't let go." His eyes burned at her, his voice rough.

"I'm sorry, Dylan."

"Me, too. More than I can say. I hurt Candee. I should have figured it out. I should have known." He looked so troubled she wanted to cup his cheek, but she held back.

"Maybe if we'd talked back then…"

He shook his head. "Wouldn't have worked. We needed perspective. We needed for what happened not to matter so much. We needed to be friends."

He was right, though she got that panicked feeling again.

She wanted to say. *Wait. Don't write us off. Maybe we're not done.*

Of course they were done. Weren't they?

"It's imprinting. That's the trouble."

"Excuse me?"

"Like with ducklings. They imprint on whatever creature they see when they hatch. A dog, a person, a goat. We were each other's first love. We got imprinted."

"Okay…"

"Plus we were young…*drenched* in hormones."

"Oh, yeah."

"Tingly and shaky and floating on air," she continued. "It felt like we'd invented sex." Even as she was explaining it away, the feeling grew, fueled by the familiar look in Dylan's eyes—the way he drank her in, every nuance—deciding the right moment to take her, kiss her, make her his own.

They were breathing slowly and noisily now, like the air scraped their lungs on the way out.

"Yeah. All that." Dylan's hands slid toward her across the table, moved in. Was he going to kiss her? Did she want that?

With every beat of her unchanged heart.

What if they *had* stayed together? What if they *were* soul mates? What kind of life might they have built together?

That poem about the two roads in a yellow wood and the one not taken came into her head, and she heard herself say, "Do you ever wonder what might have happened with us?"

"All the time," he said hoarsely.

And that was that. Like someone had shot a starting gun, they lunged for each other and kissed. Dylan's lips tasted smoky from the chicken, sweet from the drink, and like Dylan, the way he used to taste. He rose and so did she. Their chairs hit the tile with twin bangs and they slammed their bodies together, arms wrapped tight.

The kiss seemed to touch off a bonfire that roared through

her. Everything faded except Dylan's mouth, his arms, his chest pressed against hers, his hips, too, his erection insistent against her belly. She ached for more.

She never wanted to stop. She didn't dare stop. Reality would land like an avalanche, dousing the fire, making them see how foolish they were acting.

But what if it was great? What if it was healing?

Dylan broke off the kiss, leaving Tara rocking forward. "This is not a good idea. It's late. We've been drinking." Neither of them had touched the second high-test drinks she'd made. Dylan had spilled half of hers on her blouse.

"Right. Good." Better to stop now, before it got heavy. Before they went too far and there would be consequences. And there *would be* consequences. Good or bad, she didn't care to risk it, no matter what her body screamed.

She looked around, saw the dishes and picked up a plate. "I'll clean up," she forced out.

Dylan took the plate from her. "I've got it. You should go. Get some rest."

She nodded. They practically ran inside, as if they both feared if she stayed one more second they'd tear off each other's clothes in some wrongheaded grab for the best of their past.

She snatched her purse from the floor and patted Duster, who whined piteously for her to stay. Backing toward the door, she said, "The dinner was great. Beer-butt chicken… who knew?" she babbled.

Dylan gripped the edge of the door, as if to keep himself from going after her as she backed onto the terrace. "Glad you liked it." His eyes glowed, the pupils huge.

"When the insurance adjuster calls me back about where the Tesla is, we can get your mechanic out there."

"Sounds good."

"As soon as I hear, I'll call."

"Do that," he said hoarsely. "Night." He shut the door.

She stood there, staring at the door, her heart pounding. What the hell was wrong with her?

She turned, grateful for the cool October breeze on her overheated face. She looked up at the sky, the stars white pinpricks in black velvet. They'd forgotten to look at the stars.

The door flew open. "The telescope," Dylan blurted. "Venus will be bright tonight and the moon is so…" They both looked up. The moon was a huge orange ball overhead. "Big and…"

"Beautiful," she finished. She saw the same yearning in his face that she knew was plastered over hers.

She did not need this. She had a plan for her life and it did not include this man or the town that had claimed him forever. She wouldn't waste time wanting what could never be.

Even if they wanted to try, it wouldn't work. They were too different. They'd hurt each other too deeply. She would never come first with him. And he would never rest easy with her. That was that.

"We don't need a telescope to see that, do we?" she said softly.

"Guess not." He was disappointed, but also relieved, she could tell. He knew it would be a mistake, too. That made her more certain than ever.

Until she sat in her car and noticed she could smell Dylan on her skin, that heady and arousing scent that made her crave him more than ever.

It took every ounce of willpower she had to drive away.

DYLAN STARED AT the door he'd just shut against the sight of Tara beneath a golden moon. *Venus will be bright*. What an idiot.

Duster whined, his eyes full of accusation.

"How do you think *I* feel?" he said. He'd wanted her with

everything in him. Kissing her had been heaven…her sweet lips soft and giving and knowing. The electricity had been the same, the rush of heat and need.

And that was bad. He didn't want that in his life. Couldn't cope with it. Wanting her would take over his life. And he knew Tara could turn on him in a heartbeat. Even knowing she'd suffered without him, missed him, didn't change the deeper truth—she disapproved of him, his choices, his life. Sooner or later, it would come up again. She would leave him in the emotional dust. He did not want to yearn again for an impossible love.

Love didn't have to be crazy and all-consuming. In fact, it couldn't be if you wanted it to last a lifetime.

He was still reeling from realizing that Candee had been right—he *had* kept Tara in his heart, burning candles to her memory, like a fool.

Candee had paid the price for his refusal to see the truth. He'd fought for their marriage. He'd watched his parents tear theirs up like so much paper. But he'd sabotaged his without knowing. He'd been in total denial.

He was ashamed, angry at himself.

He realized he could go right back to how he'd been with Tara.

For all they'd matured, too much remained the same. Tara was still mercurial and complicated. He still felt the need to protect her, to rescue her, whether she needed it or not.

That's what helping her "investigate her case" was all about, for God's sake. He was done managing people. He'd managed his father for ten years. It was enough. The complications with the Wharton contract were giving him fits, delaying his release from the company and his father.

Dylan had no time to relive old loves. That imprint thing made sense. He needed to get past that, and quick, if he ever expected to make a life with a woman—a solid, steady life, not the crazy, white-water raft trip he'd have with Tara. And he intended to do that. It was all part of his plan.

He carried the dishes in from the patio, pausing to stare at the sky. It *was* a good night for stargazing. He remembered trading places at the eyepiece—fingers tangling, faces inches apart, her hair falling against his face, the smell of her...

Not worth it. Not even close.

He cleaned up and headed to bed. Duster leaped up like a dog half his age. "She made you feel young again, didn't she?" he said. She'd done the same to him and that wasn't good for either of them. Like the huge orange moon overhead, he didn't need a telescope to see that.

"IT'S A HOSPITAL ROOM, not a beauty parlor," Judith groused, bracing the vase of flowers against the canvas bag on the passenger-seat floor. Tara had filled the bag with cosmetics, nail polish, hair gear and a portable iPod player.

"It can't hurt and it could help wake her up."

"I think you're crazy, but it'll probably cheer up your mother. She likes things to look good. I'll bring her out when she wakes up."

"Good."

"Take it easy on the face goop. Faye wasn't much for makeup."

"I promise." She drove off, pleased when she glanced in the rearview mirror and saw Judith give a small wave.

Once in Faye's room, Tara brightened the lights, set the flowers on the counter near the mirror and got the nineties playlist she'd put together going on the iPod with speakers.

Happy with how much more cheerful the room felt, she leaned in to kiss Faye's forehead. "I'm thinking Stormy Skies eye shadow to go with your eyes. You agree?" She studied her sister's face. "Blink once for no."

Tara held her breath, hoping against hope for any sign of

life. Nothing. "Stormy Skies it is." Tara sighed. "Are you slipping away or fighting your way back, Faye?" she whispered.

Forcing herself to cheer up, she put the Sunset Crater photo into the silver frame, set it where Faye could see it, then misted Faye's sheets and pillow with the peppermint and citrus spray the store clerk said would be energizing. After that, she plugged in the flatiron and set out the cosmetics and nail polish on Faye's tray. "Makeover time," she said, and got to work, singing along with MC Hammer's "U Can't Touch This." Rita was right. Some of that nineties music was pretty bad.

When she finished with Faye's face, Tara studied the effect. "Much better. You can't even see the shadow of the bruises." It was Wednesday, nine days since the accident, eight days since Tara had arrived, and the bruises had faded substantially.

Next she worked on Faye's hair. "You won't believe what happened last night," she said, deciding to think out loud with her sister. "I had dinner at Dylan's and we almost went to bed together." She paused mid brushstroke to see if Faye had responded to that.

Nothing.

"I know. Bad idea. In the end, I was the one who stopped us. I knew it would be pointless...probably sad, really." *If it wasn't life changing.* She straightened a strand of Faye's hair. "I need to start dating. I've been lonely, but I didn't notice. That should fix it."

She finished Faye's hair, admiring the smoothness, the slight under-curl she'd achieved. "Perfect." She stared at her sister's closed eyes. She seemed so far away. "Come on, Faye," she said. "Wake up. Live. You've got music and flowers and people who love you." Her gaze snagged on the Sunset Crater picture. "Look at how happy you were, how in love. I'm sorry I didn't see that at the time."

Her sister didn't respond.

"But you weren't happy before the wreck, were you? You were worried. What was wrong? The questions are piling up and you're the only one who can answer them."

Fighting frustration, she placed Faye's hand on the tray and shook the nail polish. "Neon orange," she said. "Not your style, but it's lively, right? And you need lively stuff." She'd chosen candy-apple red lipstick for the same reason. She opened the polish, loaded the brush and reached down for Faye's hand. Faye's index finger *twitched*.

Tara gasped, dripping polish on Faye's knuckle. Her heart leaped. "Faye? Did you do that on purpose? Do it again." She stared at Faye's hand. *There*. Another twitch. Wait. Maybe not. Maybe Tara had imagined that.

Someone entered the room. "We can hear that nasty music all the way from—"

"Rita! Her finger twitched! She's waking up."

Rita moved swiftly to Faye's bedside. She hesitated, probably at the change in Faye's appearance, then picked up Faye's hand. Tara clicked off the music. "You coming back, sugar?" Rita asked softly. "Can you squeeze my hand for me?"

Nothing. Rita took her flashlight out and tested Faye's pupils. No change.

Rita did the rest of the tests, then sighed. "Sorry, hon. Transient spasms. It happens."

"So it's nothing?" Tara's heart sank. "It doesn't mean she's improving?"

Rita sat on the chair next to Tara, her eyes full of sympathy. "It's nice, you fixing her face and hair. I'm gonna need sunglasses to tolerate that nail polish, though."

Tara couldn't even manage a smile.

"How you doing?" Rita asked.

"Okay, I guess."

"It's hard, this limbo you're in. You gotta prepare yourself either way."

"I wish I'd been there for her more…before."

"We're all just human beings doing what we can."

"She was on antidepressants, Rita, and something for anxiety. I had no idea how bad off she was. I'm scared that if she was drinking that night, the alcohol mixed with the pills might have caused her to lose control of the car."

Rita blew out a breath and gave Tara an irritated look. "I don't know what it is about you that does this to me."

"What do you mean?"

Rita pushed to her feet. "I checked the labs, okay? Your sister had no alcohol in her system when she was admitted. And don't say one more word about it."

Faye hadn't been drunk. Thank God. Tara's heart lifted as she took the deepest breath she'd taken since she arrived. Her whole body felt lighter. She wanted to burst out laughing. She wanted to dance to MC Hammer.

"You have no idea what a relief that is." She jumped up and kissed Rita right on the mouth. "Thank you, thank you, a million times, thank you."

"Calm yourself down now." But Rita was smiling. "They got chocolates on sale in the gift shop, you want to thank me better than a big wet kiss. No nuts, no caramels, no coconut." With that, she was gone, leaving Tara smiling in gratitude, almost collapsing with relief.

The rumor was wrong. But what about her father? Fallon had hinted he'd been the one driving. He claimed he'd smelled alcohol. The only way to find out if her father had been drunk would be to get her mother to ask the hospital about it.

And what if he had been? That would be terrible, too. Judith would have Tara's head for suggesting the possibility to her mother.

She looked back at her sister. "I never doubted you. Not really. I'm going to find out who's lying about you and why.

Don't you worry." She was more determined than ever. She couldn't wait to tell Dylan. She started to call him, then realized she needed to hustle if she wanted her timing at Wharton to work. She needed to sit in on some of the meeting after she looked through Faye's office.

Besides, she'd rather tell Dylan in person, see the expression on his face…see him again.

It was true, she thought with dismay. She couldn't wait to see him again…maybe touch him…definitely smell him.

She glanced at Faye, who looked almost like herself with her hair done and makeup on. What would Faye tell her? *For God's sake, grow up.*

The Faye in the Sunset Crater photo would say, *Go with your heart.*

And that, she knew, she didn't dare do.

"I'M GOING TO TELL Victor we've authorized overtime to catch up on production," Dylan told his father early Wednesday morning.

"We can't afford that and you know it. You set the price too low as it is. Let 'em wait. God knows, we waited long enough for that contract." His father braced his head in his hands, clearly exhausted. He hadn't been sleeping. Dylan had gotten emails from him at two and three in the morning, always about a new idea to pursue. Since the funeral, his father had been more miserable than ever. He'd retreated more and more to the research lab, AWOL from his CEO duties.

Dylan had a sinking feeling he'd have to stay longer at Ryland than he'd intended to make sure his father was back on track again.

"We have to do what we can. Once we get the specs adjusted, we'll catch up quickly. If we don't meet our deadlines, Wharton can't meet theirs and the dominos tumble."

"Maybe you should have me speak at that damn meeting. You can be nice and accommodating and I'll tell them exactly where they went wrong."

"I'll be fine, Dad." No way would he let his father add fuel to the conflict after the exchange with Joseph at the funeral. Dylan hadn't realized Joseph had questioned the Ryland contract. With the high fail rate their testers were reporting now, he was certain all the managers would be concerned.

The delay of the Wharton management meeting where he was to speak had given Victor more time to gather data from his shift managers for Dylan to share during his presentation.

"I say no on the overtime," his father declared.

"I talked it over with Victor and we agree it's the best solution. Once the Wharton batteries get out in quantity, we'll make up for any money we lost."

"Are you forgetting whose company this is?" his father demanded.

"You signed off on the bid. My job is to supervise the operation."

His father grabbed his ring of keys from the desk and held them out. "Then you might as well hand these over to Joe Banes. Tell him to turn off the light once he's cleaned us out."

"I can't talk to you when you're like this," Dylan said, leaving before he blew up, which would only make it worse. His jaw ached from being clenched. Tara's words played in his head: *Does your father realize you saved him? Does he appreciate what you gave up for him?*

Not enough, no. But Dylan had made the right choice. He'd helped build a remarkable company. He'd pushed hard to get here. It had been a risk, letting income drop for the next quarter, but the payoff would be huge. When he faced a tough decision, Dylan found himself thinking, *What would Abbott Wharton do?*

Out in the factory, Dylan went straight to Victor's glassed-in office. "It's a go on overtime."

"Good," Victor said, holding out stapled pages. "Dale put together the figures." Dale was the Quality Assurance manager. "We doubled our tests on this lot. If Wharton fails them, maybe Sean's right. Maybe they *are* sabotaging us for a price break." He offered a grim smile. Victor and Dylan had shaken their heads more than once over his father's suspicion of all things Wharton. Dylan had advised Victor on the best approach to working with his father. He hoped to hell it would be enough.

"I'll give them the data and explain our system. If they adjust the specs like we've suggested, we should be fine."

"If Jeb Harris would let us over there to see what equipment they're using and how they're using it, we could clear this up quick."

"He says it's proprietary," Dylan reminded him. Victor thought the Wharton testing manager was a bit high and mighty. "The test results should be enough."

"We'll figure it out," Victor said, fire in his eyes. "I stand by my people and my people stand by their work."

"I appreciate how you've handled it, top to bottom, Victor." For all his flaws, his father's scrappy, underdog tenacity and grit had inspired fierce loyalty in the employees all the way down to the warehouse guys. Ryland Engineering was a good company with heart and spirit and Dylan was proud of what they'd built. He would see this through if it was the last thing he did.

At 10:00 a.m., Tara stepped into the lobby of Wharton Electronics for the first time since she was a kid, awed by the machinery and lights on the factory floor. Her father had been so proud of the place. He came alive within these walls. His voice went lighter and his eyes sparkled. That gave her a stab of grief.

The lobby was impressive, with a high ceiling, huge windows and tons of light. Her steps on the granite floor echoed as if she were in a luxury-car showroom. Photos of Wharton batteries jutted from the wall on 3-D rectangles, so bright and pretty they looked like edible jewels.

The waiting area held low, modern furniture in neon green and yellow, a sleek table and a spiky palm in a tall vase. From the table she picked up a copy of the annual report to read over, then watched a few seconds of the promotional video running on a huge flat-screen TV.

She headed for the front desk. The receptionist was on the phone. Waiting for her to finish, Tara took in the two huge oil portraits on the wall behind her. The first was of Tara's grandfather. The brass nameplate at the bottom identified him as the company's first CEO and gave his birth and death dates. Next to him was her father, who'd taken over the plant in 1985 at age forty-five, having worked his way up from the factory floor—*Whartons earn their place in this world,* he'd always said.

His father's nameplate was missing. With a jolt, she realized they'd sent it to be engraved with his death date.

Tara leaned against the counter to steady herself. She was never ready for these jolts when they hit.

She sighed. Whose painting would appear beside her father's? Who would take over as CEO? Faye, if she recovered. *Please recover. Please.* Certainly not Joseph. He didn't strike her as a leader. One of the other VPs, she guessed. Offering recommendations on the new CEO might well be one of her tasks as a consultant. The idea was hard to consider, with Faye's life hanging in the balance.

Her plan was to look around in Faye's office and her father's if possible, then drop in on the meeting an hour before lunch to ask about her tour. Sitting through some of the meeting she'd get a feel for the power players. If a tour wasn't possible today, she'd talk to employees in the cafeteria and stop by managers' offices for informal chats and generally take the temperature of the place.

The receptionist ended her call and smiled up at Tara. "Can I help you?" She hesitated. "Oh! You're Mr. Wharton's other daughter.... You're...um..."

"Tara."

"That's right. Tara. Nice to finally meet you. How is Ms. Banes? Everyone is so worried about her."

"She's stable. We're hoping for the best."

"We are, too. We really are." She paused, biting her lip. Tara assumed lots of employees were worried. She accepted the visitor badge the receptionist gave her, then took the winding wood stairs instead of the elevator, to enjoy the sun on her arms and the view of the river through the huge windows.

From the second-floor landing she surveyed the row of offices—empty and dark, since the managers were in the third-floor meeting room. Carol looked up from her desk behind a low fabric wall in front of what must be Faye's office. She smiled and waved Tara over. "I snitched the key to your father's office, too," she whispered. "His secretary takes notes in the meeting."

"Good work," Tara said.

Carol opened the door to Faye's office and they entered. Tara was transfixed by the art on the walls—whimsical collages of words and drawings incorporated into blueprint grids. "Faye's work, huh?" Tara said.

"She's very talented."

"She is." Tara realized her mother hadn't put a single one of Faye's paintings in the house. It didn't fit with the decor, of course, but the real problem was that neither of their parents had respected Faye's talent. That had always irked Tara, whose first act whenever she moved was to hang the piece Faye had made for her. She wanted another painting in her condo. If Faye recovered... *When* she recovered, Tara would ask about that.

While they waited for Faye's computer to boot, Tara flipped through Faye's paper files, the notebooks on her desk with quarterly reports, audits, the budget, cost and quality analyses, and a strategic plan—all standard for someone in Faye's position.

When they turned back to the computer, Carol frowned. "There's a password now."

"That's new?"

"Yes. Faye didn't want the hassle."

"Who would have put it on?"

"Probably Mr. Banes asked our IT guy to do it to keep me from snooping." She sighed.

Or to hide something he wanted no one to know.

"The IT guy can override it for you, but I don't know if he'd do it without Mr. Banes's okay."

"We'll leave that for now," she said, frustrated as hell and dying to know what Joseph wanted kept secret.

Her father's office was neat as a pin, his computer password-protected like the one at home. She looked through the folders in his desk drawers, thinking she might find the missing ones from home, but they were all business-related, as far as she could tell. The file cabinet was locked. "That's Lisa's doing," Carol said. "She gets very officious because he's the CEO."

That was that, Tara realized. She'd learned nothing useful, except that Joseph had likely locked down Faye's computer. On to the next part of her plan...where she hoped for more luck.

CHAPTER TEN

TARA REACHED THE TOP of the stairs to the conference room just as the elevator doors opened and out stepped…

"Dylan!" Heat bloomed in her face at how glad she was to see him. "What are you doing here?"

He raised the stack of stapled pages he held. "I'm on the agenda. You?"

"Popping in to meet the managers, maybe get a tour."

"You mean snoop around?" he whispered behind his hand.

"We call it observing workplace dynamics, but, okay, snooping."

"It's nice to see you," he said, his gaze sweeping over her with appreciation. "You look good. Very professional… and…good. Very good."

"Thanks." She'd worn a conservative gray suit and white silk blouse, but Dylan looked her over like she about to do a striptease around a pole. Her face had to be bright red. She felt feverish. "Thanks for dinner last night."

"Yeah. It was fun."

"Fun. Yes. It was that." *And so much more.* She flashed on the kiss, the fire in his eyes. She'd felt so alive, so desired, so—

"We should go in," he said, breaking the gaze.

"We should. Will I make you nervous if I sit in on your remarks?"

"You'll make me nervous, but not about my remarks." He ran his eyes down her body again, sending sparks everywhere his gaze landed, then leaned past her to hold the door open.

Everyone at the conference table—all men but one, Tara noticed—looked up as they entered. A second woman sat away from the table typing in a laptop. Lisa the secretary, she assumed.

"Tara!" Joseph lurched to his feet, looking alarmed.

"I stopped in for that tour," she said. "I wanted to say hello. I ran into Dylan in the hall."

Joseph smiled queasily. "Everyone, this is Tara Wharton, Faye's sister." He stopped, as if that was it.

"Could you introduce me?" she asked politely.

He sighed, resigned to the delay, then went around the table, giving names and titles, ending with Miriam Zeller, the Human Resources manager. "Miriam gives the tours. Miriam, would you mind?"

"Of course." Miriam rose, smiling in her direction.

"Let's wait until the lunch break," Tara said. "I'll sit in, if that's okay."

Joseph clearly wanted her gone. "We've arranged for Mr. Ryland to speak to us, so we really should—"

"I'm happy to have her listen in," Dylan said, backing Tara's play. "Maybe you could pass these out?" He held out the stack of paper to her, his eyes twinkling in conspiracy.

As she handed out the last packet, her phone vibrated. Seeing the insurance agency's name, she ducked out to take the call.

It was a secretary telling her the adjuster would not be available that day and, no, she didn't know where the car might be. Another damn delay. Fuming, Tara returned to the meeting just as Dylan asked if there were questions.

"Yeah, I've got one," Carl Goodman said. The factory manager wore a suit that he didn't seem comfortable in. He'd dressed up for the meeting, which meant corporate offices had more prestige than the factory. Interesting. "What are you going to do about the backup on production?"

Dylan responded calmly, explaining that Ryland employees were working overtime to boost output. That seemed to appease Goodman.

Dylan took more questions, sounding knowledgeable and trustworthy, making eye contact all around the table. He was good, a natural leader, and Tara was reminded again how impressive he'd been in high school. She felt a surge of attraction. He'd probably do wonders for Wharton once he could give the town his full attention.

After he'd finished speaking, he thanked everyone and turned for the door, giving Tara a wink as he left. She went hot all over. *From a wink, for God's sake.* She felt like she had some girlish crush on a rock star.

Mentally shaking that off, she tuned in to the dynamics of the meeting. It wasn't going well. Joseph was clearly uncomfortable being in charge. He allowed the same point to be made repeatedly, cut off productive discussions and managed to annoy nearly everyone. There were simple techniques she could teach him for fixing that. She was champing at the bit to try.

The informal leader seemed to be Davis Mann, the VP of Manufacturing. When a question came up, they all looked to him. He oversaw the factory operations and was Carl Goodman's boss. She needed to touch base with him for sure before she left Wharton today.

At noon, catering brought in a sandwich buffet. As people got their food, Tara moved from person to person, asking questions and listening closely to the answers as well as the interpersonal dynamics. She caught Davis Mann alone in the hall and arranged to stop by his office to talk after her tour.

At the end of the break, Miriam Zeller approached her. "Ready for that tour?"

"I don't want to keep you from the meeting." Women managers in a mostly male workplace had to work hard to stay in the loop.

"They'll tread water from here on out. To tell you the truth, I'm happy to escape the tedium."

As they headed for the elevator, she asked Miriam how she felt about being the only woman on the management team, mentioning the experiences of women she'd worked with. That started them off with a nice rapport and gave Tara a chance to explain what she did for a living.

Getting off at the second floor, they moved toward the back stairs to the factory, passing offices as they went. As they passed the bookkeeping department, a woman rushed out, stopping just before she plowed into Tara. It was Candee, Dylan's ex-wife.

"Oh. Hi," Candee said. "You're Tara."

It took her a second to respond. Why hadn't Dylan mentioned Candee worked for Wharton? "I am."

"Candee Ryland," Candee said sharply, evidently assuming Tara's delayed response meant Tara didn't know her name.

"Yes. I know. Dylan told me…" What? She flipped through what she knew about Dylan's ex-wife…they'd slept together since the divorce…she'd left him because she thought he still loved Tara…she'd sold him cookware he didn't use…given him a recipe for beer-butt chicken… None of that seemed appropriate. "Who you are," she finished lamely.

"Yeah?" Her voice spiked. "Well, he told me who *you* are, too, so we're even." She seemed to reconsider her tone. "What I mean is—"

"I know what you mean," Tara said, cutting her off in an effort to smooth the moment. Instead she'd sounded rude.

"Perfect," Candee snapped. "If you'll excuse me." She stalked away.

Miriam politely didn't ask what that was about. Tara had stepped in it again, her people skills in tatters in this town.

Miriam led Tara along a catwalk overlooking the factory floor, which seemed to sparkle with cleanliness. Fluorescent lights made the white cement floor gleam. Ventilators roared, pulling the highly flammable aluminum dust from the air, according to Miriam.

The section of the factory where the battery cells were built contained glassed-in machines like giant tollbooths lined in rows, control panels flashing colored lights. Workers there wore white suits, hairnets, paper slippers and gloves to keep down static.

In the assembly area, robotic arms and hydraulic lifts made rhythmic *whoosh* and *clunk* sounds as they put together cells, then loaded boxes of batteries onto a conveyor belt to be prepared for distribution. Workers here wore golf shirts and jeans or khakis, and she spotted Carl Goodman, minus coat and tie, talking to a technician. He'd abandoned the meeting for more important duties, she assumed.

Miriam rattled off stats on the size of the operation, units produced, the specifics of the new Wharton battery, which used nanotechnology and complicated chemicals to make lighter, faster-charging and more powerful batteries.

After that, they looked in on the R&D lab, the cafeteria and the loading dock, ending up on the tarmac waiting for a technician from the testing area—the last stop on the tour—to pick them up in an electric cart.

"I'm very impressed," Tara said.

"I know. So am I. At our price point, we're poised to sweep the market. If everything comes together as we hope." There was tension in her voice.

"I'm sure losing my father and Faye has made people uneasy. The managers seemed pretty wired."

"That was Joseph's first time running the meeting," she said diplomatically. "I'm sure that's what you picked up."

"It was more than that, I think," she said. "I understand there have been rumors of another layoff. I was told you lost a few engineers, too."

Miriam gave her a wary look. "There are always personnel shifts during a transition."

"You don't have to hold back, Miriam. I'm on your side. I want Wharton Electronics to succeed." Tara liked her and hoped she'd be an ally. "The truth is that Faye contacted me a few weeks ago about doing some consulting here."

"She did?" Miriam blew out a breath. "That's great. Joseph means well, but I'm afraid he's a bit over his head."

"That was my impression. I need him to hire me, so I wanted to lay some groundwork, if I could, with key people, especially those whose opinion he respects. I wondered about Davis Mann...?"

"Davis is great, very big picture in his thinking. Managers pay attention to what he says. The trouble is he intimidates Joseph."

"I see."

"Joseph listens to Evan Moore. You met him. He's the Research & Development VP. You might want to spend some time with him. Squeeze in some observations between his lectures on the projects they're working on. Just caring enough to listen will make him love you."

"I'll do that. Anyone else?"

"Our general counsel, Marvin Levy. His office is next to Faye's. Legal stuff scares Joseph, so he listens to Marvin with both ears. Marvin's smart, practical and thoughtful."

"I'll talk to him."

"I sound like I'm scheming against Joseph, but I'm not.

OFFICIAL OPINION POLL

Dear Reader,

Since you are a book enthusiast, we would like to know what you think.

Inside you will find a short Opinion Poll. Please participate in our poll by sharing your opinion on 3 subjects that are very important to all of us.

To thank you for your participation, we would like to send you **2 FREE BOOKS** and **2 FREE GIFTS**!

Please enjoy them with our compliments.

Sincerely,

Pam Powers

For Your Reading Pleasure...

Get 2 FREE BOOKS that have never
felt more real. It's mainstream romance with
the promise of
happy ever
after!

Free

Your 2 FREE BOOKS have a combined
cover price of $11.00 in the U.S. and
$13.00 in Canada.

Peel off sticker and place by
your completed poll on the right
page and you'll automatically
receive 2 FREE BOOKS and 2 FREE GIFTS with no
obligation to purchase anything!

*We'll send you two wonderful surprise gifts, (worth about $10),
absolutely FREE, just for trying our Romance books!
Don't miss out — **MAIL THE REPLY CARD TODAY!***

YOUR OPINION POLL
THANK-YOU FREE GIFTS INCLUDE:

▶ **2 HARLEQUIN® SUPERROMANCE® BOOKS**

▶ **2 LOVELY SURPRISE GIFTS**

OFFICIAL OPINION POLL

YOUR OPINION COUNTS!
Please check TRUE or FALSE below to express your opinion about the following statements:

Q1 Do you believe in "true love"?

"TRUE LOVE HAPPENS ONLY ONCE IN A LIFETIME."
○ TRUE
○ FALSE

Q2 Do you think marriage has any value in today's world?

"YOU CAN BE TOTALLY COMMITTED TO SOMEONE WITHOUT BEING MARRIED."
○ TRUE
○ FALSE

Q3 What kind of books do you enjoy?

"A GREAT NOVEL MUST HAVE A HAPPY ENDING."
○ TRUE
○ FALSE

YES! I have placed my sticker in the space provided below. Please send me the **2 FREE books** and **2 FREE gifts** for which I qualify. I understand that I am under no obligation to purchase anything further, as explained on the back of this card.

❏ I prefer the regular-print edition
135/336 HDL FVMU

❏ I prefer the larger-print edition
139/339 HDL FVMU

FIRST NAME   LAST NAME

ADDRESS

APT.#   CITY

STATE/PROV.   ZIP/POSTAL CODE

▶ **DETACH AND MAIL CARD TODAY!** ▶

HSR-TF-03/13
Printed in the U.S.A.
© 2012 HARLEQUIN ENTERPRISES LIMITED.

If offer card is missing write to: Harlequin Reader Service, P.O. Box 1867, Buffalo NY 14240-1867 or visit www.ReaderService.com

BUSINESS REPLY MAIL
FIRST-CLASS MAIL   PERMIT NO. 717   BUFFALO, NY

POSTAGE WILL BE PAID BY ADDRESSEE

HARLEQUIN READER SERVICE
PO BOX 1341
BUFFALO NY 14240-8571

NO POSTAGE
NECESSARY
IF MAILED
IN THE
UNITED STATES

He's good at his job. He's just not equipped to run Wharton. This is a good company. I don't want to see it fail."

"Neither do I, believe me."

Miriam studied Tara, then seemed to make a decision. "If Faye wanted you to work for us, then so do I. I'll talk to the other managers on your behalf."

"I appreciate that." Assuming she made good impressions on the attorney and the research VP, Miriam's help could set her up well for turning Joseph around. That filled her with energy and hope, something she'd been missing since she arrived.

A cart pulled up and Miriam introduced her to the driver—Matt Sutherland, assistant testing manager—a handsome man in his early thirties who colored when Tara smiled at him.

As they drove toward the testing area, which looked like a cross between an airplane hangar and a giant auto shop, Matt rattled off the kinds of testing they did—current consumption, output voltage levels, electrical noise, response time and more she didn't quite understand.

He parked outside the steel door and led her inside. To the left was a glassed-in office, followed by units of equipment with dials, meters and flashing lights. Across the space she saw cars with their hoods up, some hooked up to hoses and wires. A car's engine roared as its wheels spun against steel rollers. The air smelled of rubber and hot metal.

Matt explained they used various stimulus inputs—acceleration, temperature, wheel rotation—to ensure the battery module behaved as it should. "Very impressive," she told him, making him blush again.

"We're pretty proud of it," he said. "You should meet the boss." He led her to the office, where she saw Dylan talking to a tall gaunt man with salt-and-pepper hair wearing a blue jumpsuit.

"Dylan," she said when he noticed her. "We meet again. I swear I'm not stalking you."

"I'm not sure I believe that." He gave her that look again and it made her nerve endings throb.

"We ran into each other earlier," she explained to Matt, guessing she had blushed redder than he had.

"We're old friends," Dylan said, holding her gaze.

"From high school," she blurted, not quite able to pull away.

"Jeb Harris," the other man said, holding out a hand. "Not to interrupt." He looked amused.

"Tara Wharton," she said, shaking his hand. "You have a remarkable operation from what I've seen."

"Glad you think so. Maybe you could convince this guy." He motioned at Dylan.

"Tweak your specs and I'll be sold," Dylan said.

Jeb shook his head. The two seemed amiably annoyed with each other.

"Soon as I finish showing Ms. Wharton around, I'm taking off," Matt said to Jeb. "It's another ultrasound."

"If it's necessary," Jeb said tersely.

"It is." Matt blushed furiously, clearly nervous that he'd displeased his boss. "This way," he said to her, striding quickly away.

She hurried to join him near a car with its hood up. "This is where we install batteries for test runs," he said, glancing at his watch. A tech bolted in a battery, while another checked dials on a machine.

Matt was clearly eager to leave, and she wanted to return to the building to speak with the key managers. "I should head back, if that's okay," she said. "You need to get going, too, right? The ultrasound?"

"Yeah. My wife's twenty-four weeks along, but it's been

tough. The doctor asked to see her every two weeks." They started back toward the cart.

"It's good of you to take off work to support your wife."

"Jeb's not happy about it with us so busy, but family's the most important thing." The earnest look on his face touched Tara and made her feel guilty about her own behavior toward her family.

"Of course," she said. She wondered now if she should have given them another chance, visited despite the tension, pushed past the barriers. Maybe she was dreaming.

As they passed the office, Dylan stuck out his head. "How about Ruby's for dinner? Give us a chance to catch up. Say six?"

Catch up? They'd been together the night before, but maybe he had more news. "Sounds good," she said, secretly eager for more time with him.

"My best to your wife," Dylan said to Matt.

"Thanks," he said, not meeting Dylan's gaze. What was that about?

"Dylan knows your wife?" she asked.

"Yeah. Melissa was at a cookware party at his ex-wife's."

"Small towns, I guess," she said, still not understanding the hostility.

"He's a nice guy and all. It's just that he's selling us defective units. That's what they were arguing over, Jeb and him." He frowned.

"It's a big problem?" she asked.

"They can talk all they want, but standards are standards. Ryland buys cheap components out of Tennessee and blames the tests when they turn out bad." He glanced at her. "No offense to your friend."

"None taken." But it sounded like Dylan had his work cut out for him if what Matt said was true. Both companies had a lot riding on the project.

It was almost four o'clock when Tara got home, her head jammed with data and plans. She'd made headway with Davis Mann and the two people Miriam said Joseph trusted. It would take a couple days for the idea to percolate up to Joseph. If all went well, she wouldn't have to say a word. He would approach her.

Judith met her at the front door holding out a paper sack with a receipt stapled to it. She looked oddly pale. "The funeral guy dropped this by. He didn't want Rachel to have to fetch it. It's from the medical examiner.... It's, you know... from the body. What Mr. Wharton had on. I don't want your mother to see it."

"No. That's smart." She took the sack, fighting queasiness, and carried it to her room. She had to see what clues might be here...her father's wallet...possibly Faye's phone. Steeling herself, she yanked the sack open, popping the staple. A sour, earthy smell filled her nose—moist earth, leaves and the metallic scent of blood.

On top were her father's shoes. They were dusty, not bloody, thank God. Beneath them were tan slacks that had been cut apart. The waist area of the pants was stained with blood. The shirt below was crusty with it. So much blood. Her heart lurched in her chest. An envelope, also bloodstained, stuck out of his shirt pocket. She made out part of the return address—*CGC Gen*—before bile rose in the back of her throat. She turned her head, deciding to feel for what else was there. She touched a belt...coins...then a wallet, which she pulled out. It was clean. Thin, finely stitched and well worn. Inside she found several fresh twenties, a black American Express card, a driver's license and a few photos—her father in cap and gown, a wedding picture, a family portrait with Faye as a toddler. No pictures of Tara, but then, these shots were quite old. Her father likely hadn't changed anything since he first used the wallet.

The only other items in the wallet were two business cards. Looking at the first, she was startled to see her own name. *Her father had kept her business card.* She stared at it a long time, swallowing against a lump in her throat.

The second card was from a Randall Scott. She'd seen that name before…

In her father's desk drawer. Yeah. This time, she noticed Family Law below the name. That was code for divorce lawyer, right? On the back of the card was written an appointment from three weeks ago.

What the hell? Her father had seen a divorce attorney? Why? Had something happened?

Her mother hadn't said a word to her. Maybe she didn't know. A divorce would have devastated her mother, whose social status meant everything to her. The stigma, the gossip, would be more than she could bear.

Tara felt chilled to the bone. Her father wanted a divorce? How serious had he been? She checked the clock: four-thirty. Still business hours. She called the number, asked for the billing office and told the bookkeeper she needed to confirm the total charges on Mr. Wharton's account, holding her breath that the ruse would work.

It did. The bookkeeper told her that her father had seen the attorney at his office twice and had three phone conferences. That sounded serious, especially with her father as frugal as he was. There were no charges for filing fees, so he hadn't done anything official yet at least.

Her parents hadn't seemed close, but their marriage stood for something, a bond that mattered to the two of them. They'd been married almost forty years. Talk about standing the test of time.

But if her father was unhappy enough to take such drastic action…something terrible must have happened.

She remembered Bill Fallon and how solicitous he'd been

of her mother. And her mother had talked about him in a strange dreamy voice. What if he'd been *more* than a friend to her?

No. Her mother would not cheat on her father. That would violate the social requirements of the life her mother had chosen.

Tara didn't dare ask her mother about this. If she didn't know that her husband wanted to end the marriage, Tara would rather die than tell her. Some truths caused useless harm.

Her head spun, but slowly, as if through fog. Dread seemed to press her into the floor, compressing her lungs. She had to sort this out, make some sense of it, clear her head, decide what to do about what she'd learned.

She needed Dylan. He would listen. He would help. Thank goodness they had dinner plans. He was her port in the storm even now.

WHEN TARA STEPPED into Ruby's, Dylan felt a shift in the energy of the restaurant, similar to the way a theater audience reacted when the curtain opened. Conversations faded. Heads turned. Breaths were held. Tara's striking beauty would draw attention anywhere, especially from men, but this was different. This was Wharton.

Everyone knew her or of her. They were curious, titillated, or envious. For the first time, he imagined how difficult this would be for her. He'd always thought she made too much of her name and people's opinions of her.

Now, with what she was going through—losing her father, her sister so ill, her theories about the accident—this much scrutiny and speculation would be a trial.

He saw her hesitate, take in the room, almost shudder. Then she threw back her shoulders and strode forward, sexy and confident. A girl at the bar called to her, so she stopped to talk for a few seconds. A few feet farther and someone in a booth spoke. After that a girl he remembered from high school stopped Tara in the aisle for a hug, some words, a laugh.

When Tara finally dropped into the booth, her back to the restaurant, she looked worn out. "Sanctuary," she said in a drawn-out voice.

"I see what you mean," he said.

"It's exhausting. Even my old friends make me crazy. They treat me like a wax figure in a museum, frozen in time. They got married, had kids, have mortgages, but they talk to me like I haven't changed at all. Dana Gibbons wants to tear up the town one night. Riley Evans is sorry he can't hook me up with weed now that he's a teacher. Reed Walker said he'd dust off the Harley and hit the highway the minute his wife leaves to visit her sister. Can you believe that? He's ready to cheat on his wife for old times' sake." She shook her head. "Do I look like I want a drunken bender or a ride on a Harley to you?"

"Nope."

"Good. I'd like to think I've grown up that much."

"It's that imprint thing again, I guess."

"Well, it sucks." She took a shaky breath. "People are staring, aren't they?" They were. "I hate being in this gold-fish bowl."

He realized that this dinner would add to the rumor they were back together. Fallon had no doubt spread the word.

"We could leave. Go to my house," he said, though he didn't trust himself alone with her again. Since last night, his desire had only intensified, as foolish and shortsighted as that was.

"No. I won't be chased out." She sat taller. "Just ignore them."

"You got it." That had always been his approach when the

scrutiny got to be too much for him. It was easier for him because he was comfortable here. He knew the people, their flaws and strengths. He didn't see every look as a criticism the way Tara did.

The waitress arrived with chips and salsa to take their orders. Tara picked up the menu, scanned it, then looked up at the waitress. "So I hear Ruthie Rand makes great goat and nopalitos empanadas. I'll have that and a draft beer."

Dylan ordered the same. When the waitress left, he said, "Where'd you hear about the empanadas?"

"Ruthie's mom, Judith, is our housekeeper. Judith told me Ruthie had an offer to cook for a food truck in Tucson, but she's afraid to leave here. I figure I'll rave about the dish and hope that encourages her."

That reminded him she'd been that way in high school, too. Pushing kids with talents to go for it. "Remember Sheila Stark? Goth girl who got suspended for fighting a cheerleader?"

"Sure I remember her. She had a great voice."

"She took your advice and started a band. Might have an offer with an indie label."

"How do you know that?"

"Her sister Cherry's our receptionist."

"Good for her. Growing up here, it's easy to feel inferior. You have no real yardstick to measure your talent."

"I'd say growing up here gave her a safe place to explore her abilities, develop the confidence to take risks."

"So besides being town manager, you're head of the Chamber of Commerce?"

"I'm a member, sure, but my point is that everything you disdain about small-town life has a positive side."

"Yeah?" She grinned at him, ready to mock, except he thought he saw a light in her eyes, too. "So I say it's stifling and full of gossips and you say..."

"It's cozy and friendly." He wouldn't admit his dislike for the gossip because he knew she would pounce on any sign that he'd been wrong to stay, that he'd settled for less by remaining in Wharton.

He knew she was just as guarded with him.

"We'll have to agree to disagree," she said flatly, the light gone from her eyes. She would not bend on this. Probably not even about the bigger, better Wharton he wanted to build. That was unexpectedly disappointing to him and he found himself saying more.

"You'd be surprised how many midsize companies are looking to move to towns like Wharton. Towns that will give them more attention, where the jobs mean a lot to the community. I was at an Association of Cities and Towns meeting a month ago and started on a target list of businesses. I've been assembling proposals when I have time."

"When *do* you have time? You've got a lot going on at Ryland it sounds like. Did you work things out with Jeb?"

He stopped reaching for a chip to answer. "I convinced him to adjust the threshold on one measurement, but we're still at odds. I don't get where the hostility is coming from."

"Matt said something about Ryland using inferior parts…?"

"That's bullshit." He lowered his voice. "Sorry to bark at you. We got faulty components from a vendor on an early shipment, but that's long fixed. I overheard Matt's wife complaining about it to her cousin who's on our assembly line."

"At the cookware party, right? Matt said you met his wife there. You sure you don't want to change *friendly* to *gossipy?* Sounds like you've been stung, too."

"What matters is we work out the problem." It didn't help that his father was disengaged lately. They needed to be united in this final push to get Ryland over the hump, so Dylan could leave the place with a clear conscience.

"I hope you do," Tara said.

They dipped for salsa at the same time, the mere brush of her fingers sending a jolt of lust through him. He had it bad and it made him feel like a fool.

She swallowed, so at least he knew she'd felt something, too. "I didn't see Harvey behind the bar," she said. "He retire?"

"Couple years back, yeah."

"He used to make us great drinks, remember?"

"He used to make *you* drinks. He liked you."

"That's because he didn't dare say no to a Wharton. That was one situation I didn't mind my name."

"People liked you for you, not your name."

She shook her head. "Trust me. I had good reason to hang with the dropouts, the stoners and the lost souls. They had enough troubles they didn't give a shit what my name was."

He could argue, but he could feel her opinion was set in stone.

She took another chip and dipped it, her face troubled. "I feel bad about some of that. The way I was and how it affected my friends. Like Dana, for example. She was a B student until I got hold of her. Her grades dropped. She never went to college."

"That was her decision, not yours."

"But I made screwing off look cool. It wasn't fair. I had a safety net. I would never starve. I don't intend to ever take a dime from my family, but I know, deep down, that if disaster strikes I'm covered. That's an amazing gift I sneered at back then."

"You were young. You had reasons." At best, her parents treated her with benign neglect. At worst, deliberate cruelty. Children shouldn't have to read between the lines to know they were loved.

"Don't cut me slack, Dylan. I know the mistakes I made."

They didn't see the world the same—then or now. Maybe that couldn't be helped. Tara, like everyone else, was made up of her experiences—the moments, big and small, good and bad, that had shaped her character, her hopes and expectations, her limits and her reach.

"You looked down on me back then," she said. "Admit it."

"I thought you were wasting your abilities."

"You were such a straight arrow." She pointed a chip at him, then licked the salt off.

He had to close his eyes to handle that sight. He'd forgotten that habit of hers. "Meanwhile, you used to call me Do Right Boy," he said hoarsely.

"That's right. I was pretty mean. How did you stand me?"

"I told you why last night."

"I tickled your brain...I remember." Attraction burned in her eyes, her pupils large and gleaming. She pursed her lips, her tongue peeking at him, the way she used to before she threw herself at him, as if she were famished and he were a banquet table. Their attraction surged again. It was constantly ticking in the background, waiting for one of them to flip the switch.

The waitress arrived with their beers, breaking the unbearable tension. When she'd gone, Tara tapped her beer to his. "To being wiser."

"To that," he said, feeling more foolish every second. "So how did your snooping go?"

"Mixed. I made headway toward getting hired to consult, but I got nowhere in Faye's office. Joseph locked it down, possibly to keep Faye's assistant from seeing sensitive stuff. I'd really like to know more about the finances at Wharton." She tilted her head at him. "Which reminds me. You didn't tell me Candee worked for us."

"Yeah. She's a bookkeeper."

"I ran into her. It was awkward. I offended her, I think.

She thought I didn't know her name, then I cut her off trying to fix it."

"You were nervous. So was she."

"I'm sure that's true." She looked thoughtful. "I envy the two of you. That you're friends. You help each other, cook together, do each other favors."

"It wasn't easy, believe me. But we both wanted it, so we worked at it."

"Yeah," she said, going still. "You think we will ever be like that? You and me?"

No. He knew it instantly. It would be too difficult. He would always want more.

"You don't," she said. "I can see that. I'm not the work-for-it kind of person, am I?" She dropped her eyes to hide how hurt she was, pushing her beer forward, then sliding it back.

"It's not that," he said, stopping her hand, taking it in both of his. He'd made her feel bad about herself back then. There was the sadness of that beneath every word they said to each other.

"It's not you, Tara. It's us. The way we were. It was different with us than it ever was with Candee. Deeper somehow." He rubbed the back of her hand with his thumbs, wanting to press the truth into her.

"You think so?" she asked.

"I do."

"So we should give up on being friends?"

"No. But we have to be careful with each other, not get ourselves into tempting situations."

"That makes sense," she said, looking down at his hands holding hers so tightly. He didn't want to let go. They lifted their eyes to each other. Her lips parted, about to speak.

"Watch it! Hot!" The waitress had arrived, holding their food.

They yanked their hands apart, the server's words truer than she knew.

She set down the dishes and left. The aroma of spicy beef and buttery pastry filled the air.

"Smells great," Tara said, clearly relieved for the interruption. She seemed as alarmed by the push-pull between them as he felt.

"Yum," Tara said, licking her lips after the first bite. "These are delicious. I've never tasted anything like it."

"So Wharton does have something you like. First, the empanadas. Next, the whole town."

"Even you can't believe that."

"Wait until you taste the flan." He didn't know why he kept pushing her, trying to convince her, but he could no more stop himself than he could stop the fire in his blood when he looked at her.

She laughed, the familiar liquid honey sound he remembered so well. "You're funnier than you used to be," she said. "I like that."

"Good," he said, entirely too pleased. He remembered that she'd lightened the heaviness of his life back then. She'd kept him on his toes, challenged him. He felt the same thing now, he realized, and he liked it. He had to remember that when he got serious about someone. She needed to...*tickle his brain*.

"Do you think if I apologized to Candee, she would give me some insights into the company's finances?" Tara said after they'd eaten more.

"Candee's a cool head. She'd be discreet. I'll talk to her."

"That'd be great. Thanks."

"Don't thank me yet. She'll probably drag you to her next party. I think it's candles."

She groaned, then grinned. "I'll go if you go."

"Candles? No way. I'm holding out for power tools."

"Why? You love candles. Remember that time your parents went on an overnight and you made a path to the bed with tea candles?"

"And Duster knocked them into the curtains, which went up in flames? Of course I remember that."

"We were beating back the flames with wet towels, the smoke alarm squealing. Good times, huh?"

"To you maybe. Though my parents were so busy fighting they didn't seem to care what happened to the curtains."

"Yeah. That was hard on you—your parents' breakup." Tara put down her fork. "And, actually, I just found out that my father wanted to divorce my mother."

"What?"

"Yeah." She wiped her mouth with a napkin. "We got my dad's personal effects and I went through his wallet looking for clues. I found an appointment card with a divorce lawyer. I called the office and they told me Dad had met with the guy several times." She looked bewildered.

"Damn."

"I know. It blew me away. I mean, I knew they weren't close, but it's tearing me up inside. I don't understand why."

"Because they're your parents. They're supposed to be together. They just took a jackhammer to the foundation of your life."

"Exactly!" She looked at him with gratitude. "I knew you'd understand. That's it. It's like my life's been shaken up in a bag and dumped out, pieces falling everywhere. I don't know what's true anymore."

"And you feel helpless."

"I do. That, too. I don't think my mother knows, thank God. But I can't figure out why all of a sudden Dad would do this. Something happened, don't you think? Maybe Dad found out about Bill Fallon hitting on my mother... Maybe that night, Bill Fallon was with Mom instead of at poker... Maybe he was coming back when the accident happened...

That could be what he's hiding and why my mother seems so messed up."

Her eyes were frantic, and he could tell the speculation was distracting her from the pain and confusion she felt.

"Sounds kind of far-fetched, don't you think?"

But she didn't hear him. "What if Faye found out? Maybe her *let it go* text was about the divorce. Maybe that's why they were together that night. Maybe that's why she saw a therapist. She would be even more upset than I am." Her eyes darted like her words. "The poker guys! They *have* to know something. You said you'd talk to one of them, remember? That's important."

"I said I would if I could figure out the right approach."

"I still don't know where the car is. Maybe you could ask Fallon. Surely he knows. Also, you should confirm that they did collect the evidence. While you're at it, check the photos."

"I can't hound the man, Tara."

She locked gazes with him, finally acknowledging he was part of this conversation. "*Hound* the man? You mean make sure he does his *job?* They could junk the car any day, Dylan. We can't waste time."

"If I push, he'll dig in his heels."

"I don't care how small the town, police are supposed to investigate. The law is the law. And you're his *boss*. You could fire him."

Dylan had to work with Fallon after Tara was gone. He didn't need more enmity than already existed. He wanted no trouble from Fallon until he retired. "We're not tracking a suspect, Tara. We have no reason to believe a crime has been committed. Fallon will do what I asked, don't worry."

She looked at him in a way he remembered with dread, as if he'd betrayed her. "And if we find evidence that a crime has been committed? What then? Will we pursue it? Or cover it up?"

"Come on, Tara."

She stared at him, clearly fighting the urge to argue. She sat back, then spoke in a voice of forced calm. "Okay. You won't push him. However, I think we should get a different mechanic to check the car. If Tony Carmichael serviced my father's cars, like you said, he might not admit that the brakes failed."

"Tony's honest. He's worked on our cars forever."

"He's human. Humans don't like to admit failure. And with all this foot-dragging, I think I should hire an accident expert. They'll have forensic mechanics who'll know what to look for in the engine. Better yet, tell Fallon I'm bringing in experts and maybe he'll snap to and do his job. Unless he's guilty, of course, and then he'll—"

"Hold it." Dylan raised his hands. "The only thing Bill Fallon is guilty of is lazy police work. You agreed we'd find out what we could before you call out the artillery."

"You said you'd help me," she said, anger crackling in her eyes.

"I *am* helping you. I'm trying to be the voice of reason. But you don't trust me. I can see that. Nobody's innocent to you. Not even me."

"I get it," she said, her voice low with held-back fury. "Your job is to babysit me until I get tired of spinning my wheels and give up and leave. That's it, isn't it? You and Bill Fallon probably worked it all out, had a good laugh over me being so frantic."

"That's ridiculous."

"I should have known."

"Known what?" he spat out, angry now, too.

"That you're part of this town. You don't see the corruption, the stupidity, the smugness. You put up with it. You go along. Well, I won't. I'll do what has to be done on my own."

She got up, bumping the table so the flatware rattled, and stalked off, every eye in the place following her.

He let a few seconds pass, then went after her, ignoring the looks, imagining the comments. *Can you believe he's still chasing that heartbreaker? Does he have no dignity?* Not when it came to Tara. She was going through hell. He couldn't abandon her now.

CHAPTER ELEVEN

"TARA, WAIT!"

Dylan's voice stopped Tara just as she realized she'd blindly marched two blocks in the wrong direction for her car. She turned and headed back, meeting Dylan outside Ruby's entrance.

"What?" she demanded, crossing her arms, her emotions snarled up, her mind racing. She was angry, frustrated and out of control. She'd been wrong in some of what she'd said. She'd overdone it again like she'd done in Bill Fallon's office. She wasn't sure she wanted Dylan to point that out right now.

"I'm on your side, Tara," he said, low, holding her gaze, his eyes hot with conviction. "Disagreeing with you doesn't make me corrupt or a sellout or whatever you think I am."

She fought to control her breathing, tried to calm down, to hear the sense in his words. "I know that, Dylan. You're a good person." She'd fallen back on the knee-jerk negativity and defensiveness that used to rule her.

"I'm not against you and neither is the town."

"It feels that way," she said. "Everywhere I turn I get stalled."

"You're frustrated and impatient. I get that, but you can't accuse every person who fidgets, won't answer a question or gets defensive of trying to kill your father, sister or both."

"And you can't blindly defend them all."

"You're right. But I won't assume the worst about them, either. People keep secrets. Sure. They lie. They cover up their mistakes. But not every person and not all the time. I know these people. I know how they think, what they're after, what they're capable of. Give me some credit, Tara."

What he said made sense. Her mind had been buzzing with doubts and suspicions and worries, like a fly blocked by a window. "It crowds in on me sometimes and I respond the way I used to."

"You're under a lot of pressure."

"Yeah." Something else dawned on her. "I'm also afraid I'll find out terrible things about my parents, Dylan. Things I don't want to know. I have to push on before I lose my nerve. I have to know the truth, even if it hurts."

"We'll find out the truth, Tara. I promise."

"Okay." She inhaled a breath, holding it in, letting it out slowly, releasing her anger at the same time. Dylan stood quietly, waiting for her to sort her thoughts. He was so good at that. When she felt normal, she said, "Don't you get sick of being right?"

"Never. You?"

"No way." She liked this easy teasing between them. It was better than it had been when they were younger. They were both old enough to be able to laugh at themselves and each other.

Dylan smiled abruptly. He was looking over her shoulder.

"What's so funny?" She turned to see what had amused him in the middle of their argument. It was a bench and a desert willow in a sidewalk planter. She still didn't get the joke.

"Don't you remember that time with Duster?"

Then it hit her. "This is the planter I fell into. The tree's so much bigger."

"I warned you he wouldn't hold his *stay* when the ice-cream truck came."

"It was worth a try," she said. In his rush to get to the

truck, Duster had knocked her into the peat moss around the freshly planted sapling.

Every inch of this town held memories for her and Dylan—silly, romantic, sweet and sad. She had to resist them. The stakes were too high. If she let memories, or Dylan's praise of the town, sink in, seduce her, she might be tempted to stay, to forget how hard she'd fought to make her way into the bigger world.

"Now what?" she said, totally uncertain of the next step. That never happened to her in her real life.

"We go back for the flan," Dylan said, nodding toward the café window.

"Are you nuts? Half the town saw me stomp out. If I go back in they'll think you won the fight."

"If we go back, we both win."

She rolled her eyes. "Please. This is not a *Lifetime* movie."

"Couldn't resist." He grinned.

"How do you stand this? Everybody watching your every move?"

"I don't give them that much power over me."

"Okay, Dr. Phil. Guess I'm not as mature as you." She sighed. "I do have to tell the waitress to tell Ruthie her empanadas are the best ever. She should take that food truck job in Tucson."

"After you." He motioned for her to walk ahead of him.

"I wouldn't mind taking the Walk of Shame if we'd actually *done* something to make it worthwhile."

"That could be arranged," he said, spots of gold flaring in his dark eyes like two struck matches, tilting his chin, as if to kiss her.

Her stomach dropped. Desire tightened some muscles, softened others. She was usually the one who threw out the dare. But here was Dylan waiting for her to take him up on it.

For a few seconds, she considered kissing him, sliding into that rush of pleasure and seeing where it would take them.

Then she thought of the gawking crowd—Wharton at its worst—and the urge evaporated like steam.

Tara walked in front of him, head high, wondering if he'd been serious. Did he really want the entire town to think they were together? Did he want to *be* together? Or had he known she would turn him down?

Later, after the caramel glory of Ruthie's flan had melted in their mouths, when they told each other good-night, she felt like she'd ducked trouble and missed out on a dream at the same time.

TARA ROSE EARLY Thursday morning, braced for trouble, she wasn't sure what kind. Dylan? No. She'd walked away from him. Faye? No change there. Then she remembered. *The will.* Today they went to Tucson to see Norton Marshall, their estate attorney, to go over her father's will.

She set off for her run, welcoming the chill in the air because it cleared her head. She thought about Dylan. He'd come after her, ignored the onlookers and promised to help her despite her bristles and accusations. He was a strong person, solid in his beliefs. He had what it took to survive in Wharton—to thrive really. She admired him for that, respected him.

And she *wanted* him. Oh, how she wanted him.

Tara pushed the thoughts away—again—as she headed up the hill to the house, breathing hard, energized by the exercise. She showered and made a few client contacts, then Judith met her in the hallway with a tray of breakfast. "Your mother's in the sunroom working on that charity event. Now's your chance to help her. Make her eat while you're at it."

Tara took the tray and found her mother at the antique

desk, talking on the phone, her back toward Tara. On a card table beside her mother were neatly placed file folders, stapled pages and a table layout with names sketched in.

"That would be lovely, Margaret," her mother said. "I'll put you down for a table then?" She listened. "Oh, well, that's kind of you. We're doing very well, thank you." Hanging up, her mother pressed the phone to her chest, her shoulders shaking with suppressed sobs. After a few seconds, she took a shuddering breath, consulted her paper, cleared her throat and made another call. Tara stood there, stunned by her mother's struggle and her determination.

"Yes. Natalie? It's Rachel Wharton calling," she said, her voice cool and smooth. "It's regarding the Harvest Dinner Dance to raise money for the food kitchen?" Tara could see over her mother's shoulder that the call list was long, with few names checked off.

When her mother hung up, Tara said, "Mom?"

Her mother's head whipped around. Her nose was red, her eyes puffy. "Don't sneak up on me like that!" Her eyes danced, frantic and miserable.

"Here's breakfast." Tara made room for the tray on the table. "Take a break."

"I'm nearly two weeks behind on the dinner," she said, turning back to her list.

"How about if I make those calls? I've got time."

"You couldn't possibly." She sniffed. "You don't know these people or their families or the donations they've made in the past."

"So write me notes." Tara pulled the list closer.

"No." Her mother took it back. "These are my friends. They can't turn me down. You're a virtual stranger." She glanced at the list. "Beverly Crowley's the next call. She'd likely hang up on you."

"Because of the protest? Really?"

"She'd *like* to hang up on me, but she doesn't dare. I'm too well-connected. So instead she refuses to look me in the eye."

"That was twelve years ago, Mom."

"You threatened the Crowleys' livelihood. People don't forget that."

"Their livelihood? The whole town shops at their store. They were rolling in it. All we did was get him to treat his employees fairly—"

"Enough." Her mother raised her hands. "You can't even admit you were wrong now, after ten years. You haven't changed a bit."

Tara bristled, then calmed herself. Her mother was displacing her grief and anxiety on Tara, something she'd done to Dylan just last night. Maybe she had more in common with her mother than Tara had realized.

"What can I do instead?" Tara said.

"Nothing. Go about your business."

Tara picked up the folder labeled Silent Auction and flipped it open to a list of businesses. "I can call these companies for donations. How's that?"

Her mother firmly took back the folder.

"You need help and I'm offering it," she said, trying to be kind, but anger lined her words. "I'm your daughter. We should be able to help each other. Or at least talk to each other. Instead you keep shutting me out."

"I don't have time for one of your scenes, Tara," her mother snapped, abruptly angry. "You're here for a few days. This is my life. This is my home. I have to make my way through this on my own. Don't pretend to help me."

Her mother's words stung. *Still.* Tara clenched her fists and her jaw. Her mother didn't *want* to make peace. Tara's fantasy of a tearful reconciliation, a loving mother-daughter bond, was just that, a fantasy. Her mother was the same per-

son she'd always been, except with years of built-up resentment of her AWOL daughter. What did Tara expect?

Heavy with disappointment, she breathed in the delicious
aroma of the food Judith had prepared. Judith wasn't put off
by Tara's mother's bristles. She went about her business, taking care of Tara's mother as best she could.

The tray held a delicate-looking omelet and fresh straw-
berries, along with a latte and orange juice. She had to take
her mother as she was. That had to be enough. "You really
should eat, Mom," she said quietly, all hostility gone. "Do it
for Judith. She's worried about you."

Her mother glanced at the food, then at Tara, then out the
window. She seemed to be thinking hard. Finally she turned
to Tara. "All right. You can do the auction calls. I *am* running out of time." She slowly pushed the file toward Tara,
then stopped. "But only if you can be diplomatic."

"I can do that. I'm good at it. I have clients, remember?"

"That's right. Your sister said you're quite good. Okay."
She pushed the file the rest of the way to Tara and gave it a
pat. That was it. The closest thing to a peace offering Tara
would get from her mother. Permission to harass local businesses for donations. At the moment, that was enough for
Tara.

TARA SAT BESIDE Faye's bed, her heart full and aching. She'd
come straight from the reading of the will to the hospital.
Joseph was driving her mother home. It troubled Tara how
little time her mother spent with Faye. Was it her guilt over
the argument she'd had that night with Faye? Did she think
Faye had been so upset she'd driven poorly? Or was it the
horror at the possibility of Faye dying? She would expect her
mother to show at least as much courage as she'd displayed
making phone calls about a stupid society event.

It's how she copes. She sees it as her job.

Tara was getting better at accepting people for who they were, good and bad, she thought. That was a tiny point of pride amid her mistakes. Besides, in the lawyer's office just now, she'd learned something about her father that had touched her deeply, opened her up to new realizations.

Tara took her sister's hand, the orange nail polish gleaming. "We went over Dad's will today. I wish you'd been there."

Tara had been surprised to learn how little money her family had. "Dad sold all his stocks to invest in the company. Did you know that? He was worried, wasn't he? You all were."

She pressed Faye's hand to her own cheek. "Mom will be okay. She owns the house, free and clear. There's the life insurance, of course. The car accident settlement is likely to be huge, too." Her mother had sat like a soldier, barely speaking, the entire meeting. Only her hands twisting in her lap showed her distress.

"You and Mom own the company," Tara said to Faye. The ownership was to *be divided evenly between and among Rachel Ann Kingsley Wharton and any Wharton child who has made a valuable contribution to the success of Wharton Electronics.* The lawyer had apologized to Tara, saying he had invited her father to update his will numerous times, but that her father had declined.

"No money for me, Faye, but that's how I wanted it." She put Faye's hand back down. "Did he know you wanted to hire me? Would he have wanted that? He kept my card. At least I have that."

And there was something else. Something that made her grin. "He gave you the ship bottles, of course, but you won't believe what he gave me. His library. All those books. He noticed that I was a big reader, too. I can't believe that. *And...* the antique shotgun. The one he wouldn't use for fear it might break? He must have known I'd learned to shoot. The guy who owned the range must have told him."

She swallowed the lump in her throat. "Can you believe that? You probably can. You were always generous with him. But I can't. And I just wish he'd said one word to me. About my business. About my interests. Hell, about my marksmanship." One kind word would have meant so much to her.

That's not his way. She didn't need Faye to tell her that.

Her parents were her parents. She could write them off or she could accept them as they were. She'd decided to accept them, warts and all.

And her father had gifted her with two of his most valuable possessions. There was always that card in his wallet, too. That had to be enough.

Her cell phone rang. She saw it was Dylan.

"The Tesla's at Roadrunner Wrecking on the outskirts of Tucson," he said without even saying hello.

Her mind switched gears instantly. "How'd you find out?"

"I had my secretary pull up the bill from the yard where Wharton P.D. tows vehicles and called on the off chance they would know where the car had gone from there. Turns out it's still on the lot. Your insurance company has a contract with them."

"Great detective work, Dylan. Thank you." At last they could get somewhere.

"So, I'm on my way there right now with Tony Carmichael and—"

"I'll meet you there. I'm at the hospital with Faye, so I'm close," she said, her nerves jumping at the prospect.

"The car will be smashed up. It might be...gory."

"I need to be there."

"I can't talk you out of it?"

"Not a chance."

He sighed. "You know I had to try."

"I know you did."

"I'm bringing a camera to take stills and video of the car and Tony's comments."

"Good idea. We can study it later or show it to Fallon or any experts we deal with." And if the scene was too much for Tara, she'd be able to look at the stills and footage when she felt braver. "We make a good team, Dylan."

"Yeah…"

"When I'm not stomping out of restaurants and calling you a sellout."

"Nobody's perfect."

She smiled. It reassured her that they could get past their arguments more easily. That wouldn't be the case if they were sleeping together, she knew. They would be too tense with each other, weighing every word for a double meaning, a change in feeling. Something.

With the address in the GPS, Roadrunner Wrecking was a snap to find and in a half hour, she met Dylan and Tony Carmichael at the high chain-link fence that marked the entrance to the salvage yard. Tony was a stocky man in overalls and a Grateful Dead T-shirt, a long blond ponytail pulled back by a do-rag of the American flag. Dylan introduced them and Tara shook his rough palm with her nerve-clammy one. "We appreciate you taking time for this," she said. "We'll pay you, of course."

"No big deal. It's a beautiful machine. I serviced her a couple weeks ago. I'd like to see how she held up under pressure."

"Let's go take a look," Dylan said. He picked up a wheeled cart, probably to look at the undercarriage, and Tony grabbed a toolbox and a jack. They met the manager in his tiny office and the guy led them to a cement slab with several wrecked cars. "Adjuster did his thing," he said. "I expected demo orders by now, but that's the insurance company's call. They

pay us either way. That's it." He pointed at a dark blue vehicle. "You need me, I'm in my office."

Tara gasped at the battered car. She refused to picture
how it had gotten that way. She was determined to be brave.

Tony pried up the hood, bracing it open with the crowbar. Tara and Dylan joined him, Dylan holding the camera,
running video, she assumed.

The engine was surprisingly clean, though much of it was
bent and crumpled. "Looks pretty jammed up," Tony said.
"Not sure how much I can see without a cutting torch and
major equipment."

"Really?" Tara asked, disappointed.

"The radiator's been shoved into the block," Tony said,
banging on the metal with a wrench, "so I can't get at the
pistons." He tapped the lid of a crunched-up black box behind the battery. She saw the edge of a label as bright as the
nail polish she'd used on Faye. "The controls are electronic.
I'd need to check the programming to see if it fouled up or
shorted out."

"We're looking for anything that might have malfunctioned or been tampered with," Tara said, finding it hard
to speak.

"Brakes, drive train, steering," Dylan said.

"I'll do what I can," Tony said. He turned to look through
his toolbox. Tara and Dylan stepped back and surveyed the
car. What remained of the windshield was a mosaic of shat-
tered safety glass. The other windows had only pebbled
chunks remaining. The dented driver's door hung from its
hinges. "How could anyone have survived?" she said. She felt
dizzy and inhaled quickly, but oxygen seemed to elude her.

"You sure you want to be here?" Dylan asked.

She nodded, but she couldn't face the interior yet. "Let's
check the back bumper for dents." If she kept moving, she'd
do better.

They found part of the bumper missing, the rest crushed. Both taillights were broken. "They must have been hit from behind. Something tore that bumper apart. And look at the dent."

"The damage could have happened when it tumbled downhill."

"But a collision would explain the speed when the car hit the barrier." She knelt to look closer and saw scrapes of pale-blue paint. "Take pictures of this," she said, excited by the find. "This could be from the car that hit them."

Dylan dropped to a crouch and snapped shots. "It could be the primer under the Tesla's topcoat, too."

"We need to see the missing piece of bumper. It would have more paint scrapes. I hope it didn't fall off when the car got towed. If it was at the crash site, Fallon should have it in evidence."

"I'll see what he's got," Dylan said.

"He parks at town hall, right? Could you check his car for dents or scrapes? I know you don't think he did anything, but he *was* at the scene...."

"He drives his cruiser for personal use. Police cars get pretty beat-up." He looked at her face. "I'll check," he said finally.

"Thanks." He'd meant it when he said he'd help, even when he didn't agree with her. She felt a surge of gratitude.

The trunk latch had been sprung. Dylan helped her try to lift it. With a shriek of metal against metal, it rose. She smelled sweet pickles. Then she saw the trunk was scattered with the contents of a plastic sack from Crowley's. Cans, tortilla chips, a jar of olives, a broken jar of salsa and two broken bottles. She turned over a piece with a label. Pinch. Her father's brand of scotch. "*This* is why the car smelled of liquor," she said. "No one was drunk. He bought whiskey at the store."

"It's a possibility, certainly," Dylan said. Dylan kept holding back on agreeing with any of her conclusions. She knew he thought she was overstating things and assuming the worst. He was helping her. That was enough.

They checked the photos Dylan had taken, making sure they were in focus and well lit. Their gazes met and held.

"We need to look at the interior," she said shakily.

"I can do it. You can take a walk."

"I need to see for myself," she said.

"Right." He braced her with a hand to her back and they headed for the driver's side of the car. She locked her mind into fact-finding mode, not allowing horror or panic to interfere with the examination of the car.

Inside, side and front airbags sagged and a white dust coated every surface. "The powder's from the airbags," Dylan explained. There was no blood visible. Whew.

She noticed the placement of the seats. "The driver's seat is too far back for Faye's short legs. Dad must have been driving."

"The EMTs might have moved the seat to get the driver out."

"But both of them were outside the car, according to Fallon." She pictured the ragged pool of dark soil where her father's blood must have mingled with Faye's, and where she'd found Faye's missing shoe. Her vision swirled.

"Tara?" Dylan reached for her.

"I'm all right." She shifted her gaze to the passenger seat. "Less foot room there. See." Then she caught sight of a few strands of fiber hanging from the broken safety glass still in the window. She looked closer, squinted. Not fiber. Hair. Dark, curly hair. Faye's hair. Tara gulped and stepped back, bumping into Dylan, turning toward him. "It's Faye's hair," she gasped. "It's caught in the passenger window. She wasn't driving. There's the proof." Her stomach churned and she tasted bile. She refused to throw up again. "Think I'll take that walk. Get pictures." She stumbled off, blindly weaving among the broken vehicles stacked and scattered throughout the salvage yard, taking deep breaths, forcing her stomach to settle down.

Tara had walked a long way before she felt normal again. When she returned, Tony was rolling out from under the car. He handed up Dylan's camera, then got to his feet.

"Brake lines look okay," he said, wiping his hands on a red rag. "Oil pan's dented from striking the railing, I would guess."

"Can you tell if the brakes were slammed?" Tara asked. "There were no skid marks on the highway near the rail."

"No way to tell. Discs are smooth, pads fine. The mechanism's functional. Hang on." He looked in the driver's side. "Emergency brake's on. There should have been skid marks."

She hadn't noticed the emergency brake. Thank God Tony was here.

"So the emergency brake didn't hold?" Dylan asked.

"The parts look fine. Something overrode the brakes. The accelerator might have jammed. Some circuitry went haywire."

"Or they got hit from behind," Tara said. "Could that explain it?"

"Don't know the physics on that. I could check the circuitry in my shop. Do more with the engine, too. Be good to check for any recalls on the car."

"We'll get it towed to your place," she said. "Would that work?"

"It should." Tony nodded, then left them to gather his tools.

"You were right about Tony. He's good," she said to Dylan. "We're finally getting somewhere. We can talk it over tonight. Want to grab supper?"

"Sorry. I've got a meeting, Tara."

"Oh, sure."

"I need to convince the town council to annex more land on the outskirts of town. It'll mean taxes to fund utilities. I've got the votes even without the mayor, but the more support the better off we'll be."

"You don't have to explain it to me. I know you're busy." She was surprised at how disappointed she was.

Dylan frowned. "I'm busy, yeah. Maybe too busy. What are you doing tomorrow?"

"Not much. Getting the car towed. Visiting Faye. Making calls for Mom's charity banquet. Some client work. Waiting for Joseph to hire me."

"Sounds like a busy morning. Could you free up the afternoon? I've got an idea. I'll pick you up at one. Wear jeans and athletic shoes."

"What are we doing?" Her heart lifted with delight.

"Trust me."

"I almost do."

Sadness shadowed Dylan's smile. Trust between them was a fragile thing. Maybe it always would be.

CHAPTER TWELVE

DYLAN PRESSED THE call button on the Wharton gate. Tara had sounded so bereft when he couldn't have dinner with her that he'd taken off a half day to make it up to her. He hadn't realized how much of his free time had been tied up in meetings. He deserved a life, too, he realized.

He looked up at the house. Impressive, if out of place in the desert. *Mount Vernon, Arizona,* was what Tara used to call it.

"What?" The voice from the speaker was Judith's, the Wharton's gruff housekeeper.

"Dylan Ryland for Tara."

The gate swung open and he drove through. He had to ring the doorbell twice before someone answered the door. It was Tara, a toothbrush in her hand, foam on her lips. "Sorry," she said. "Judith, for God's sake, why didn't you get the door?"

"I'm busy here," Judith grumbled, passing by with a laundry basket.

"Just need to spit and run a brush through my hair." She dashed for the stairs, taking them two at a time. He couldn't help but watch her butt. The jeans were criminally tight.

"Ahem." Judith jabbed a thumb toward the sitting room. He went there, a chastised teenager again. He'd been waiting a few minutes when someone came around the corner. He expected Tara, but it was her mother. "Dylan Ryland. What brings you here?"

"He came for me," Tara said, popping into the room.

"Am I dressed right?" She wore a gray jersey shirt that hung slightly off her shoulders, jeans and lightweight hiking shoes. With her hair pulled back, her face free of makeup, she looked great. "Perfect."

"For a homeless woman," her mother said. "But that makes you a matched set." She looked him over in his worn jeans, faded Wharton Raiders T-shirt and scuffed Timberlands. "What are you two up to?"

"Dylan has something planned," Tara said, her eyes lit with pleasure. Rachel's eyebrows lifted. She clearly thought something was going on between them. He knew the gossip had flown after their fight at Ruby's. Candee had called him early this morning after a friend told her. Victor Lansing had joked that he appreciated the sacrifices Dylan was willing to make to solve the Wharton problem.

He was grateful Tara hadn't taken him up on his dare about the kiss, though he'd been certain she wouldn't, not in the Wharton fishbowl. He still wasn't sure why he'd said that, why his heart had flipped at the prospect, why for a few seconds there he didn't care who knew they still had feelings for each other.

"Have you eaten, Mom?" Tara asked.

"I'm not hungry."

"You can't skip meals. You know that."

"What have we come to when Tara thinks she has to look after me?" Rachel said to him. "It's a lost cause, but maybe that's the appeal."

"I asked Judith to make you some chamomile tea," Tara said.

"You two go have your homeless fun."

Dylan was surprised to see the affection on Rachel's face when she looked at her daughter.

They left and got into the car.

"I have news," Tara said as he pulled onto the highway.

"This morning at the hospital, Joseph said he wants to hire me as a consultant."

"How did you manage that?"

"I did my homework, convinced people who had influence with Joseph that hiring me would be smart. Legally it would be a hedge against litigation regarding fiduciary duty and oversight."

"That's a mouthful."

"That's what I thought, but the legal argument was Joseph's tipping point. So, he warns me that he will not tolerate group hugs or feel-good mission statements, then he asks me to start on Monday."

"That was fast. Will he cooperate with you?"

"I think so. I told him I would be his eyes and ears, that my role was to calm the waters, reduce conflict and uncertainty. That seemed to relieve him. He really needs a buffer between him and people."

"Sounds like you'll do that for him."

"Yeah. In fact, he got choked up. He told me that Faye had been like that with employees and that he missed her, that it's been hard to be at Wharton without her. I was very touched."

"If you got Joe Banes to open up, you're a miracle worker."

"Not really. It's all smoke and mirrors."

"I doubt that."

She looked out the window for a few seconds, then back at him. "You're right. I mock myself because what I do sometimes scares me. I charge a fortune and clients expect miracles. So far I've delivered, but it's a high-wire act. I have to get the vibe, connect with the true leaders, deduce the unspoken conflicts, coax people to trust each other, and there are a dozen ways it can all fall apart at any time."

"Sounds complicated."

"It is. There are predictable patterns, but each company is unique."

"And you love it."

"I do. Very much. If I keep growing, I'll need to bring on a partner soon. First, I'll need to recover from being away so long, but if I can help Wharton, it's worth everything to me."

"On that subject, I talked to Candee about giving you some insights into the business department. She wants the three of us to talk it over." He cleared his throat, not looking forward to the meeting.

"So…a three-way?" Tara grinned.

"I doubt it will be that fun." Tara had been right. Candee had been upset by their meeting. He hoped Candee wouldn't give Tara hell when they met. "She suggested Monday night at my house."

"Sounds good."

"I hope it will be." He hoped it would be brief. The less time Tara and Candee spent together, the less chance they'd get on each other's nerves, hurt anyone's feelings or turn on him as the common enemy.

"Things are coming together," she said sounding happy. "I'll be working at Wharton, looking into what's happening there. Once Tony gets the car to his shop to check it, we'll know what caused the wreck."

"There's a glitch there. The salvage guy said your insurance company has to sign off before he'll release the car."

"Damn," she said. "I have to get that adjuster on the phone. That's all there is to it." She blew out a breath. "One step forward, two steps back."

"I did talk to one of the poker players for you," Dylan said. "Mitch Bender was at the meeting last night, so I asked him about your father."

"What did he say?" She turned to face him in her seat, eager and nervous, honing in on him.

"He said that Abbott seemed agitated. He lost three hands straight, which was unusual, then he left in the middle of a game to take a call—also odd, since he usually ignored his cell phone and got irritated when the other guys interrupted a game taking phone calls. A little later, he took a break and went to the john, but they could hear him talking on the phone. He left without speaking to any of them."

"The call must have upset him. Maybe it was from Faye. Maybe she called him, rather than the other way around. Had he been drinking? Did you ask Mitch that?"

"He hadn't noticed, but Bill Fallon called him the next morning and told him that if anyone official asked about Abbott, he should say that Abbott had had his usual iced tea. That seemed odd to Mitch."

"So Fallon *did* think Dad was drunk. It's still weird that he was right there at the scene. I don't buy his story about the medicine run for his wife."

"Maybe the first call your father got came from Fallon. Maybe Fallon wanted to meet your father somewhere."

"To talk about Mom, maybe? I don't know. There are too many possibilities."

"Which is why we need to know more before we—"

"Accuse anyone. Got it. You made your point last night." She shot him a look.

"Like I said, I never get tired of being right."

"So how did your meeting go?" she asked him.

"Not bad. The mayor's an obstacle right now. We need the right candidate to take his place. I've got to keep Troy from jumping into the race. My ace in the hole is that he hates politics. He wants to work for the town, not a bunch of constituents ready to recall him."

"Will the timing work? The election and your shift to full-time manager?"

"Good question." He'd begun to worry, too, with his father behaving as he had been. He shook his head. "Forget that. We're supposed to be relaxing." He took the turnoff toward the river.

"Wait. Are we going to the river for a picnic?"

"We'll eat eventually," he said.

"Then is it a hike? It's beautiful this time of year."

"Kind of," he said, smiling in advance, knowing she'd love his idea, certain it would be exactly what they both needed, a chance to enjoy some harmless fun together. He parked in the lower picnic area. A path wound around the hill to a series of caves. There were several trails down to the river from there.

He got out and headed for the back of the Land Rover.

By the time Tara joined him, he'd donned his helmet, grabbed his gun and held out hers.

"Paintball?" She laughed out loud. "You're kidding!"

"The range closed down a few years back, but I bought up some pellets. I figured we could rock-hop and use the caves and outcroppings for cover. What do you think?"

"I think you're brilliant." Her voice was lighter than he'd heard since she'd returned to Wharton. He'd forgotten how good it felt to make her happy.

"The paint's mud-colored and biodegradable."

"That is so you. Set up a wild stunt, but protect the environment." Her admiration warmed him. For all that he understood her, she understood him, too. And he realized he hadn't felt that connection with anyone in ten years, not even with Candee.

She took the cartridge he offered her. "I'm rusty," she warned.

"It's like riding a bike."

"I think that's what they say about sex, isn't it?"

"That, too." Their gazes tangled. Each time this happened, the urge became stronger and the voice of reason weaker.

"I brought sweats and towels in case we land in the river."

He raised a hand. "Do not call me Do Right Boy. You'll thank me when you're shivering."

"Fair enough."

He took out the two bags of paint pellets and handed her one.

"That all you got?" she said.

"I won't need half this to beat you."

She pretended to aim at his chest, then blew smoke from the end of her gun, a very sexy move that sent a jolt through his equipment, made him want to yank her to him and kiss her hard. Thank God, they'd be in constant motion for a while.

"Bring it on," he said, but she needed the win more than he did, so he intended to lose. "I figure we'd play capture the flag." He paused. "Except I forgot the flags."

"Who needs flags? Let's make it interesting. Let's call it Capture the Underwear. My bra and your boxers."

"Really?"

"Sure." She reached inside the sleeves of her shirt, unhooked her bra and pulled it out through the sleeve opening.

"I could never figure out how you did that," he said.

"You were always too busy watching my boobs to notice my technique."

"It's a guy thing." He tried not to stare at her softly swaying breasts as she waved her bra in front of his face. It was black and lacy and she was laughing at him.

But when he undid his belt, the laughter died on her lips and she sucked in a breath. "Uh, I'll…" She spun her finger to signify turning, then made the move.

He smiled. She wasn't managing her sexual responses any better than he was.

Dylan took off his boxers, grateful they weren't threadbare, then put his pants back on.

They tied their unmentionables to two sticks.

Tara shook her bra flag at him. "Take a good look. You won't see this again until after I've snatched yours."

But he was distracted by the shape of her nipples through the soft fabric. He wanted to touch them, watch her eyes burn in response, hear her breathing hitch, her body tremble.

She snapped her fingers. "You in there, Dylan? I just said I'd own you."

"Uh, yeah." He cleared his throat—and his mind. "We'll see about that."

They set distance boundaries, planted their flags and began the battle, chasing each other back and forth across the narrow bend of the river, hopping rocks, voices echoing against the hills on either side as they yelled, shrieked, and howled, shot and missed, ducking behind boulders, lunging around tree trunks, slipping into the river with sharp gasps at the cold.

He felt eighteen again. Tara's face, when he caught glimpses of it, was totally intent, totally delighted, animated and happy and so *young*.

Half an hour into the game, he spotted her flag, but stayed clear until he heard her yell that she'd found his. She emerged from some trees waving his underwear in triumph. "You're mine!" she called to him.

He just smiled. She was blotched with paint and splashed with river water so that her shirt clung to her shape. He was grateful when she crossed her arms to rub them for warmth, blocking his view.

"Let's get some dry clothes," he said, thinking the roomy sweats would hide her curves well, though Tara could make a garbage bag with leg holes look sexy.

They dressed back to back.

"That was really fun," she said, turning to smile at him.

He noticed a gray streak in her hair. "You've got some paint here." He wiped it with a towel, standing close, smelling her perfume, feeling her eyes on him, tugged again into her magnetic field.

"I'm starved," she said shakily, stepping back to break the hold they had on each other. "You said there was a picnic?"

"I did."

"Let's eat up on the ridge." She headed up the path toward the tables near the caves. He grabbed the ice chest and the Mexican blanket he planned to use as a tablecloth and followed, catching up with her in the second cave. "This is the one, isn't it?" she said in a breathless voice. "From that storm?"

"Yeah." They'd made love here one August during a monsoon. The memory hit him hard. Maybe he should have picked a more neutral spot, but then he couldn't think of a place that didn't hold memories for them.

"There was lightning and that great smell of rain and creosote and the river."

"I remember."

"The light was rust and gold—almost supernatural. I felt like we were Adam and Eve in the garden."

Making love with the storm all around, naked, sheltered in the cave and in each other's arms, it had been almost mystical.

"Let's eat in here," she said.

"Sure." He could hardly say *no, it makes me think of you naked*. He set the ice chest on the smooth stone floor and together they shook out the blanket, then sat on it.

As he opened the cooler, she said, "I remember you tasted like German chocolate cake and vinegar chips." Grinning, he held out the bag of vinegar chips and a plastic-lidded bakery box of German chocolate cupcakes.

"You didn't! You are so sentimental."

"I remembered that you liked them," he said, but their gazes locked, and he realized it had more to do with the memory of that time. What the hell did he think he was doing? They were alone in the cave and he could almost hear the rumble of thunder.

His subconscious had been working overtime.

She handed him a cupcake, took one herself, then dug into the chips bag, holding out her full palm so he could take some.

Watching each other, they bit into the cake then ate a chip. "Mmm," she said.

"Yeah." The flavors of salt, vinegar, chocolate and coconut blended well.

"I have to check." She leaned in and kissed him softly, running her tongue along his lips. She sat back. It had been a quick, friendly kiss, nothing like the one at his house, but he could hardly see for how much he wanted more.

"Well?" he managed.

"Tastes the same…maybe better," she said softly, her pupils huge, her hair trembling on her shoulders.

And he wasn't quite done. "My turn." He leaned in and took her face in his hands, kissing her more intently. She gave a little moan and returned the favor. He pulled her closer until they were chest to chest, the rush of it blasting through him, the need for her, the hunger. She tasted sweet and salty and like her.

She broke off again, fighting for breath, her eyes sparkling with blue fire, the way they got when she was aroused beyond reason. "Why can't we leave each other alone?" She sounded desperate. Her words vibrated in the air, almost alive, raising goose bumps on his skin.

"I wish to hell I knew," he said. Ten years and a lifetime later, he wanted this woman like no other before or since.

"Why are we here? In this exact place?"

"I didn't think it through clearly."

"I think you did, Dylan. I think deep down you knew ex-

actly what you were doing. You have instincts, too. Maybe
we need this. To do this."

She pushed him back onto the blanket and landed over
him, her eyes big, her mouth soft, lips parted. "I can hardly
think for all this *wanting*. It's too much with everything else
going on. You know?"

"I do. I know." He wanted her. He wanted to be inside
her. He rose and rolled her onto her back, so he was on top
looking down at her.

"Oh." Her eyes widened, their blue glowing up at him ea-
gerly. "What did you say about the gawkers last night? You
don't give them power over you? Maybe we're giving this
too much power, making it too big a deal."

"You don't think it's a big deal?" His hips pressed against
her, his erection against her belly, her chest heaving with
harsh breaths. She was flailing around for a rationale to do
what they both wanted. The desire rumbled through him, an
idling engine ready to roar to life.

"I know it is," she said, then frowned, "but denying it,
fighting it so hard, makes us do stupid things. Like this.
We're supposed to be having fun, blowing off steam, but
we're in a cave where we made love, torturing ourselves, denying ourselves, getting all wound up." She licked her lips,
her tongue sticking to the dry surface. He wanted to wet
them with his own, meet her tongue with his. Lust surged,
washing away all the barriers he kept flinging up.

Her eyes darted across his face, seeking his agreement. "If
we quit fighting and just do it, the pressure will evaporate.
We'll be ourselves again. We can concentrate. Our minds
will be clear." She paused. "I mean it can't possibly be as
good as we're imagining, right?"

That was the problem. "What if it's better?"

"You think it could be?" Her eyes flashed emotion after
emotion—hope, alarm, despair, hope again.

"It could be." He paused. "And that's not helpful." It would stoke the self-destructive urge he had to strap himself into Tara's emotional roller coaster, take his chances on the drops and twists and hair-raising turns.

He was too old for that. Too wise. The thrill wasn't worth the crash. And there would be a crash. For all she'd matured, Tara was the same demanding, difficult, quick-release girl she'd been as a teenager. And he was the same all-in rescuer scrambling to be everything she needed and not quite making the grade.

"What do you mean?" Her eyes searched his, a blazing blue.

"I think we're safer staying friends," he said.

Already, without sex, they'd been slipping into old habits, old ways of being together—good and bad. No matter what emotional safeguards they tried to build in, when she left, he would suffer. He knew himself that well.

She *would* leave. He couldn't forget that. It wasn't just geography standing between them. They wanted different things, they saw the world differently and they had a long-standing, gut-level distrust of each other.

He didn't have time for a heartbreak. Not with the last phase of his work at Ryland at a crucial point, not with his town leadership dream about to become real.

He didn't need fresh feelings for Tara getting in the way of building a life with a woman—a life built on trust and common goals and mutual respect. He was closing in on thirty. He didn't have time for make-believe.

"I see your point," she said. She was hurt, he saw, but trying to hide it. She'd suggested sex and he'd declined. She had interpreted that as him not wanting her as much as she wanted him. That had been the crux of the sense of betrayal over his not going to college with her.

So he had to explain. "I'm not into casual sex and casual

is the last thing I feel about you. I ruined my marriage because of how I felt about you, Tara."

She studied him, deciding whether or not he meant what he'd just said. He'd told her the truth and it hadn't been easy.

"I believe you," she said softly. They were lying exactly as they had been, his hands in her hair, their bodies together, faces inches from a kiss. Without moving at all, Tara withdrew from him. Desire faded from her eyes.

It hurt like hell, so he sat up and turned to the basket. "You hungry?"

"Starving," she said, her voice breathy with relief.

He brought out the rest of the food—crostini with three kinds of spread, Bing cherries, a couple of sodas. They both avoided the cupcakes and chips.

Layering some fig-and-prosciutto spread onto a piece of bread, Tara said, "So we went over my dad's will yesterday."

"Yeah?"

She paused. "There was no money for me, but I knew that going in. The thing is…he gave me his library. All his books."

"That's nice, I guess." Didn't sound like much to him.

"Don't you get it? He noticed that I love to read." He hated that she settled for the man's crumbs. But he had no right to judge. His relationship with his parents hadn't been easy, either. Parents were supposed to love you no matter what, but when he'd chosen his father over his mother, a chasm grew between Dylan and his mother that existed to this day.

Love could be fragile. He'd seen that vividly then. He'd seen it with his mother and with Tara. It was a lesson that had registered down deep.

Hell, part of the reason he'd stayed with his father might have been to prove that he loved him.

"Also, he gave me his antique shotgun," Tara was saying, so he tuned back in. "That means he found out I was shooting…" She swallowed hard, clearly struggling. "It's sweet and awful at the same time. He could have talked to me. Written a note or an email…something." She smiled sadly.

"Your father—"

"It's okay. I get it. He is who he is. My mom, too. I have to accept her as she is and go from there."

He was startled by the change in her attitude. His heart filled with tenderness and he touched her cheek, wishing he could say something to make her feel better. "Sounds like you're a work-at-it person after all."

"That means a lot to hear you say that." She kissed his palm. Their eyes locked and the air between them crackled.

Dylan pulled away, more alarmed than he'd been by their physical connection. He cared for her. He admired her courage, her determination, her big heart. She was trying to make things right with her parents, giving them both far more credit than they deserved.

They finished eating, packed up and drove home in a companionable silence. At her house, she got out of the car and came to his window. Her eyes were clear. She had color in her cheeks and a calm expression on her face.

"Thanks so much. I know you gave up work to spend the afternoon with me. I feel lots better. You always know what I need."

"It's good to see you happy."

"You're a great guy, Dylan. I see that more and more. I don't think I realized what I had when I had you." In her eyes, he saw longing and regret in a flash like lightning in the monsoon they'd watched from that cave long ago. She leaned in for a quick kiss, then backed up and waved at him.

He watched her in the rearview. She looked lonely standing in front of that huge house in those baggy sweats, arms folded as if against a chill, though the day was warm.

He knew how she felt. He was lonely, too, and filled with regret. He could taste it on his lips—German chocolate, vinegar chips and Tara.

CHAPTER THIRTEEN

TARA HUNG HER DAMP, paint-spattered clothes on the drying rack in the laundry room so they wouldn't mildew before Judith did laundry, her heart in turmoil.

Dylan. He'd said his feelings for her were serious, that they'd killed his marriage to Candee. When he'd said they were better as friends, Tara's first reaction was hurt that he could set her aside as he had done years ago for what he found more important. But that was the old Tara, the girl eaten alive by her insecurities, the one who demanded all-consuming love because she didn't love herself.

The more mature Tara understood him and agreed...except that she'd wanted him so much. When he'd touched her cheek, looking at her with such tenderness and pride, she'd felt lifted up, floating on air.

There was attraction, sure, but so much more.

Was she still in love with him?

The possibility hit her like a paintball bullet in the sternum, sharp, hard and bruising. It scared her. How could she still be lost in that teenage fantasy of perfect love? What if she never got past it? What if she was locked forever dreaming of the impossible?

She flipped off the light with a snap and headed down the hall.

"Tara?" her mother called to her from the sunroom, where she stood with a list in her hand, her eyes red-rimmed, her face swollen. She'd been crying. "Good Lord, you look even more homeless than when you left," she snapped. "Is that mud in your hair?"

Tara bristled, then realized this was how her mother told her she cared. On impulse, Tara put her arms around her mother and hugged her. "I love you, too, Mom."

Her mother backed out of the hug. "Have you been drinking?"

Swept up in new affection, Tara said, "Of course not. You don't have to hide how you feel, Mom, or put on a face for me."

"What is *with* you?" Her mother sounded vicious. "Why are you so extreme? On or off, black or white, thrilled or enraged. You're so *difficult*. You've always been difficult. That's your trouble."

Hurt coiled around Tara's heart. Just when she'd thought they were making some headway. She could hardly breathe for the pain. She'd tried, but her mother always rebuffed her.

"No, Mom," she snapped back. "My trouble is that you wish I'd never been born. I was a mistake. We both know that."

Her mother stared at her. "No child is a mistake," she said in a low voice. "You'll see when you have your own."

"What makes you think I want any?" She did, though. In her heart of hearts, once she proved to herself that she was capable of that level of love.

"You'll do what you're called upon to do. One step and then the next." She thrust the folder at Tara. "These calls won't make themselves. Call Raven's Dry Cleaning right away. They close early. It's the Jewish Sabbath." She turned on her heels and walked away.

Tara stood there, reeling. She should probably be angry, but she realized she wasn't. *No child is a mistake.* Somehow that soothed her—balm to the sting—and eased the lonely hollow she'd always felt inside knowing that she was *not wanted*.

For the first time, it occurred to her that her mother might have doubted herself, worried she wasn't up to motherhood, that she'd done the best she could with what she had, who she was.

Her mother had assumed Tara would have children. She had more faith in Tara than Tara did in herself. That touched Tara.

Something bloomed in her, a new sturdiness, a new confidence. All from the smallest hint of honesty from her mother. Coming from her mother, she realized, that was big. Very big.

Buoyed by the feeling, she decided her first call would be to the insurance adjuster. She was determined to reach him this time. When she told the secretary she needed to touch base with the adjuster *before she took any legal action,* he was suddenly on the phone.

"I understand you have some concerns, Ms. Wharton," he said, cutting her off before she could say more than hello, his voice icy, "but I have been in contact with your family's attorney, and I assumed he would answer your questions. Since that seems not to be the case, I'll repeat what I told him. I've examined and rated the car and taken statements from the law enforcement officer who first responded to the scene, a Mr. Bill Fallon, chief of the Wharton P.D. There were no witnesses. As the case proceeds we'll work with your attorney regarding the settlement of the bodily injury claims. That's all I can tell you at this time."

"Did you take photos at the accident site? Did you examine the engine?"

"I determined the level of damage and coverage pertinence. This is a run-of-the-mill, single-car loss. There was no need for more."

"Run-of-the-mill? My father is dead, my sister in a coma."

There was a pause while he inhaled. "I simply meant that the circumstances are clear. We're not disputing coverage, as there are no SLIs—Suspicious Loss Indicators—signs that the driver, policyholder or car owner committed fraud related to the policy."

"There is plenty that's suspicious about this accident. We believe there's evidence the car was struck from behind and possibly that the engine was tampered with. The emergency brake was engaged, but there were no skid marks. Something malfunctioned."

"There was a collision? Chief Fallon did not mention this."

"No, because he's actively covering up some aspects of the accident."

"We haven't yet received his report."

"Which won't tell you a thing. What we need is for you to release the car to us so we can have the engine fully examined."

"Hmm," he said. "With a settlement of this size, we, of course, are interested in correctly assessing responsibility…"

"So you'll release the car to our mechanic?"

"No, but I will submit the case to our SIU—Special Investigation Unit. You'll need to email me a narrative description of the evidence, along with any photographs. If there was malfeasance, we'll want to subrogate the perpetrator."

"What does that mean?"

"Seek to recover our settlement costs from the person who committed the fraud. If the SIU deems it worthy, an investigator will do in-person interviews, compare statements, take pictures, contract with a collision reconstructionist and anything else we need to resolve the case."

This was exactly what she was after. Excited, she said, "How soon before we see the investigator?"

"That depends on backlog, the significance of the settlement, the cost of the investigation compared with the likelihood that we'll prove our case."

Tara did her best to convince him that urgent action was needed and when she hung up, she sent him the narrative and photos. Just in case, Tara Google-searched *collision reconstructionist,* then called a company in L.A. she found online. The Wharton name, famous in engineering circles, snagged the expert's interest, and once he'd charged $500 to her credit card, he promised he'd get back to her in a day or two with his Level I analysis, which wouldn't hold up in court, but might impress the insurance company's investigators.

After that, adrenalized from the conversations, she did more online research, finding no reports of acceleration errors or brake failures for the Tesla, which also had great safety ratings. Finished, she shut the lid of her laptop. As far as the car went, all she could do now was wait.

She called Dylan to fill him in, trying to ignore the way her heart lifted when he answered, how his voice in her ear sent goose bumps of pleasure down her arms, how they both seemed to scramble for any topic to prolong the conversation, the intimacy of their laughter, the pauses when they just breathed at each other, how good it felt to be connected to him, how smart he was, how kind, how supportive, and how delighted he seemed by every word she spoke.

They were *friends.* They'd decided. They'd been certain. But they were talking to each other like a couple just falling in love. And she couldn't wait to see him Monday night when she would talk to Candee.

After that, Tara got busy with her mother's calls. She would double the donations from the previous year easily. It was almost laughable, the fact that CEOs trusted Tara to help them with decisions controlling the lives of thousands of employees, yet her mother didn't believe her capable of asking for a few measly donations from small-town businesses. It boggled the mind. She refused to let it get to her. She was bigger than that.

Tara sighed. It wore her out how much she had to be *bigger than* since she'd returned to her family, Dylan and this town.

No child is a mistake. There had been a flash of fire in her mother's eyes, a set of her jaw that still moved Tara.

One step and then the next.

Absolutely right.

"SHE'S NOT HERE yet, is she?" Candee said when Dylan opened the door to her Monday evening.

"Not yet. You look nice." She'd dressed for a date in a short, sexy dress and heels, with her hair up. She'd fussed for Tara, which gave him a pang.

She beamed. "When I ran into her at Wharton I looked like crap. I don't want her to think you married some loser."

"You're not a loser, Candee, and you never look like crap." Maybe when she got to know Tara, Candee would stop seeing her as this impossible ideal. Or maybe she'd sense his growing feelings for her and it would be so much worse. Dread tightened his muscles.

Duster came over to greet her and she patted him absently. "Now, what are you serving?" She looked toward the kitchen. "Wait. No food?"

"This is a meeting, not a party. There's beer." He intended to stay stone-cold sober to keep the conversation on track and away from awkward topics.

"That's no way to host." She looked him over. "Not a T-shirt. Please put on something more respectful."

He rolled his eyes, but he went to change if it made Candee more comfortable. The doorbell rang as he was buttoning a blue oxford shirt and when he came out, Candee had let Tara in. She wore jeans and a short-sleeved yellow shirt that shimmered in the light. Silk or satin. Something that looked liquid.

Tara crouched down for Duster to put his paws on her shoulder and do the kiss trick.

"That's cool," Candee said, but she looked a little startled. Duster never did tricks for Candee, as much as he loved her.

"I taught him that in high school," Tara said with a shrug, catching Candee's tone and clearly trying to minimize the damage. "Old dog, old trick."

"I put out snacks," Candee said. She motioned at the cocktail table, which held the German chocolate cupcakes on a plate, the vinegar chips in a bowl. *Great.*

Tara gave a surprised laugh.

"It's all he had," Candee said, puzzled by the reaction. "To drink there's beer…"

"No, no. The snacks are fine." She shot a look at Dylan, who smiled sheepishly.

"What's the joke?" Candee demanded, clearly feeling left out.

"It's not a joke," Tara said. "It's—"

"Leftovers from a picnic," he finally said, knowing their delay in explaining made it sound more significant than it should.

"A picnic. How fun," Candee said flatly. Had Dylan and Candee ever picnicked? Not that he could recall.

"I needed a break, so we had a paintball battle. It was a thing from high school," Tara added, trying to make it sound light, but it sounded intimate and exclusive. "Anyway, I really appreciate you talking to me about Wharton's finances. I know it's an imposition."

After a pause, Candee said, "I came as a favor to Dylan." She shot him a look, definitely pissed. "I'll get us beers," she said, walking away, her hips twitching angrily. Uh-oh. Bad start.

When she left the room, Tara mouthed *I'm sorry* at the same time he did.

Candee came back with three bottles. She held out one to him, twisted the lids on the other two and handed one to Tara.

She lifted her bottle for a toast. "To old friends," she said, a twinkle of mischief in her eye. Hmm. He twisted the lid from his beer. Foam squirted everywhere, dousing his shirt and the floor.

Both women burst out laughing.

"Dammit, Candee."

"Good one," Tara said.

"Couldn't resist. You go change. I'll wipe up."

He would put on a new shirt quick. Leaving them alone together was dangerous.

CANDEE WIPED UP the spill, then dropped onto the sofa and grabbed a potato chip, shooting Tara a challenging look as she ate it.

Tara sat at the other end of the couch, eating a chip, too. The stunt had been aimed at Tara, as well, she knew. They'd made Candee feel left out talking about the picnic, referencing high school, even Duster's trick.

She decided to be direct. "I want to apologize to you for the other day. I sounded rude, I know. I was caught off guard."

Candee shrugged, then sipped her beer, but Tara saw by the shift in her posture that Candee had needed the apology.

"Dylan talks about you a lot," she added. "It's obvious how much he cares about you and—"

"Don't butter me up," Candee said, setting down her beer with a click. "If you want him, you can have him. It's not my concern. We've been divorced for years." Her tone told a different story.

"That's just it. I don't want him." Candee huffed a skeptical breath. "Well, there's attraction, yes, but we agreed not to act on it."

"Whatever you say."

"It's the truth."

"Come on. I saw how you looked at each other. All that intimate smirking, that guilty-thrill look. I'm not an idiot."

Tara's face heated. "Well, we shouldn't be doing that. There's no point to it."

Candee watched her for a few seconds, then finally gave a snorting laugh. "I don't know why I'm picking on you. I'm over Dylan. I finally am." She shook her head. "It's just habit. Knee-jerk stuff."

Relieved to hear her say that, Tara said, "I know what you mean. I've been doing that since I came back to town."

"Yeah?"

"Yeah. Being a brat…hypersensitive to every slight… thinking the worst of people…"

"Making googly eyes at Dylan?"

She laughed. "That, too."

A sad look crossed Candee's face. "He never looked at me like that. If I'd realized that before the wedding, I wouldn't have wanted to marry him."

"I'm sorry it didn't work out," Tara said. "I don't know if this makes you feel better or not, but I was jealous of you when I heard you two were married. He committed his life to you, which was far more than he did with me."

"Yeah?" Candee looked her over, sharp assessment in her gaze. Tara liked her. She was a straight shooter. She dropped her gaze to the floor, took a drink of her beer. "He wanted it to work. I know that," she said finally, softly. "He fought like hell to hang on to me, but I wanted the real thing, not leftovers, you know?" She looked at Tara, this time her eyes were soft and open.

"I do. I really do." She felt a snap as they connected with

each other. "I admire you both for staying friends. That can't have been easy."

"It wasn't. Not at first. It's easier when I stay away from the wedding album." She gave a sheepish smile.

"For me, it's the German chocolate cupcakes." She picked one up and bit off the frosting.

Candee picked up one herself and began to eat it, a thoughtful expression on her face. When she turned to Tara, her expression held mischief. "Well, all I can say is lucky for you, I no longer want to scratch your eyes out."

Tara stopped chewing and lowered the cupcake from her mouth, startled to realize how pissed Candee must have been at her.

"I'm kidding," she said, grinning. "I'm more of a hair puller."

Tara burst out laughing. "I like how you think."

Candee smiled. "The truth is…I'm seeing a guy. His name's Adam. Dylan doesn't know yet. He's perfect for me. At first I got scared because I kept comparing him to Dylan. That horrified me because of Dylan doing that to me with you."

"I can imagine."

"But after a little while, my Adam memories pushed the Dylan ones out the window. Now when I'm with him, I'm totally with him."

"That's good."

"Yeah. Now I have to tell Dylan."

"He'll be happy for you, I'm sure."

"I hope so." She took another bite of cupcake. After she'd swallowed, she said, "You have a boyfriend?"

"Not at the moment." She peeled away the cupcake paper. "I need to get on that. I didn't realize I was so lonely. I have this great condo, but I treat it like a hotel. I'm living like a guest in my own life." She stopped abruptly. "I don't know why I said that. I hardly know you."

"You know enough."

"I guess so."

Suddenly Duster jumped between them, dropping his head on Tara's lap, flapping his tail on Candee's.

"Duster just declared us friends," Candee said.

"Smart dog."

"Yeah," she said, "though he never did any tricks for me."

As if in response, Duster got up and reversed his position so his head was on Candee's lap, his backside on Tara's.

"It's okay," Candee said. "I forgive you, Duster."

They smiled at each other over the dog. Finally Candee said, "So...do you hate those preppy shirts he wears as much as I do?"

They talked easily then, filling the distance between them with new camaraderie.

When Dylan came back, they were laughing.

"What's so funny?" Dylan asked warily.

"You," Candee said. "We were talking about you and *The Wire*."

"Candee says you do the dialogue with voices. I told her about the time you sang the theme song on karaoke."

"Great. Need a Sharpie to draw a target on my chest?"

Candee seemed to consider the idea. "Nah. I like that shirt. What do you think?" she asked Tara.

It was a light blue silk and Dylan looked gorgeous in it. "Not bad. You know they do have markers that are washable."

"Oooh, good one." Candee clicked her beer against Tara's.

Dylan dropped into the love seat, his face red, though he seemed relieved. Maybe because Candee hadn't gouged out Tara's eyes. "Did you two go over the Wharton situation yet?"

"Not yet, no." Tara looked at Candee. "You up for this?"

"If I can help, I will. Tell me what's going on."

"What we discuss can't go beyond this room," Tara said. "I don't want to add to any rumors at Wharton. Today was my first day working there and I don't want to get Joseph's guard up."

"I'll keep it quiet. Don't worry about that."

"What I hope you can help me with is any irregularities in the financial pictures. My sister, my father and Joseph Banes were heard to be arguing in the days before the accident. I'm guessing it was related to cash-flow or taxes. Joseph's behavior has been odd. He locked down my sister's computer unexpectedly and might have taken files from my father's home office. I need to know if he's doing something questionable or illegal.

Candee nodded, thinking. "I know they asked for an extension on the quarterly tax payment. I heard my boss talking to Mr. Banes about it. That means penalties and interest. No one's happy about that. Maybe that's what the dispute was about. We had to put off the auditors, too."

"Could be. But I'd like to know for sure."

"I can look through my boss's emails when he's at lunch, if you want. See what's come to him from Mr. Banes or Ms. Banes."

"That would be great. As long as you don't jeopardize your job. I've hit a lot of stone walls."

"No sweat. He hits wrong keys a lot and asks me to restore his defaults. So I'm covered. Here's another thing…I can get our IT guy to unlock your sister's computer."

"Would he tell Joseph?"

"Not if I ask him not to. We dated for a while."

"I didn't know that," Dylan said.

"I don't tell you everything," she said. "You're not my dad."

"I don't expect you to. I was surprised, that's all."

"Surprised anyone would date me? Is that it?"

"No. That's not it." Dylan was totally puzzled by Candee's reaction, but Tara knew it was her nervousness about Adam. "Why are you getting so sensitive all of a sudden?"

"Why are you getting so nosy?"

Tara figured she could help out a little. "Hey, you two, you're making me think you're not friends anymore."

"Of course we are," Dylan said.

"So you're glad Candee's dating, right? You want her to find someone who will make her happy?"

"Absolutely." He looked at Candee. "More than anything."

"So you can get me off your back, right?" But she was smiling.

"Hell, no," Tara threw in. "Where would he get great recipes like that beer-butt chicken? It was delicious."

"He cooked for you? Wow." Candee's eyebrows lifted. "Now that's interesting."

"We had to talk through the case, so he cooked supper," Tara said, but she was blushing and so was Dylan. "The point is, that you wish each other well, and Dylan would be happy to hear you'd found someone special, Candee." She leveled her gaze at Candee.

"Okay," she said. "Now that you mention it, there is a guy I met. Adam Baylor. I met him at a Home Parties Association meeting. He's the regional director. We've been dating for a month and I like him a lot."

"Oh." Dylan blinked, not speaking, clearly surprised.

Tara kicked his foot. "And…?"

He got it. "And that's great. I'm happy for you, Candee."

"You are?" She looked doubtful.

"I am." Dylan had adjusted to the news and his answer was clearly true. "Very much so."

"Told you," Tara said.

"You did." Candee gave Tara a high-five and blew out a breath. "I'm glad that's over."

"So…you two discussed this?" Dylan asked, totally puzzled by the conversation. "While I was…"

"Changing your shirt, right," Candee said. "That's how we roll, right, Tara?" She snapped her fingers quickly.

Tara laughed. She really did like Candee. "Anyway, I appreciate your help at Wharton. Anything you find out, give me a call." She gave Candee her cell number. "I can't thank you enough."

"Oh, I think you can. Come to my candle party next week."

"A candle party?" Dylan had been right about this.

"They're a blast. We have all kinds—tea, pillars, tapers, scented, unscented. Something for everyone. You'll like my friends. Plus, you can meet Adam. He'll be there. So will Dylan, right?"

"Me? Uh—" He looked like he'd rather eat glass shards.

"You have to come. Melissa Sutherland's cousin will be there—Jessica, one of your shipping clerks? You know her?"

"No, I don't."

"She's cute and she just broke up with her boyfriend."

Dylan held up a hand. "I'll buy candles, but no setups. I'm not interested."

"No?" She looked from Dylan to Tara and back, drawing conclusions that Tara could guess at and hoped Candee wouldn't voice. "Fine by me," she finally said. "You're tied up at the moment."

"I'm not—" Dylan started to object, but his face glowed red.

"Whatever," Candee said. "I leave you to it then." She jumped up and they walked her to the door. "Adam wants to try out some samples he got for this new home sales opportunity. Sex toys! Bye." Then she was gone.

Dylan shut the door and they looked at each other.

"I'm glad she's got a guy, but that last bit was too much information."

"*Are* you glad?" Tara asked. "You hesitated."

"I was surprised she hadn't mentioned it earlier. It's a relief. Sometimes I got the feeling she was still holding out hope for us."

"You're pretty tough to get over," Tara said. "Speaking from experience."

"So are you," he said, and their eyes locked. Here they were again, alone at his house, and the attraction hummed like a wire between them.

"Candee thinks we're still hung up on each other," Tara said.

"She wouldn't be wrong."

"No, she wouldn't. I should go," Tara said. They'd accomplished their purpose.

"You could. Or you could finish your beer and your cupcake." He nodded at the table.

Then she thought of a legitimate reason to stay. "Actually there's something else we could discuss."

"Great." They moved to the sofa and sat, close, bodies leaning in. "What's up?"

"It looks like you and I will be working together."

"Yeah?"

"Our operations VP asked me to mediate the conflict between our testing department and your engineers."

Dylan tensed. "How did that get decided?"

"It was after I mediated an ongoing dispute between our assembly-line manager and the shipping manager."

"That's great, I'm sure, but our disagreement is based on technical issues."

"Partly, for sure. You all have the answers between you. My job will be to manage the meeting in a way that allows the real issues to surface, get discussed, then options offered and selected."

"Sounds good in theory. And I'm sure you're good at what you do, but the issue is that we've done all we can by boosting our testing and increasing production. Our process is different than Wharton's. It's apples to oranges. We're at loggerheads. Jeb says their procedures and equipment are proprietary, so we're shut out."

"I see what you mean." She thought about that. "How about this? What if we brought the Wharton engineers out to Ryland and you could show them your processes. After the tour, we'd meet and discuss the situation."

Dylan considered that. "It's worth a try. I'm at my wit's end."

"Let's do that. I'll talk to Jeb, you fill in your guys, then we'll set up the visit."

"It's a plan." He smiled. "So you got shipping talking to assembly? I gotta say that's impressive. I hope you can do the same for us."

"That's my hope," she said.

"It's crucial to the company that we get this sorted out. A lot hangs in the balance."

"I realize that. I do." That put lots of pressure on her. Joseph would be evaluating her based on how this came out, she knew, and Dylan's company's future hung in the balance. She knew she was good. She knew her processes worked. She would trust them and herself.

Time to go. There was no reason to stay except to torture themselves. Just as she leaned forward to stand, Dylan put his arm across the back of the sofa, nonverbally urging her to stay. She leaned back.

"You two sure covered a lot of ground while I put on a clean shirt," he said.

"When you tell the truth, things move fast. I like Candee. She gives you hell."

"You would like that." He squeezed her shoulder, setting off a charge along her nerves, pops and flashes going every which way. She noticed the crinkles outside his eyes, the square line of his jaw, the way a lock of hair hung over his forehead, the crisp line of his lips. He seemed to be taking her in, too.

"Here we are again," she said softly. The minute they were alone together, their connection kicked in.

"Here we are." Embers flared beneath the smoky gray of his eyes. Her own body seemed to be liquefying.

"I should go home."

"Do you want to?" he asked in that low, sexy voice.

"No. I don't." Why lie?

"I don't want you to leave." He touched a strand of her hair.

"We're playing with fire." She started to tremble.

"I realize that."

Tara knew that look, recognized the tilt of his head, the parting of his lips. The next move was obvious: his lips hot on hers, his hands searing her through her clothes. All she had to do was shift slightly forward, offer herself, and they would surrender to each other, to the yearning they'd felt since they had seen each other again.

Her cell phone buzzed. Just like the day of the funeral on the hummingbird terrace, she took out her phone and saw Rita's cell number on the display. She almost laughed. "You won't believe this, but it's Rita again. She's got a sixth sense for keeping me out of trouble with you."

Dylan fell back, away from her. Smiling, she said, "Hi, Rita! What's up?"

"You'll want to get here as quick as you can," Rita said flatly. "Faye went into cardiac arrest. They revived her, but she's not stable. Her husband and your mother are on their way."

Tara's entire body went electric. "Is she dying?" Her voice cracked.

"Just get here. Are you safe to drive?"

"Am I safe to drive…?" She caught Dylan's gaze.

"I'll take you," he said.

Ice cold, her head buzzing, she told Rita she'd be there and hung up. "Faye's heart stopped," she said, her tongue thick in her mouth. "They brought her back, but they don't know if she'll live."

"Let's go," he said, standing, giving her a hand to help her up. He gave her her purse, then guided her into his garage and held the door for her to climb up into his SUV. She was glad he was with her. Faye and Dylan had been heart and home to her. Tonight she might lose one of them forever.

CHAPTER FOURTEEN

DYLAN PUSHED THE SUV above the speed limit, but Tara leaned forward, silently urging him to go faster. He roared through yellow lights and took turns so fast his tires squealed. It was warm in the car, but Tara was shaking with chills, gulping big breaths, her vision edged with gray. Every muscle was tight, as if her body believed that as long as she held on, Faye would, too. *Don't die, Faye. Don't die. Please don't leave me.* The words were a mantra, a prayer in her head.

"If I lose her, I don't know what I'll do," she said, staring straight ahead.

"She's getting the best care there is. They'll save her if they can."

Tara hung on to his words, needing them to be true. *Hurry! Hurry!* She twisted her fingers in her lap as if that would make the wheels turn faster. Dizzy from lack of oxygen, she gulped more air, but it didn't seem to help. She felt like she was breathing *for* Faye.

Dylan parked near the emergency entrance and they dashed inside, then had to wait for the elevator. She kept jabbing the call button as if that would make the slowest elevator on the planet get there sooner.

Dylan took her hand and squeezed it. "Whatever you need from me, you've got it. Anything." His eyes brimmed with worry...and love.

Throat too tight to speak, she nodded. She felt abruptly

steadier, stronger somehow, and her breathing evened out. *She wasn't alone.* Dylan was with her.

In the ICU waiting room, Joseph and Rachel rose from their chairs to greet them, both ghostly pale.

"They found an aneurysm," Joseph said. "She's in surgery now."

"How long?" Tara's voice cracked.

Dylan put his arm around her shoulder and squeezed.

"No idea. We're waiting for the surgeon to come out," Joseph said.

Dylan walked Tara to a chair and they sat together. There were a half-dozen people in the waiting area, talking, reading or looking dazed. Dylan still held her hand. He rubbed slow circles on her back. That contact seemed to be the only thing that kept her sane.

They waited, the minutes ticking by like hours. Tara's mother stared stonily ahead, her hair trembling from the tension in her thin body. Joseph fidgeted and paced, arms and legs disjointed as if he couldn't feel them.

Finally a man in green scrubs stepped into the waiting area. "Joseph Banes?" He spoke to the room. Joseph stopped in his tracks. "That's me."

The rest of them jumped to their feet.

"It went as well as we could expect," the doctor said. "She's stable for now."

"Is she still in danger?" Tara asked, her voice a thin thread of sound.

"Not immediately, no." That was as encouraging as the man was going to get, Tara realized. Faye was alive. Tara had to hang on to that. As long as Faye breathed, there was hope.

"Can we see her?" Tara asked.

"Briefly, yes. If the ICU nurses give you the go-ahead."

Joseph and Rachel went in first, her mother's movements almost zombie-like. When they returned a few minutes later,

Tara and Dylan took their place at Faye's bedside. She looked terrible, her skin gray, all makeup gone, an elastic mark outlining her face from the paper cap she'd worn during the surgery. The gauze pad across her collarbone was stained with blood and Betadine. As if he could read Tara's discomfort, Dylan folded under a blood-streaked section of sheet.

Tara picked up Faye's hand. "Fight your way back, Faye. Don't die. Please, don't die." Her voice trembled. She sounded like a desperate child, but she didn't care. When the nurse asked them to leave, she let Dylan guide her into the empty hall.

"What if she dies?" she asked him.

"You'll handle it," he said, brushing her hair from her cheek. "You're tough and brave. You'll do what you need to do. And you have me. Don't forget that. I'm here. Always."

"You are," she said. His steady gaze, his calm support made her feel like she could handle anything. "You are here." Her heart filled up and spilled over. "I love you, Dylan. I never stopped loving you."

He sucked in a breath, startled. "Same here. The more I deny it, the more I know it's true." They held each other's gaze, letting their words sink in, grab hold, change everything between them.

When they rejoined the others, Joseph stood. "Your mother needs to go home," he said to them. "Would you take her? I'll stay the night."

Tara saw that her mother looked ready to collapse. She made Joseph promise to call if anything changed, then they took her mother to Dylan's Land Rover. Her mother seemed totally wrecked. All the way back, Tara tried to get her mother to talk, but nothing worked. At the house, Tara went around to help her mother step down from the SUV. She shook off her arm and got out shakily.

"I'll make you some tea," Tara said. "We'll get through this together."

"No, we won't. I won't have it. Not from you, I won't." Her mother's eyes flashed fire. "I won't have you hovering over me, pitying me. You don't want to be here. You don't belong here. Please go. Leave me in peace." She stalked up the stairs.

Judith was coming down to meet her. "We'll be fine, Tara," Judith said, her voice kind.

"I have to get my car," she said, still shocked by her mother's words.

"Go on then," Judith said.

Tara climbed into the front seat, numb and stung, grateful when Dylan drove off without a word. They were silent as they drove, though she felt his eyes on her often. She clenched all her muscles, fisted her hands, holding in her emotions. Her mother wanted her gone. She would not bend, would not forgive.

Dylan pulled up beside her car in his driveway. "Stay with me, Tara," he said, his eyes holding hers. "Don't go back there tonight."

He wanted her with him, she knew that, but she was certain he was afraid she'd go back and confront her mother, and that would be a disaster.

"I'll tell Judith," she said, pulling out her phone.

"You're smart to stay," Judith said, then added softly, "I don't know what got into her. I really don't. She's glad you're here. I know that."

Things were pretty bad when Judith felt the need to comfort Tara.

Inside the house, Tara turned to Dylan. His gaze held kindness and concern. "There's a guest room, if you'd like. It's got workout equipment, but the sheets are clean."

She shook her head. "I want to sleep with you." Tonight she needed to be held, to feel loved, to feel alive. She might lose her sister. She'd lost what little bit of her mother's love she thought she'd had. She wasn't about to lose Dylan, too. She needed him, needed his touch. In his arms, she would feel safe, she would fit, she would be home.

Dylan pulled her close and kissed her, sweeping her away from her fear and sorrow. Duster dropped to his belly beside them with a sigh.

Tara melted into the moment, lost at last in the physical intimacy of finally being with Dylan again. The embrace felt old and new at the same time. Dylan's lips were warm and giving. She welcomed his tongue, the slow slide of his lips on hers, the urgency of him against her stomach. Her body responded, aching, tingling, burning.

It was such a relief not to fight this anymore. Dylan broke off the kiss, still holding her close. "You're sure this is what you want?"

"I'm sure."

"Good." Dylan bent and swung her into his arms, then turned for the hall. Duster rose and followed them. In the door to his bedroom, Dylan stopped. "I have condoms, if—"

"I'm on the pill," she said. She'd loved that Dylan always made sure they were protected, no matter how wild or frantic they were. He'd been that way with her. No matter how high she flew, Dylan was a steady hand on the kite string.

He leaned down to kiss her again. She closed her mind against the near loss of her sister, her mother's cruelty, the accident, the troubles at Wharton, everything but her body coming alive in Dylan's arms—the man she still loved, who loved her still.

She breathed him in—his spicy cologne and that sweet smell of his skin, stronger now, as if physical desire drew honey from his pores.

Desire flooded her in slow, thick waves, dissolving every ounce of resistance.

This was Dylan, who understood her, who knew her body as well as his own, who knew how to please her. She could let go, trust his mouth and hands and body to give her what she wanted. She yearned to be part of him, for him to be part of her, so close they hardly knew where one body ended and the other began.

DYLAN HAD MEANT only to offer Tara a safe place to stay after her mother's verbal attack. Instead he was taking her to bed. He held her sweet body in his arms, kissed her soft mouth. It seemed crazy and utterly right at once.

In his room, he set her on her feet, then helped her out of her top and slacks. Tara kicked off her shoes. He drank her in—beautiful, long-limbed, wearing white lace panties and bra. Her eyes glittered, her lips were puffy from his assault. He wanted her now, all of her, more than he wanted his next breath.

He couldn't take his eyes off the swell of her breasts above the lace, or the way her stomach muscles shivered, anticipating his touch. He whipped off his shirt, tossed it away.

She held his face in both hands and pressed her lips there, sliding, teasing, her tongue easing in, exploring him. "I've missed your taste and the sweet smell of you." She kissed him more intently, pulling at him, as if to draw life itself from his mouth. At the same time, she undid his zipper, then pushed his pants and boxers down with her hands, then her foot.

He kicked his pants away, and pulled her closer, spreading his fingers to hold more of her ribs and back.

Tara jumped up, wrapping her legs around his waist. He cupped her bottom and turned for the bed, reaching down to rip the covers out of the way. He laid her on the sheet. She was in his bed, the woman who'd filled his dreams, whose body was heaven to him.

Leaning over her, he unclipped her bra and cupped her impossibly soft breasts, the nipples pink, pebbled with arousal. He lifted one to his mouth, ran his tongue around its surface, while she shuddered and gasped.

"That feels…so…good," she said.

He wanted to be inside her, to make her come, to come himself. It was a pulse in his head, a throb along his nerves. He fought to get control, to take it slow. He ran his fingers over her through her panties.

She moaned, then reached for him, her fingers tight around his shaft, making him hers.

They moved in rhythm, fingers and lips and hips, like they'd been together all this time, as if they'd never stopped making love, taking each other higher and higher. Somewhere in his half-gone brain he knew he was carried away, making far too much of the moment, but he didn't care. Lust surged through him, unstoppable as the blood in his veins.

"Get…inside…me." She was struggling to get her panties off. He helped her, throwing them to the floor. She bent her knees and guided him between her thighs. He looked into her eyes, saw how much she wanted this…wanted him. She used to whisper in his ear, *You're my home.*

He'd wanted to be. The idea swelled in him, enflaming the primal need to protect her, to keep her safe and well, to sacrifice his own life for hers if he had to.

With that thought, he thrust into her soft slickness, feeling a pleasure so intense he couldn't catch his breath.

"Oh…" She closed her eyes, her lips parted. "I remember this," she whispered, then opened her eyes. "I remember you. All of me remembers all of you."

He fought to respond, but words failed him. All he could think about was merging with her, becoming one with her. He pulled out, then pushed in, amazed that each time he felt more.

Dylan forced himself to go slow, to focus on every sensation. He wouldn't miss a single gasp, a blink of her blue eyes. He would feel every muscle twitch, drink in every kiss, hear every mew and sigh.

She made him want to do more, take her higher, make it last longer. She wrapped her legs around him, digging in with her heels, lifting her hips with each thrust. He knew she was close, so he went still to let the pressure build, make the release more intense.

She gripped his backside with both hands. She never wanted to wait. She pushed down as she lifted her hips, again and again. He couldn't resist, not after all the waiting and wanting he'd endured already.

When he kicked into gear, she bucked up, eyes wide, pupils huge and black, giving herself over to him. That was the hottest part. That Tara, so scared to be close, so slow to trust, trusted him, let go with him, only him.

Her breath hitched. She was nearly there. His body picked up the cue and tightened for the last push over. There it was, that look she got when she came. He'd missed that, dreamed of it far too often. "Oh, I'm…" She gasped.

"I know you are," he said as she exploded. Her release caught him, carried him with her, the rushing wave almost too much to stand.

He couldn't believe the wonder he felt, the joy of sharing this with Tara, the girl he'd first loved, the woman he still did.

TARA'S CLIMAX HIT so hard that every inch of her body, every fiber of her being felt it, throbbed with it. *This.* This was what stopped hearts, launched ships, made the world go 'round. She felt it in her body and in her heart.

They'd climaxed together. She'd forgotten how natural that had always been for them.

She felt like she'd returned home from a harrowing trip. In a way, she had. All of it—Faye's coma, her near death, her father's death, her mother's harsh words, even the old pain of losing Dylan—rose up in a huge wave of emotion, which broke free in a sharp sob. She had held back so much for so long, hidden the pain even from herself, that she couldn't help the outburst.

Dylan pulled her onto his chest and rubbed her back in slow circles, and let her cry. He didn't ask her what was wrong. He let her be. However she was, that was fine with him.

Tara lifted her head to be sure he still wore that look, that tender acceptance of her, no matter what. Yeah. There it was. "I thought I made it up," she said, still choked up. "That look you have." She couldn't even describe it, except that it made her feel loved and safe and *known*.

"I know what you mean." They stayed like that for a few minutes. Abruptly Dylan's eyes went distant. Was he pulling away?

No. Don't. Not yet. Her heart turned over in her chest. She wasn't ready to back away. She needed him too much right now.

"You want to call the hospital?" Dylan said. "Make sure nothing's changed. I don't want you to worry."

Oh. Whew. He'd merely turned his thoughts to their situation. He wasn't backing away, leaving her. No cause for panic.

"Yes. My phone's in the living room." She started to get up.

"I'll get it. I need to get you food anyway." He kissed her forehead and climbed out of bed. He was gorgeous in the lamplight, broad shoulders, prominent muscles, graceful movements.

"You remembered how hungry I get?"

"I remember everything about you, Tara," he said roughly,

his eyes glistening with longing…sorrow…regret. As if he hadn't wanted that to be true, but was helpless to prevent it.

She knew exactly how he felt.

What now? She couldn't keep the thought from her mind. Being in Dylan's bed tonight was about Faye nearly dying, about the turmoil of these days in Wharton, and about the love they still held for each other.

She couldn't count on this. She shouldn't.

She squeezed her eyes shut, squeezed back that thought. They deserved this moment, this pleasure and relief, the feeling of being understood, loved, the feeling of home.

I get to have this. We both do. No regrets.

What about tomorrow? And the day after that? If they worked at it, could they get past the pain they'd caused each other? Could they start fresh?

She felt so right in his arms; she didn't want it to ever be wrong.

A HALF HOUR LATER, Dylan balled up the last cupcake wrapper and tossed it onto the nightstand before settling back around Tara. Against all odds, he had her in his bed. He tucked her more firmly against his chest, one hand on her breast, breathing in her smell, feeling every inch of her body against every inch of his. He hadn't been wrong about how good they'd been together. Now he felt fully alive, fully awake for the first time in years.

Now what?

He'd been so clear before that being with her would only arouse impossible hopes. Their relationship was a dead-end. A dead-end wrapped in pain.

But they loved each other. That had been important. And making love had been healing. Could they end it with that? Stop now? Let that be enough?

Who was he kidding? He'd never get enough of her. He

pushed away the thought. For now, he had her in his arms. He would enjoy that for all it was worth. He'd deal with tomorrow tomorrow.

He woke to Duster licking his face, the smell of Tara in his bed and a note: *Gone to see Faye. Thank you for last night. I'll call from Wharton. Tara.*

Thank you for last night? Like he'd done her a favor? Damn.

At least he didn't have to wonder whether they'd be together again tonight. Clearly that was that.

His cell phone rang. It was her.

"Faye's back in her room, Dylan. She's stable again. It's such a relief. You have no idea how much better I feel."

"I'm glad to hear that," he said, his anger fading in the face of her delight.

"Me, too. I can breathe again. And think. I'm on my way to Wharton to set up that field trip to Ryland. Let your guys know, okay?"

"Okay…"

"Is something wrong? Was my note too terse? I didn't mean it to be."

"No. It was fine." He sighed. He couldn't be angry at her. She didn't know how to handle this any better than he did. They'd figure it out together.

"So, can we meet for lunch and talk?" she asked.

He thought through his day and realized it wasn't possible. "I'm sorry. I have a meeting." He had to convince Troy Waller not to run for mayor, to wait for Dylan to hire him. The man seemed to doubt Dylan's commitment to his plan.

"Oh. Then…supper?"

This was the day he usually stayed late to go over production figures before he met with Victor and his father in the morning, but he didn't want to disappoint Tara again.

"Sure. Supper at my house." He'd throw together spaghetti. He owed them both that much. And after supper? Would she stay the night? He'd see if she brought a suitcase.

CHAPTER FIFTEEN

TARA BLEW OUT A BREATH. It was 6:00 p.m. She needed to get over to Dylan's for the dinner he'd offered to make her. Her main accomplishment today had been to convince Jeb Harris to take a crew to Ryland Engineering the next morning for a field trip.

She'd coordinated with Dylan, who'd sounded mildly hopeful, though it was hard to tell after that awkward phone call in the morning. She hadn't been able to figure out what to say in her note about their night together, so she'd been breezy and Dylan had sounded hesitant.

They'd had reasons to be together last night, but now? Did they dare continue? The very fact she was so freaked out told her they should back off. Maybe you never got over the pain of the past. Her mother certainly wasn't willing to, and maybe Tara was kidding herself that it was possible for her and Dylan.

Where could a relationship between them go, anyway? She'd leave and he'd stay. Long-distance romances were hopeless. She never wanted to feel the hurt of their first breakup again, so why prolong the end and risk more hurt?

As she headed down the hall, she noticed Joseph's office light was on. He'd come in at noon, after spending the night at the hospital with Faye.

She tapped on the door, then peeked in.

Joseph was slumped in his chair, tie open, a pint bottle of Wild Turkey on his desk beside a few paper cones from the water cooler. He held one, she saw. "Still here?" he asked her, head wobbling, clearly drunk. "Aren't you the dedicated consultant. Cheers." He lifted the cone, sloshing whiskey on his desk, then drank it, making a face.

"Whiskey neat is no fun," he said. "It looks so manly in the movies when men drown their sorrows. Maybe if I bought the good stuff like Abbott, but that's…not…me. Guard the pennies and the dollars take care of themselves." He balled up the cone and tossed it toward the trash can, missing by a mile.

"Did something happen, Joseph?" she asked.

"It's about to," he said, picking up an iPhone near his hand. "This is Faye's phone. I've been carrying it around since they gave it to me at the hospital, scared to look at it. But last night she almost died, soooo I charged it up. I hadda see."

Tara sank into a chair. "Why are you afraid to look at her phone?" Her neck hairs began to prickle.

"Because as long as I didn't look, I could pretend she still loved me. The proof she doesn't is right here." He shook the phone.

"What kind of proof?" A chill raised goose bumps.

"Messages, texts, the guy's number."

"What guy?"

"She was having an affair," he said, getting choked up.

"No way," Tara said. "Not Faye." Faye was steady and loyal. She would never do such a thing.

"She hadn't been herself. Distant. Preoccupied. Hardly talking to me except to argue."

"What did you argue about?"

"The taxes. I delayed payment. Abbott and Faye were angry about the penalties and the interest. They never listened to me. Never. I told them we should kill the Ryland contract, cut our losses, but no, it's too damned symbolic. I told them we should outsource, that manufacturing was too expensive. Oh, no, gotta be loyal…town's counting on us… whatever." He shook his head.

"I disappointed her," he said grimly. "I let her down. That's it. That's why. She wanted kids. But I had…problems."

"Like what?" she asked gently. This might tell her more about the accident. She held her breath, her heart pounding.

"Number one…slow sperm… Number two…recessive gene for a neurological disorder. That's what did it. The straw that broke my back. She talked to a gen…et…ics counselor. Then she stopped talking to me." He was slurring, spacing out syllables, running words together. He tried to pour himself another drink, but couldn't get the cones pulled apart.

"So she found a guy with better genes and better sperm." He waved the phone. "It's all here."

"What makes you say that? Is there a message?"

"Two new numbers. So far, I called one. It's a divorce attorney." His face crumpled. "She didn't even try. She gave up on me just…like…that." He snapped a finger.

That made no sense to Tara, not with the kind of person Faye was. "And the other number?"

"Has to be *him*. I got drunk before I called him. Figured I could give him hell that way."

So he was only guessing. At least that.

"I think she met him at Vito's that night. She told Abbott, I think. Maybe Abbott didn't want her to do it—divorce me, I mean—cuz she sent him a text."

"Nothing changes. Let it go," Tara said. "I saw it on Dad's phone."

"Why would she cut me off like that?" He looked at her, his eyes full of passion. "I'd do anything for her. *Anything. She's…my…life.*"

"What happened that night? After you quarreled with Faye?"

His eyes were red embers. "She said she was meeting Abbott at Vito's. Abbott. Right. I'm not an idiot. She saw Abbott every day. Besides, we weren't even eating pasta. She bought low-carb ketchup, for heaven's sake."

"Were you angry that night?" she asked, afraid he'd done something terrible after all. "Did you do something, Joseph? Something you regret?" Had he run them off the road in a fit of fury, jealousy and fear? *Please, no.*

"Of course I did something I regret. Wouldn't you?" He took two harsh breaths. "I bought a Bundt cake and a gallon of ice cream and ate myself sick, then fell asleep watching Animal Planet. Bill Fallon woke me up when he called about the accident."

Joseph hadn't caused the crash. Thank God. Abruptly a thought came to her. "Wait. Was the divorce attorney Randall Scott?"

"Did she tell you, too? Abbott *and* you?"

"No. My father met with the guy. He had the card in his wallet."

"Abbott set it up? He hated me that much?"

"No, Joseph. Calm down. It was my father who was looking into divorce. *He* met with Randall Scott, not Faye."

"Why did Faye have the number on her phone?"

"No idea. Maybe she knew Scott and asked him to take Dad as a client. What I do know is that she would never divorce you out of the blue like that."

"You think that's it? Abbott was divorcing Rachel? Really? That would be so great!"

"I wouldn't say it was *great,* Joseph. A divorce is not great, but I'm sure you're relieved it wasn't Faye."

"Yeah…that."

"Faye wouldn't have cheated on you, either. She would have asked you to go to marriage counseling first. She—" She stopped, realizing a possibility. "I bet I know who's at that other number. Dial it. Put it on speaker."

Warily he did what she asked. The message machine kicked in right away. *You've reached the office of Dr. Eli Finch...*

"He's a psychiatrist," she said. "Faye went to him for depression and anxiety, and he prescribed her some pills."

Joseph's eyes went wide. "How did you know that?"

"Her iPad had a note about picking up prescriptions, so I got them and called the doctor's number."

"She wasn't having an affair? You're sure?" She'd never seen him look so wide-eyed and happy. He'd been in agony over this, which explained his moodiness, how much he'd fidgeted whenever she asked him questions. He thought he'd disappointed Faye enough to send her into the arms of another man.

"I'm as sure as I can be."

"Thank God." He fell back in his chair. Gradually, the wide-open look of relief on his face changed to determination and he sat straight up and locked gazes with her. "I know you think Faye shouldn't have married me, but I swear to you that if she wakes up, I'll prove you wrong."

"You don't have to prove it. I already know I was wrong. Faye loved you. She chose you. And I had no business second-guessing her."

"Now I need to hear Faye say that." Abruptly, his face crumpled and he buried it in his arms on his desk and sobbed his heart out. Joseph's love for Faye was clearer to Tara than ever. In a few minutes, once he'd collected himself, Tara offered to drive him home.

After that, she headed to Dylan's house for supper, nervous about seeing him and what they would say to each other.

All the reasons they couldn't sleep together again swirled in her brain, but the minute she saw his face in the doorway, she just threw her arms around him, so glad to see him, so happy to be with him after a long, difficult day.

He stiffened slightly before he returned the hug. Uh-oh. He wanted to put on the brakes. She let go and backed up. "Smells great," she said to cover for her impulsive move, really glad she'd left her suitcase out in the car. He clearly intended them to share a supper, not a bed.

"Nothing fancy. Just spaghetti." He smiled, but it didn't reach his eyes.

"I'm sure you had work you should be doing instead, so I appreciate it." She was losing him again. She felt that twist of pain, the swirl and drop like her insides were dissolving.

To hide her reaction, she crouched to greet Duster.

"I checked Fallon's cruiser for you," Dylan said.

"You did?" She stood, grateful for the change of subject.

"No dents or scrapes. So he didn't hit the car. I got him to show me the evidence. He complained it was a waste of storage and man hours, but he dumped out the boxes for me. No bumper piece."

"Shoot. Maybe it's still at the site. I hoped to email a photo of the bumper to the accident expert. I expect his call any time." She tried to focus on the case and ignore her sinking heart, the lump in her throat, the way her eyes burned.

"Let's eat, huh?" he said, leading her to the kitchen. They sat at the table, both of them awkward, it seemed. Dylan served spaghetti, set out salad bowls and garlic bread.

"Sorry I'm a little late," she said. "I had to drive Joseph home. He was drunk."

"What?" He put down his fork.

"I know. We had the strangest conversation...." She told him the story haltingly, her mind not on the words. Dylan seemed to be only half listening, too. "So, all that odd behavior was out of guilt." She stopped, unable to stand it anymore, and braced her hands on the table. "You think last night was a mistake, right? That why you're acting like this?"

"Acting like what?"

"Distant…preoccupied…uncomfortable."

"It wasn't a mistake," he said firmly. "It was amazing."

"I think so, too," she said, her heart jumping into her throat, relief pouring through her. "It was exactly what I needed."

"That's good. That's what I wanted. To be what you needed. To—"

"Dylan, don't try to tell me that was pity sex." She grinned.

He burst out laughing. "God, no. I wanted you more than my next breath. Come here." He got up from the table and reached for her, wrapping her into a hug. He looked at her. "I don't know what to do now."

"Me, neither."

"I mean there's no future for us. We both know that."

He was right, but it stung how swiftly he'd concluded that. He could at least express regret. "We're on different paths," she said.

"If we were wise, we'd stop now, before we get more involved, before either of us gets hurt."

"Right," she said, deeply disappointed.

"If we were wise, that is," he repeated. His gaze deepened. "The trouble is I'm feeling more foolish by the minute. I want more time with you."

"Me, too," Tara said, her heart singing. "Maybe we can be together until I leave? Or if there's a natural stopping place…"

"I like where you're going with this."

Was that even possible? How could it be that easy? She could get hurt. So could he.

But when Dylan lowered his mouth to kiss her, holding her so tight she could hardly breathe, kissing her like he'd die if he had to stop, she was willing to risk it. They *were* wiser in some ways, after all.

Dylan broke off the kiss to murmur in her ear, "I've got a spare toothbrush in my kit bag. New."

"No need," she murmured back. "My suitcase is in the car."

He laughed a big belly laugh. "That's my girl."

THE NEXT MORNING at nine, Dylan watched Tara and her team enter the Ryland lobby. How she managed to look alert after making love half the night then leaving at dawn to see Faye before work was beyond him.

When he'd watched her get into her car, her hair lit by the pale orange of the rising sun, he'd had the unsettling feeling she wouldn't be back. They'd certainly made love like it was the last time. Even as they'd agreed to be together for a while, they'd both held back. Neither wanted to get hurt or hurt the other. Maybe they'd been kidding themselves to even want to try.

He wanted a settled life in Wharton and that was the last thing Tara wanted. She couldn't wait to escape the place. Beyond that, she seemed afraid of love. He sure as hell didn't want to live on the razor's edge of rejection.

Get your head in the game, he told himself as Tara approached. This was a vital business meeting. Ryland Engineering's survival hung in the balance. He smiled politely and held out a hand for Tara to shake, one professional to another.

Her gaze flickered and her body softened, sending a charge through him. She was remembering last night, too. He almost yanked her to him and kissed her like nothing else mattered, hoping that would make it so.

Behind Tara, the Wharton team approached—Jeb Harris, Matt Sutherland and two technicians. Behind Dylan stood Victor Lansing and Dale Danvers, his Quality Assurance manager, along with two techs.

Dylan led them all toward the factory. He glanced in his

father's office. Empty again. He'd asked his father to make an appearance to show his commitment to solving the problem. There was a risk that his father would say something blunt, but Dylan had laid out the plan to him. When push came to shove, his father did the right thing.

They passed through the factory doors. A tenth the size of the Wharton plant, it rivaled Wharton in efficiency and output, in his opinion. If they were paying attention, the Wharton crew would see it was a tight operation. He hoped that would help convince them to look seriously at what had to be errors in their testing protocols.

As they walked the length of the plant, Dylan showed them where the surface-mounted components were soldered to circuit boards, the reflow ovens where the connections were sealed, and where they programmed the units, emphasizing the double checks, the extra testing they'd implemented. Harris seemed impressed. Sutherland, who'd so helpfully suggested Ryland find a better supplier, walked with his arms folded, frowning.

After the tour, they gathered in a conference room for the meeting.

There were snacks and coffee—Tara's idea, so the men could see each other as people, not simply obstacles.

Tara called the meeting to order and went over the ground rules she'd written on a newsprint tablet: *listen first, assume good intentions, no attacks, no blanket statements, offer solutions, be specific.*

Just as she finished, Dylan's father walked in.

Dylan introduced him to the Wharton team and Tara.

"The prodigal daughter returns," his father said. "I understand they've put you to work over there. Does that mean you plan to stay?"

"For a while, yes," she said. "I hope to make a contribution." She didn't respond to the light mockery in his father's tone. She was a professional, for sure, and he admired her for that. Her plan for the meeting was solid, too.

His dad sat in the chair Dylan had saved for him, but he seemed edgy, restless. Dylan's gut tightened. He caught his father's eye. *Don't screw this up.*

As the men began their discussion, Tara did a good job of guiding the conversation, drawing out important points, emphasizing areas of agreement and enforcing the ground rules.

Eventually they reached the crux of the conflict—the failure rate of Ryland's parts. Jeb claimed the bad units caused power surges, suggesting Ryland's suppliers had provided shoddy components. Victor pointed out that even if the parts were bad, which they weren't, it would require an extreme torque or a huge jolt to cause the surge they described. Finally Victor said that they needed to see the Wharton tests performed, period.

Jeb went on his rant about all the proprietary equipment and processes, how a visit wouldn't be possible.

Then Tara asked about showing the Ryland team selected tests, setting aside the proprietary items.

Trapped by his own objection, Jeb Harris had no choice but to agree. Matt Sutherland's jaw dropped, clearly surprised by the concession.

Abruptly his father stood. "I can't believe we are begging to see the tests we supposedly failed. What are you hiding over there, Jeb? Rigged tests? Sabotage?"

"Mr. Ryland," Tara interrupted firmly, "you missed the discussion of ground rules, but you'll need to reframe your comments. No accusations. No presumptions or blanket statements."

"This is my business, my building and my reputation at stake, I'll make whatever statements I want, blanket or otherwise."

"We're working it out," Dylan said. "Let us finish."

"Those so-called power surges are bogus," his father said, brushing off Dylan's objection. "I'm driving around with one of those so-called duds in my own car. So are you, son, by the way."

"What?" Dylan said.

"I changed out your battery when you had your car serviced. I put one in Candee's Prius, too. A couple others."

Dylan was furious, but he held his tongue.

"Have you had any power surges, son?" his father demanded. "No, you haven't. No one else has, either. We're the best vendor you've got, Jeb, and we won't offer our part for less than the dirt-cheap price Abbott extorted from my son, who has this fairy story in his head that Abbott and I could sing kumbaya around the campfire again." He shot Dylan a glare, his eyes on fire.

"Abbott Wharton was a stubborn, arrogant man who expected the world to bend to his will. In the end, he didn't get that, did he? No. The world had its way with him and now he's gone."

There were gasps, looks were exchanged and dead silence fell over the room.

"Abbott Wharton robbed me once. He won't rob me again. I promise you that. I'm finished with what I have to say." His father stalked from the room.

Dylan looked at the stunned faces around the table. His father had just killed the compromise they'd nearly reached.

Victor got up. "We stand by our product," he said, then turned to leave, Dale and the techs following. Victor had taken the test failures personally. He'd been downing heavy-duty antacids since the troubles began.

"That was unfortunate," Tara said, red spots on her cheeks. "But we'll straighten this out and follow up about a visit."

"I won't kowtow to those assholes," Jeb said and took

his team out of the room, leaving Tara and Dylan staring at each other.

"What the hell was that?" Tara said.

"I'm sorry. I talked to him about being conciliatory, but—"

"Conciliatory? He dropped a bomb and stomped out like a child. He ruined everything. We were this close to an agreement."

"I know. I'll straighten it out. I'll settle our guys down and apologize to Jeb."

"Your father's the one who should apologize. That was unforgivable."

"Abbott's death has been hard on him. He's not been himself."

"I seriously doubt that, Dylan. He basically said my father got what he deserved."

"That's not what he meant." He wanted to throttle his father for saying something so clumsy, but Tara was far too eager to criticize the man.

"I would have asked him to leave, but I was afraid he'd hit me."

"Come on. He would never do that. I don't blame you for being angry. Dad blew it. I get that. Why make it worse?"

"I don't see how it could be any worse. So is this your *job?* Follow after him and clean up his messes? How can you stand it?"

"Tara, stop." She was furious. He could see that. She thought his father was still exploiting him, using him, that Dylan was blindly loyal to the man. He was not about to defend himself or his father to her. And he didn't want to hear more hateful words from her.

They stared at each other for long seconds. Tara seemed to collect herself, set aside her personal feelings and shift into professional mode. "Okay," she said. "You're right. That's water under the bridge. What can we do to salvage this?"

Whew. They were a team again, working together to save the contract between their two companies and, as it turned out, Dylan's long-held dream. That was the most important thing here.

But things had shifted between them. That brief exchange was a loud and clear reminder of all that stood between them. He'd been right. This morning at dawn, they really had been saying goodbye for good.

CHAPTER SIXTEEN

LEAVING DYLAN AFTER they'd worked out their plan, Tara paused in the Ryland lobby to calm down. The entire time they'd talked, she'd battled her outrage at Sean Ryland's stunt, her disappointment that Dylan was still making excuses for the man and the terrible sadness that washed over her when she realized she and Dylan were done.

They both knew it would end. They'd set limits. They'd agreed they had no future. Still, she'd wanted *more*. She'd had a secret hope.

She was a fool.

She took a final calming breath and was about to leave when she remembered her phone had buzzed with a message. She dialed voice mail, her gaze snagging on the whimsical sculpture in front of her—a fountain of floating circuit boards, each with a splash of orange—the Ryland Engineering logo. The peach-colored walls were a good match.

When the first message started, she jolted. It was the accident expert from L.A. She listened as he rattled off his conclusions.

There was a lot of jargon about vectors and drag and torque, but the key point was "there was a collision of some kind, possibly tangential, but the surge in acceleration in evidence would require another factor…possibly a malfunction in the electrical system."

Okay, she thought, sorting through what she'd heard. *The*

car had been hit and a part had malfunctioned. Something electrical. There'd been a surge.

Her gaze kept snagging on the sculpture. All those logos. She'd seen them before. On the Ryland tour maybe?

Wait. She remembered. *The Tesla.* Tony had banged on a box he said he'd need to check. She'd seen the edge of the logo. Thinking harder, she realized the car had had a Wharton Electronics battery, too. The Tesla factory-installed battery had been changed out.

The Wharton test crew claimed the faulty Ryland units caused *power surges*. The Ryland people maintained that a major jolt or blow would be needed to cause the surge.

Like a collision?

A crash and a malfunction added up to the cause of the crash. It explained all the evidence. Her heart racing, she worked it out in her mind. Had Tony changed out the battery? He hadn't mentioned it when they'd looked at the crushed engine. Why not?

Calling information for the number for Auto Angels, she had him on the phone in seconds. "I haven't gotten the okay to tow the Tesla to your place yet," she said, "but I was wondering if you'd installed the Wharton battery."

"Nope. Not me. I would have, if he'd asked. I get busy. He probably didn't want to wait. Maybe one of his own techs. Could have been Mr. Ryland, now that I think about it."

"Sean Ryland?"

"Yeah. He uses my shop. I know he put a Wharton battery in his own car. Maybe Abbott asked him to do it. Why?"

"Just wondering. Thanks," she said, hanging up. Chills ran down her arms and her mind flew, conclusions clicking one after the other like so many dominoes. *Sean Ryland had installed the faulty part.*

Of course. He'd put one in Dylan's car, Candee's *and a few others*. Like her father's Tesla? He'd wanted to prove the parts were fine. Except this one had failed…and killed her father.

Her skin buzzing, her entire body crackling with electricity, she turned back toward the Ryland offices to find out the truth. She passed the startled receptionist, took the hall with long strides, found Sean's office and entered without knocking.

The man sat at his desk, chair facing the window. When he turned, she saw a handkerchief dotted with blood was wrapped around one palm. He'd broken the glass on a picture frame. The photo lay among glass shards on his desk—the same picture her father kept under his desk glass—the two men excited about their jet engine part.

"You killed my father," she blurted, her anger exploding.

His head jolted back, clearly shocked.

"That never occurred to you? That the faulty part you put in his car caused the wreck? Are you that pigheaded?"

"What the hell are you talking about?"

"You admitted you put the parts on people's cars without telling them. We all heard you. You risked their *lives* out of stubborn pride. And my father died because of it. My sister's in a coma, thanks to you." She was shaking with rage. She wanted to attack the man, who sat in his chair shaking his head, a superior look on his face.

"I never touched Abbott's car," he said. "You just calm down about that. I offered to, sure, but he couldn't risk being proved wrong."

"So you installed it anyway. Don't you have any remorse? Don't you care? Or did you hate him so much you're glad he's dead? He got what he deserved, right?"

Sean lunged to his feet. "If you were a man I'd knock you flat."

"Go for it!" she yelled. "What's a punch in the jaw compared with murder?" She was out of control, saying too much, being vicious, but a storm raged inside her at this man, who'd harmed her family, harmed his own son.

"What are you doing here?" he said in a low, malevolent tone. "You think being here makes up for betraying your family. Get out. Go back to your important life. Leave us alone. Leave my son alone. Haven't you done enough damage to him?"

"Me? If anyone's done any damage to Dylan, it's you—keeping him here to clean up your mess. You were so bitter. So hateful. Blaming my father for your mistakes. You—"

"What the hell's going on in here?" Dylan stood in the doorway, clearly upset, looking from one to the other.

"She accused me of killing Abbott," Sean said, pointing at her.

"What?" Dylan stared at her, eyes wide, disbelieving.

"He put a faulty circuit in the Tesla like he did in your car. The accident expert said there was a collision and that there had to be some other malfunction to cause that kind of acceleration. A Ryland unit was in the Tesla. I saw it myself. Tony didn't put it in. He said your father might have."

"Did you do that?" Dylan asked his father.

"My own son," Sean said in a disgusted tone. "No, I didn't. Now get out of my office before I do something I'll regret."

"This isn't over," Tara said to him. "Count on it."

"We need to talk," Dylan said to his father, then held the door for Tara. He passed her, walking fast. She had to half run to catch up with him in the lobby. He kept going out to the parking lot before he turned on her. "Murder, Tara? You accused my father of murder? I know you hate him, but that's too much even for you."

"He put the part in, Dylan. He had motive and opportunity. The Tesla was in the shop. Tony says your dad works on cars there. He admitted he put the part in a few cars, including yours, without telling the owners. He wanted to prove his point. And that part caused the wreck. The part and a collision."

"He wouldn't lie about that"

"Can you be that blind? Of course he would. He had a point to prove. He risked lives to do it—yours, Candee's, my father's, my sister's, who knows how many others? He caused the wreck and he's too stubborn to admit it."

"Someone else put the part in, Tara. Another mechanic. Maybe someone at Wharton. It wasn't him."

She looked into his impassive face and realized the truth. "You'll always take his side. He threw a tantrum that all but destroyed your contract with Wharton, but you excuse it, explain it away, refused to admit he's wrong." She stopped to catch her breath, furious, dizzy from lack of oxygen.

"That's enough, Tara. I know you want someone to blame and I know you'd love it to be my father, the man you blame for our breakup, the man you despise, but it's not true."

"You wouldn't believe it if he signed a confession."

"My father wouldn't lie. You want the truth, but only if it's ugly. You want to justify your hatred of this town and everyone in it. You accused Bill Fallon, Greg Pescatore, Joseph, now my father. Who's next? Your mother? Me? Why not me? Wharton caused my father trouble. Maybe I put the faulty unit in his car. Maybe I drove him off the highway. Why not?"

She'd never seen him so angry before. "You're exaggerating to make my position look ridiculous."

"I don't need to exaggerate. You have a chip on your shoulder the size of this town. You're angry at me because I stayed, because I helped my father."

"Your father bullied you, manipulated you. He robbed you of college, dragged you into his company and kept you here to keep him from self-destructing again. You fell for it, you're still falling for it, because you think if you don't do what he wants he won't love you anymore. Parents are *supposed* to love you, no matter what. You don't have to earn their love."

"You don't know what you're talking about," he said, but she could tell that her words had struck a nerve. "How could you?"

"You mean with *my* parents, who don't love me? No, you mean because I don't know how to love. I'm not capable of love."

"That's not what I said."

"It's what you think, though."

"No. It's what *you* think, Tara. And you use that as an excuse to keep people at arm's length, to reject them before they reject you. You had no right to make me choose. I loved my father and I loved you. He needed me more."

"Don't you get it? He'll *always* need you more." She felt so lost suddenly, so sad. It seemed hopeless. They were both trapped in their past.

"My father is flawed. I know that. His bitterness tore our family apart, okay? But he's still my father. I love him and he loves me. I work around his flaws. I focus on the good. That's what you do for the people you love. You don't set impossible standards, then write them off when they can't meet them."

"That's what you think I do, isn't it? I write people off."

"I could never make you happy, Tara. You know that. You'd always be braced for me to fail you. I can't live like that, constantly having to prove my love, always about to lose you."

"And I can't live with someone who thinks that of me, who has so little respect or trust."

"Exactly," he said. He felt the same about her. They were stuck.

They looked at each other in silence for a long time as their words settled around them like dry leaves after a gust.

Her fingers and toes felt numb, her chest hollow, her brain fuzzy.

It was over. In a way it was a relief. They'd ended it before they could hurt each other more than either of them could bear.

"What do we do now?" Dylan asked softly, his eyes so sad she wanted to cup his cheek, tell him never mind, she'd be the love he needed her to be and he'd be hers. But that wasn't possible.

She looked out across the parking lot, then back at the front of the building. "We go back to work," she said, fighting with everything in her to do the sensible thing, to do what she'd promised herself and her sister she would do. "Can we do that? Or is that over, too?"

"My father did not put that part in your father's car. We don't even know if the part caused the accident. That's all speculation, Tara."

She let his words sink in, as painful as that was. "You're right. It could have been a tech at Wharton who put it in," she said softly. "Tony mentioned that, too." She herself had seen batteries being installed in the testing area. "I did assume the worst."

Dylan blew out a breath. "So let's find out who did the installation and whether or not the part was faulty."

"For that, I have to get the insurance company to release the car so we can have the part tested."

"If we can find the serial number in any of the Tesla photos I took, we could check it against the list of units Wharton has reported as bad."

"So, you'll still help me?"

"We both want the truth, Tara. If the unit was bad, if it contributed to the accident, then Ryland Engineering has to admit fault and deal with the consequences."

"I hadn't thought that far," she said. That could be catastrophic for Dylan's company. The insurance agency would likely sue Ryland for damages. When it came out that a Ryland part had killed the CEO of Wharton Electronics, there would be brutal media coverage. Dylan stood ready to do the right thing. Pride filled her. He was a good, honorable man.

"We need to look into this quietly," she said. "We can't afford any rumors until we know the whole story."

"Jeb is willing to sit down with Dale and me," he said. "I was on the phone with him when you got into it with my father."

"You could check for the serial number while you're there, right? Without raising eyebrows?"

"Should be easy enough. We'll be looking at their lists anyway, looking for patterns."

"If I come along, say, as a facilitator, I should be able to casually ask about any installation on my father's car."

"Sounds like a plan," Dylan said.

"Yeah." She had a flicker of the good feeling about working with him. "And I want you to know that if there is a problem, if Ryland Engineering is at fault, I'll help you with a crisis plan to deal with the fallout."

"If you're as good as I think you are that should help. We're not going down without a fight, that's for sure."

"I'll do all I can to make sure that doesn't happen."

"I know you will." They held each other's gaze for a long moment, saying goodbye to what they'd shared. The next time they saw each other, their intimacy would be gone.

"I'll check the pictures for the serial number. I want to look for the bumper at the crash site, just in case. There was a collision, for sure. We still need to find out who hit the car."

"We'll touch base later then?" Dylan said. "Pin down the details before we meet at the Wharton test lab?"

"Sure."

"You'll need to pick up your things. There's a key under the back mat."

"Oh. Right." He wanted all signs of her gone when he returned home. She didn't blame him. "I want to say good-bye to Duster." It was for the best. They were done with each other.

"Yeah." He swallowed hard, then blinked, clearly fighting emotion.

The sight made tears spring to her eyes, but she was not going to cry. Why cry when you were doing what had to be done?

"CAN I TALK to you a minute?" Victor stopped Dylan in the hall on his way to have it out with his father.

"Sure," he said, forcing himself to focus on Victor. "If it's about the meeting, I'm going to take Dale over to Wharton and actually look at the test data, so—"

"It's not that." The man looked almost sheepish. "I thought you should know I'm looking at making a move."

"A move?"

"Taking another job. There's a plant in Phoenix that needs a manager. It'd be a lateral move, but it's a good opportunity."

Dylan stiffened. He'd counted on Victor to fill his shoes. "We talked about you taking over when I leave."

"I appreciate the thought, but…" He fidgeted with his cap, finally looking at Dylan. "Hell, we both know that's not going to happen. You and your dad are…" He interlocked his fingers and tugged, as if they wouldn't pull apart.

"It's not like that. I have a plan. Dad knows I'm leaving."

"This is your company. It's got your name on it. Your father depends on you. He brushes me off like a fly."

He'd seen his father be brusque with Victor, that was true. "Dad can be difficult. Abbott's death has been hard for him, I think."

"What's hard for him is you threatening to leave once production ramps up. He's been throwing wrenches—figuratively—left and right. You don't know that?"

He stared at Victor, a man he'd always trusted. Could that be true? The idea made room for itself in his head.

"Think about it. That was when he started harping at the line workers, throwing shots when we had our management meetings. All that crap about how we need a new direction, that we have tunnel vision, no imagination."

"That was about the Wharton contract, the specs being too tight."

"He was fine with the contract at first. He didn't start bitching until you told him you wanted to leave."

Dylan thought back. The first argument he could recall was not long after he'd broken the word to his dad. "Damn. You're right." The pieces snapped together. How had he missed that?

Still, despite what Tara said, his father wasn't a conniving person. "He might not even realize that's what he's doing," Dylan said.

"Hard to know. He shoots from the hip."

"I need to talk with him, that's for sure. Can you give me a week before you take the job? I don't want to lose you if we can straighten this out."

"Yeah. I told them I'd need some time. I'd like to stay, but not if I have to fight for authority, Dylan."

"I understand."

"Good luck." Touching the edge of his cap in a quick salute, Victor turned and left.

Dylan stood for a few seconds, stunned that he'd missed something so obvious. Victor thought he and his father were locked together, that Dylan would never leave the company.

He'd already concluded he'd have to stay longer to get his father back on track after Abbott's death.

He'll always need you more. That's what Tara had said.

Troy Waller had told him point-blank at lunch that he was running for mayor after all. *I can't wait around for you,* he'd said. Troy didn't believe Dylan would quit Ryland Engineering, either.

Dylan felt like an idiot. He *had* been blind. Not to the extent Tara claimed, but blind enough. Damn.

There would never be the perfect time to leave. The sailing would never be smooth, the ground would never be solid. Dylan had to go anyway.

Frankly he knew his father wasn't having much fun working with him, either. They argued constantly. If Victor was ever to get the respect he deserved, then Dylan had to get out of the way so the two men could figure out a working relationship. He took a deep breath and headed into his father's office. They had a lot to talk about.

His father stood at the window. When he turned, Dylan noticed his hand was wrapped. Then he saw the broken glass on the desk. He'd smashed the picture of him and Abbott. The man definitely had a childish streak.

"You back to apologize?" his father asked.

"No, I'm not."

"She poisoned your mind that much? How could you think that I would harm Abbott? For all his crimes, he was my friend." His voice dropped and went hoarse. "Good God, son."

Dylan would not soften. Not now. "I know you didn't put the part in his car. I told Tara that. It doesn't change the fact that you put them in my car and Candee's without telling us. You risked our lives, Dad."

"That's bullshit. There's nothing wrong with those parts."

"One of them was in Abbott's Tesla. If it's faulty, then it contributed to the accident. And if it was, then Ryland Engineering is in big trouble. Tara and I are going to find out the truth."

"Tara? She doesn't want the truth. She wants to destroy us! You don't see that? Her mother's probably in on it, too." His eyes looked wild. "She called me that night, you know. Said she needed to talk to me, that it was important that she talk to me first. She never showed."

"Why didn't you tell me this?"

"Why did it matter? I never saw the woman." His father's eyes blazed. "That's not the first time Rachel Wharton said one thing and did the other."

"What does that mean?"

"Not important."

He glared at his father, sick to death of his twisted emotions and confused motivations. "I'll tell you what is important—the contract with Wharton which you practically cost us."

"Maybe that's for the best."

"No, Dad. It's not for the best. I don't know why you want to kill it, and it doesn't really matter because we need the contract. I won't lose it if there's any way to save it. And here's something else. I'm leaving the company. I'll stay until this business with the bad parts is resolved, one way or the other. I'll see us through whatever comes of the Tesla wreck investigation. In the meantime, Victor's going to take over most of my duties."

"What the hell are you talking about?"

"It's been ten years, Dad. I'm proud of what I've accomplished here. But I'm done. I need to move on. You need me to move on. You have to step up to the plate and lead the company, stop throwing stones into the works. Victor will do great in my place. Better, in fact, since he's an engineer, too."

"You're that angry at me." His father looked totally betrayed. He seemed to sink into himself. "You'd just walk out on me."

Dylan fought the urge to rescue him, to take it back, to promise to always be there. He knew that wasn't good for either of them. He felt the empty ache he'd felt at eighteen seeing his father so ruined. Maybe Tara had a point. Maybe he thought he had to rescue his father or lose the man's love.

"I'm not angry. I'm just determined. It's time, Dad. For both of us."

"I didn't know you were so unhappy here."

"We both need a break from each other."

His father looked down. "I know I'm not the easiest guy to work with."

"No, you're not. And maybe I put up with too much from you over the years. You can do better. You'll have to when Victor takes over. He's not as easygoing as I am. And you can't afford to lose him. That's certain."

His father looked at him. His eyes showed hurt, but Dylan saw a flicker of acceptance. "I didn't raise you to let people down."

"You raised me to believe in myself, to go after my dream. And that's what I'm doing. I love you, Dad. I respect you. You're a brilliant engineer. This is for the best."

"So you say," his dad said, but there was no energy behind his mockery.

"Right now, I'm going to talk to Dale about getting the testing mess fixed, once and for all. And you're going to change out those drive assemblies you put in my car, Candee's car and anybody else's car."

"They're not broken, Dylan. I'd bet my life on it."

"You bet all our lives on it, Dad. You'd better hope the part on Abbott's car wasn't faulty or you've not only lost a bet, you've your company helped kill a man and put a woman in a coma."

At home, a few hours later, when he dropped onto the couch with a beer, the enormity of what had happened rolled over him.

The possibility that a Ryland part might have killed Abbott Wharton was almost more than he could bear. If it were true, it might well sink the company.

It had been hard to hurt his father, to hear him say Dylan was letting him down, but the decision was right. Dylan knew that. His father would see that…or he wouldn't. Dylan would live with it, either way. If his father quit loving him, he'd live with that, too.

And then there was Tara. Their argument and their breakup. He sighed. In some ways, that hurt most of all. He ached all over, inside and out. It hurt to breathe.

Sensing his distress, Duster hauled his arthritic bones onto the couch and rested his muzzle on Dylan's lap, tucking his head under Dylan's hand. He seemed to think if Dylan petted him, Dylan would feel better.

"Won't work, pal. I don't think I'll feel better for a long, long time."

Dylan and Tara had shared only two nights, but it felt like they'd said no to a lifetime together, to happiness, to a closeness he'd never known before.

Not the closeness of teenagers marveling at the wonder of being in love for the first time, but an adult intimacy, a true connection, a lifelong bond.

Too much stood between them. Too little held them together. He was almost grateful to have a work problem to focus on, anything to keep him from feeling the heartbreak that waited to plow him under.

CHAPTER SEVENTEEN

TARA SAT BESIDE DYLAN at a small table in Wharton's testing office. With them were Dale Danvers and Jeb Harris. Jeb and Dale knew only of the first part of the mission—to look for patterns in part failures. Tara had been able to read the serial number on one of Dylan's engine close-ups, so they planned to look for it among the failed parts lists.

Tara glanced at Dylan. He looked as awful as she felt. His eyes were red and haunted. He was unshaven, his face gray with exhaustion. She hadn't been able to talk to him, but she guessed his misery wasn't just about the possibility that a Ryland part had caused the wreck.

She'd missed him terribly last night. At midnight, she'd gotten all the way to her car, ready to drive to him before she realized how foolish that would be. This wasn't a romantic movie where you forgot all that was wrong between you and figured love would find a way. Love couldn't find a way past a dead-end.

"You okay?" Dylan asked her. "What happened to your hand?"

She looked at the scrapes on her knuckles. "From the thorn bush." She'd found the bumper in a thick bush and had to pull it out. It had had dents and scrapes, and streaks of light blue paint—definite signs it had been hit. She'd put a call in to the insurance agent, hoping what she'd learned from the reconstructionist and figured out herself would trigger an investigation.

"The reports on the failed devices." Jeb set two thick notebooks of printouts on the table. Dylan took one, Dale the other. "Here's my analysis." Jeb presented Tara with several pages of colored graphs and charts with percentages of failures on each date for the past month. The graph showed a steady line, except for a few sharp dips.

Dylan was holding the slip of paper on which she'd written the serial number, while he scanned the report pages. After a while he traded books with Dale. When he'd finished he caught Tara's eye and shook his head. Not so far.

"These reports only go back a month," Dylan said to Jeb.

"We recycle every four weeks. Haven't you got enough there?"

"I'd like to see the earlier results, when we did have a component problem. For comparison purposes."

"It's on the computer," Jeb said with a sigh. "Archived."

Dylan and Tara looked over Jeb's shoulder as he clicked through screens.

"Also, we'd like to take a few of the failed parts to test them ourselves," Dylan said.

Jeb shot him a glare. "I'm only tolerating this so-called *review* because our lawyer ordered me to. You aren't the only people who stand by their work."

"We know that, Jeb," Tara said. "It will reassure the Ryland team that Wharton has nothing to hide."

Jeb shook his head, irritated, but going along…so far. "I'll tell Matt to hold a couple from the recycle load. He's due to haul it out today."

"Thanks, Jeb," Dylan said. "We appreciate that."

"I want this fixed as much as you do. And, for the record, I don't buy that your father installed our rejects in any damn car that's still on the road."

Tara saw that as her cue. "Do you guys put Wharton batteries in your own cars, by the way?"

"Some do. We put them in free for employees. Here's the first week," he said, motioning at the screen for Dylan.

"Because my father had one put in his Tesla," she continued, her heart racing. "I assume it was done here? He's an employee, after all." She held her breath, waiting for the answer.

"It's possible. I didn't see it." He kept his attention on the screen.

Matt Sutherland stuck his head in the door. When he saw the visitors, he stiffened, which caught Tara's attention. "What's going on?"

"They're reviewing our test reports," Jeb said.

Matt blanched. What was that about? Tara got a prickle. She tried to catch Dylan's eye, but he was glued to the screen.

"Grab a couple of yesterday's duds for them," Jeb said to Matt.

"But they're already loaded on the truck," he said, almost panicky.

"Then pull a few off," Jeb said, turning to look at his assistant. "What's with you?"

"Nothing. Stuff at home, I guess. We have an appointment this afternoon, so—"

"That's twice this week," Jeb snapped.

"I know. I'm sorry. It's her blood pressure. They're worried about it. Tuesday was the hospital tour, so that was the extra time."

"At least book the appointments on days you're not supervising. I don't have time to run your shifts and mine, Matt."

"I'll try. We're stuck with Thursday appointments because of the doctor's schedule."

Thursdays. Tara felt a jolt. She looked down at the graph before her. The days with hardly any faulty parts were Thursdays. She looked at Tuesday, the day Matt had been at the hospital. *A dip.* Electricity sizzled through her. The high error rates took place when Matt was in charge. Could he have manipulated the tests to make Ryland look bad?

He was acting jumpy about the bad units, too.

"You know if anyone put a battery in Abbott Wharton's car?" Jeb asked him.

"Abbott Wharton?" Now the pink in his cheeks flooded his face. "He would go to his own mechanic, wouldn't he? Tony Carmichael? Out at Auto Angels? He does most of the e-cars in town."

That was a lot of information, as if he was trying to shift attention away from the guilty party. Had *Matt* installed the part? And if he had, so what? Why hide it? Unless he knew the part was faulty....

"Carmichael didn't do it," Jeb said tiredly. "That's the point."

"Then I don't know," Matt said. "I need to get back to the tests." He was gone in an instant. That had been odd. Was he just guilty about missing a shift?

Dale flipped the book closed then looked at Jeb. "I know the equipment's off-limits, but I need to see your calibrations to get what's going on."

"Ah, hell. Let's go." Jeb Jeb's willingness to investigate made Tara certain he'd meant it when he said he wanted this worked out. Tara and Dylan were alone in the office.

"Look at this chart," Tara said. "There are dips in error rates whenever Matt's off."

"Yeah?"

"Yes. Every Thursday. And the Tuesday he mentioned the hospital visit?" She tapped the dip.

"Hmm. You think Matt messed with the readings? Boosted the fail rate?"

"It fits. Plus, when he saw us here, heard we were looking things over, he got upset."

"He sure as hell didn't want us checking the rejects," Dylan said.

"Right. Because he knew they weren't duds. If it's true, then the fail rate is bogus, Dylan. There's nothing wrong with the Ryland assembly."

Dylan leaned back in his chair, running his hands down his face. "Damn. That would save us." He smiled, his face cleared of worry for a few seconds. "Now how do we prove it?" He rolled closer to the desk, leaning in, giving her that jolt, making her miss him in the middle of the investigation.

"Let's show this to Jeb," Tara said. "Let him test the units Matt's about to haul away for himself. That should get him on our side."

"Jeb's a decent guy. He'll do the right thing."

"So, have you checked all the numbers? Is the Tesla part there?"

"Not yet. I've got a few more screens to look at." Dylan went back to the monitor, searching more numbers. After a few seconds, he said, "Damn. It's here. From the first failed lot, back when we had bad components from our Tennessee supplier." His face was gray, his eyes bereft of hope. "It was our part. We caused the wreck, Tara."

"I'm sorry, Dylan. I am." She felt sick about it.

"I hope you were serious about that crisis plan." All his relief had been replaced by gloom.

"Don't forget it wasn't just the part. The car got hit from behind. We still need to find who that was." She paused, as a thought occurred to her. "There's something else. Matt acted weird when Jeb asked if he knew who put the part on the Tesla. I'd bet money it was Matt."

"How do you figure?"

"He was trying to deflect the blame to Tony Carmichael, giving us too many details. That suggests he's hiding guilt—his or someone else's."

"Why hide that he put on the part?"

"Because he knew it was faulty when he installed it," she said slowly, as the realization hit her.

"But most of the rejects weren't bad and he knows it."

"So he did it deliberately. Why? To harm my father? I can't believe that. It required a crash to activate the circuitry flaw."

"Maybe he wanted to harm *Ryland*," Dylan said slowly. "You saw how hostile he was during the meeting."

"And he brought up your bad supplier the day I took the tour. He even mentioned the plant in Tennessee."

"Yeah. But what would he get out of that? He has relatives who work for Ryland. Friends, too. If Wharton dropped us as a supplier, Wharton's production would suffer, as well."

"Why then?" They looked at each other, both thinking it through. "Wait a second," she said. "I remember something. At the funeral, Faye's assistant told me about the factory manager who got fired. She said Pescatore had told people Wharton was going to shut down the factory and outsource assembly to a plant in *Kentucky*. Maybe she meant *Tennessee*."

"If Wharton outsourced, Matt and a hell of a lot of other people would lose their jobs. Maybe he wanted to discredit the Tennessee plant, keep Wharton from sending work there."

"It's a decent theory. The only way to know is to talk to Matt."

"Why would he admit any of it?"

"Because we'll ask the right questions at the right time in the right way."

"This is your area, Tara. I'll follow your lead."

His confidence in her felt good.

Dale and Jeb returned to the office at that moment, Dale looking frustrated, Jeb triumphant. "I don't get it," Dale said.

"The calibrations look good. I don't know what the problem is."

"Like I said, we stand by our work," Jeb said.

"I need to get back, if that's all right," Dale said to Dylan.

"Yeah. Go ahead. We'll keep working here for a while."

As soon as Dale left, Dylan and Tara laid out their case for Jeb. He listened, looked at the chart, shook his head in puzzlement. "I know you're showing me my own data, but it sounds crazy."

"That's why you need to grab some rejects before they get recycled and test them yourself," Dylan said.

"Guess so."

"We'd like to talk to Matt, if we can," Tara said. "See if we can get him to explain his thinking. That okay with you?"

Jeb looked at them both. "I sure as hell can't talk to him right now. I'll tear him a new one. Tell him I said to forget the recycling for now."

"Will do. Thanks, Jeb," Dylan said.

"Just figure it out. We've got production quotas to hit."

Tara grabbed the digital recorder she used to capture thoughts when she was driving, and handed it to Dylan. "Put this in your shirt pocket. We'll record what he tells us."

They spotted Matt walking into a small hangar near some panel trucks. They set off at a lope, strategizing as they went. Closer, Tara saw palettes of parts stacked beside one of the trucks.

"Go time," she said.

Dylan turned on the recorder and they went inside and found Matt bent over, shifting crates around. "Matt?" Dylan called to him.

"Huh?" He jolted and turned, looking guilty as hell, a dusty box in his hand. "I got the part you want." He flushed.

"No need. We'll grab a couple from your stack outside."

"No," he blurted, which told Tara their theory was right. "This is what you want." He thrust the box at Dylan.

"Because these are actually bad," Dylan asked, "while the others are perfectly good?" Dylan was playing bad cop. Tara would show sympathy when the time felt right.

Matt flinched, his eyes darting everywhere, desperate for escape.

"You put a bad unit in Abbott's car, didn't you, Matt?"

"I don't know what you're talking about," he said flatly, his eyes going cold, his jaw locked.

"Don't bother to lie. We can prove it." Not true, but it clearly terrified Matt, who went white except for red blotches on his neck.

Tara's instincts fired up. It was time for her to speak. "We know you didn't mean for anyone to get hurt," she said. "Whatever you did, you did for everyone's good, to save jobs and help people. We know you're that kind of guy." She spoke slowly and warmly, hoping to draw him in with her sympathy.

He softened slightly and swallowed.

"You go to the doctor with your wife, Matt, even when your boss hassles you. You'd do anything for your family. You're a family man. I admire that. And Wharton's your family, too. You felt like it was your duty to save them. Because family counts." Those were the words he'd used in the electric cart that day.

His eyes shot to hers, almost proud. He was breathing fast and shallow, scared, but also strengthened by her kind description of his motives.

She didn't speak, waiting for his confession to bubble up.

"I had to do something," he finally said. "Pescatore said they were going to outsource assembly. He saw the proposal on the fax machine. TGR Manufacturing in Tennessee. He got fired for spilling the beans."

His jaw muscle twitched, his eyes gleamed with fervor. "We work hard. Everybody on the line. The whole plant. We put together a good product. They wanted to go cheaper. It was Banes pushing it. I knew it would ruin us. It would ruin the whole town."

"So you had to fix it somehow," Tara said, urging him on.

He nodded once. "You get what you pay for. Cheap vendors make cheap products. I had to prove TGR was a bad company. I had to monkey with the tests. I had no choice. It would have happened anyway, later on. All Ryland had to do was admit it was TGR's fault, then find a better supplier. Nobody would get hurt. Easy."

He ran his hands through his hair, then jammed them on his hips, looking down. He swallowed, glanced at Dylan, then Tara. "When Mr. Wharton drove out here a couple weeks ago, it was after hours. I'd come back after the doctor's appointment to catch up on reports. He said he had a wager going with Sean Ryland about the Ryland assembly. He asked me to put one on."

It had been her father who requested the installation, after all, Tara realized. She'd been wrong to attack Dylan's father.

"I got this great idea. If I put in a bad unit, he'd give Sean Ryland hell and that would be the end of the debate." His voice took on a desperate, panicked quality. "I'd saved a few bad ones so I could match the calibrations on the tests I messed with. So I put one in. All that should have happened was a stall. That's all. Not a wreck. It couldn't cause a wreck. Like the Ryland guy said, it couldn't get dangerous without a torque or collision. When he was killed, I couldn't believe it. I never meant for anyone to get hurt."

He blinked hard, looking away, his face crumpled as he fought tears.

Tara looked at Dylan, whose mouth was a grim line, his eyes full of sorrow. She felt the same way, burning with outrage, swamped with sadness. Such a waste. Such a tragedy. So many people hurt. And all over a rumor. Her father would never have closed down Wharton.

"What's going to happen to me?" Matt asked, looking like a prisoner about to be hanged. "I swear I didn't know this could happen."

"We need you to repeat your story for the police," Dylan said. "And we want a statement certifying that the drive assembly units Ryland provided Wharton Electronics were functional, that you rigged the test results. Agreed?"

"Whatever you say," he said miserably. "I'm done for no matter what. Jeb will fire me. With the baby coming, I don't know what we'll do."

"One step at a time, Matt," Tara said, realizing she'd echoed her mother's advice about having a child. "First, tell the truth, then deal with the consequences." Her heart went out to him, but he'd done a terrible thing. "My father would never have closed the factory. The company and the people who worked for him meant too much to him. He sacrificed all his earnings and investments to keep it going until the profits from the new battery came in. You should have asked about the rumor, not taken it as truth."

Matt hung his head. He'd been scared. People did stupid things when they were scared. She'd seen it over and over in her work. "Can I call my wife, tell her where I am? She'll have to go to the doctor alone."

Dylan and Tara stepped away to give him privacy while he broke the bad news to his poor wife. "I'll drive him in, Tara. You can get going."

"This shouldn't have happened," she said. "It wouldn't have if Wharton management had kept its employees informed. That's what I would have told Faye if I'd really listened and tried to help. I might have prevented the accident after all." Guilt washed through her and she bit her lip.

"One piece of advice can't turn a company around, Tara."

"I know that. I still regret not doing my part."

"Now we have to go forward, make things right where we can."

She nodded, grateful for Dylan's steady presence, his reasonable words. "Matt's confession will bring an investigator out here for sure. We can email the tape we just got. If we're lucky, the investigators will figure out who hit the car. They do in-person interviews. Someone needs to pin Fallon down."

"We may never know what happened, Tara. You have to be prepared for that."

"Maybe when Faye wakes up, she'll tell us." The possibility seemed far away and Tara's chest felt hollow and hopeless for a moment. She forced herself to stick with what she could do, not what she hoped for.

"I hate to say this, but my father was right," Dylan said. "We *were* being sabotaged by Wharton testers."

"And I owe him an apology for what I accused him of." Dylan had been right. She had been too eager to blame his father. "Wharton wronged your company. We need to set up a meeting to discuss how to correct that."

"That will be good. I think we just saved Ryland Engineering. If you hadn't pushed for the truth, we would likely have lost the Wharton contract. I owe you for that, Tara. I'll always be grateful."

"We made a good team," she said, trying to smile. "Mostly. Except when I was naming suspects right and left."

"That's true." He smiled, then got serious. "But you made me see one thing. I have worked long enough with my father. I need to get on with what I want. Since it looks like the company will survive, I can leave when I planned."

"I said some harsh things. I exaggerated. I know that."

"There was enough truth in what you to get me thinking and a conversation I had with Victor made it even clearer.

I told my father I'll be leaving the business as soon as it's feasible."

"I'm glad then," she said, emotion rising in a wave inside her. "If that's what you want for yourself."

"It is."

Hearing him declare his independence from his father made her proud of him. He'd listened to her rant and calmly sorted the wheat from the chaff. She loved him more than ever. She'd said unfair things to him, and she hated herself for that.

"When I came here, I thought I was a better person," she said. "I thought I'd gotten past the bad feelings, the bad attitude, but I guess not. I guess I couldn't get past the imprint."

"That's not the whole story, Tara. You've done a lot. You put up with some pretty terrible things here, but you've kept your head most of the time. You've reached out to your mother, accepted her on her own terms. Your parents left you guessing growing up. It takes a big person to see past that."

"Thank you, Dylan." She tensed against the urge to cry. "That means a lot coming from you."

"You do know how to love," he said in a rough voice, his eyes burning at her. "Once you believe that, there will be no stopping you."

"Goodbye, Dylan." She rose on tiptoe and kissed his cheek, embarrassed to see she'd left a tear on Dylan's cheek. She wiped it away with her palm, turned and nearly ran for her car, blinking back the rest of her tears. She had no time to cry.

Tara had meetings to schedule, key people to inform and plans to make, including how to start a meaningful dialogue between Wharton management and its employees. She had a big job ahead of her. She would do her best. For Faye. For her father. For the company. Hell, she just might make a worthy contribution to Wharton Electronics, after all.

She was pretty sure her father would be proud.

AFTER AN EXHAUSTING afternoon at Wharton, Tara went to the hospital to tell Faye about the breakthrough. She sat in the chair and took Faye's pale hand, noticing the nail polish was still bright. Her sister hadn't been able to twitch a finger, let alone chip a nail.

Faye had been unconscious for seventeen days. How long could she last? Every day that passed without change made it more likely that Faye would die. The thought nearly killed Tara. She fought down the choked feeling, the ache in her throat, and gave Faye the news.

"We know what happened to you. A bad part was put in Dad's car to prove a point that didn't need to be proved. All that's left is to learn who bumped your car. The insurance company will be sending out an investigator anyday." The adjuster had put in an expedited request.

"We'll fix what's wrong at Wharton, too. I'm here, and I'll stay until things are right again. Please wake up and help me." Her sister's eyes seemed shadowed to Tara. She continued to waste away beneath the sheets. Unable to stand the sight, Tara glanced away. Her gaze snagged on the photo of the two sisters and their mother, Faye in love and happy.

"We couldn't make it work, Faye. Dylan and I. We've hurt each other too much. Dylan's here forever and I can't wait to leave." She swallowed hard, the pain of the breakup burning through her more powerfully than ever.

"What would you tell me, Faye? Am I right or wrong?"

When you love someone, you forgive them. Faye had told her that about her father and the ruined model ship. Love was supposed to open your heart, make new things possible.

But wasn't Tara too crippled? *You know how to love,* Dylan had said so fervently that she knew he believed it.

Could it possibly be true? When Dylan had broken her heart the first time, Tara had built walls against anyone who might hurt her. She told herself she was being smart, staying focused on her career, on the things she could control, but the truth was she'd been afraid. Afraid to risk her heart.

Tears slid down her cheeks. *Not again.* She'd lost it with Dylan already today. But sitting with Faye, knowing her sister accepted her for who she was, she decided to let go. She cried for Faye, for her father and her mother, for all the mistakes and misjudgments she'd made, and for losing Dylan all over again.

A tear dripped onto Faye's hand. When she reached to wipe it off, her sister's hand twitched. Tara froze. "Faye? Did you do that? Are you awake? Move your hand again." She'd made that request so often, getting nothing back, she was totally blown away when Faye's finger lifted again.

"Oh, my God! You did it. You moved. On purpose!" Tara grabbed her hand, holding it loosely. "Can you squeeze?"

There was the tiniest bit of pressure, but it was there.

Faye was waking up. Tara didn't need Rita and her flashlight to know that. She pushed the call button. When a voice asked what she needed, she yelled the news. Nurses came running. Rita checked the responses, then grinned at Tara. "She had to come back, girl, to turn off that bad music."

"Whatever it took," she said. "I can't believe she's waking up."

Faye groaned and turned her head.

"Faye? Can you hear me?" Tara said.

Nothing.

"Will she be able to talk?" she asked Rita.

"It happens different ways," Rita said. "Be patient."

"I can do that. I can be patient. You bet." She grabbed

her phone and called Joseph. He was so silent at first she thought he'd hung up on her. Then she heard a gasp and knew he was crying.

"She loves you, Joseph. Come see her. You'll start fresh. You'll try harder. You'll ask more questions and listen more closely."

Why can't you do that with Dylan?

Next, she called her mother. "Faye's awake, Mom. She's coming back to us." Her mother made a choked sound. She almost sounded more upset than relieved. So odd. Tara told her that Joseph would be picking her up, then clicked off.

Finally she called Dylan and told him.

He got choked up, too, but in a happy way. "Thank God, Tara. I'm so glad. Dad's here, too. We're both glad. I'll be there as soon as I can."

She was relieved he'd assumed she'd want him here. He'd supported her from the beginning. He should be here for the happy ending.

She clicked off the phone.

The neurologist arrived and told Tara some sobering things about Faye's recovery—the difficulties she might have with speech, memory and mobility. It wouldn't be easy, but Faye had fought her way back to life. She would fight her way back to full function.

"I knew you would make it. You're the strongest person I know." Faye was coming back to her. This time, she would listen, be there for Faye the way Faye had always been there for her.

When Joseph arrived, he lunged for his wife. "Faye," he choked out, pushing back her hair, kissing her forehead, looking at her with pure adoration. Tara had underestimated Joseph by miles.

Had she underestimated Dylan? Herself?

Tara noticed her mother hadn't come in. "You picked up Mom, right?"

"Still in the hall." He kept staring at Faye, as if he feared that he might miss a word or a look if he turned his head for even a second.

Tara went to find her mother. She stood a foot from the door, frozen, a terrified look on her face.

"It's okay, Mom. Come talk to her."

"I don't know what to say…how to make it right."

"Make what right? Your quarrel? Faye won't care."

Her mother didn't move.

"The neurologist said she likely won't remember the accident or the hours before it for a while, maybe never," she said to jolt her from her trance.

"She…might not…remember?" her mother said haltingly, hopefully.

Tara pulled her arm. "Come and see her."

Slowly her mother came into the room. Joseph stood and motioned for Rachel to take the bedside chair.

She sat stiffly. "Faye…" she said so softly Tara could hardly hear her. "I'm so sorry. More sorry than I can say." Her mother did not sound happy at all.

Tara had the terrible feeling that rather than praying for Faye to wake up, her mother had been dreading the possibility. Tara's instincts flared.

"What's going on, Mom?" Tara asked. When she shifted her body to better see her mother, the movement knocked the Sunset Crater photo down. Picking it up, she noticed Faye's foot near the heart-shaped dent in the fender of the powder-blue Mercedes. *Powder-blue*.

She pictured her mother's car in the garage, where she saw it each time she pulled in and out. There was no dent, heart-shaped or otherwise. When Tara had arrived, her mother's car had been in the shop. She'd assumed it was an auto shop. "The Mercedes was at the *body* shop, wasn't it?" she asked abruptly.

Her mother blinked at her, her muscles so tight that her hair shivered.

"You were the one," Tara said, her mouth so dry her tongue stuck to her lips. "You hit the car, didn't you?" Her mother had acted strangely, but Tara had never considered this possibility. Holding her breath, she waited for her mother's answer, knowing already that she was right.

CHAPTER EIGHTEEN

"IT WAS JUST A TAP," Tara's mother replied breathlessly. "I wanted to pass...get them to stop, you know? Anyone would have." Her cool dignity was gone. Her words ran together. "I brushed the bumper...had to swerve so I wouldn't crash... I was dizzy...I had taken one of my pills. I'd had a gimlet, too. I was so upset from Faye...you have no idea...." She stopped and gave Tara a pleading look, then swallowed. "I pulled over. When they didn't drive by, I knew something was wrong, like maybe they'd stopped for me, so I ran back and saw the barrier had been bent."

"You caused the crash," Tara said softly. "It was you." She still couldn't believe it or understand that this shaky, scared confession was coming from the the same dignified, emotionally restrained woman she'd grown up with.

"I called Bill. He told me not to go down there, that I couldn't help, that he would take care of it, that paramedics would be on their way in seconds. I wasn't thinking. My head was not clear. Everything was fuzzy. You have to understand."

Tara's body rocked back, as if her mother's words had physically pushed her. "So you drove away? Left them there?" Her mother had abandoned her dead husband and dying daughter. Tara felt dizzy with shock and disappointment. Her mother had hit them and run away.

"Bill was the officer in charge of the scene. That's how he

explained it. What he said was the law. I might cause more injury. He told me that."

Excuses? That's all her mother had? She was fuzzy and obeyed Bill Fallon like a child? "How could you?" Tara took quick breaths, fought down the desire to rail at her mother, to shake her, make her see what she'd done.

Get the truth. That was what mattered now. She had to let her mother talk. There would be time for outrage later. "Why were you trying to stop them?" she said finally in a calmer voice. "Why were you so upset that you took drugs and had a drink?"

Her mother stared at her, her face white, gulping for air, as if she might vomit. Joseph stood behind her, his jaw hanging, as horrified as Tara was.

"You need to tell me," Tara said. "Too much goes unsaid in our house."

Her mother gulped, but didn't speak.

"Why were you chasing Dad and Faye? Where were they going?"

"They were coming to see me, weren't they, Rachel?" The voice from the doorway made them all turn. It was Sean Ryland. His tone had been personal, almost intimate. Dylan stood beside him, eyebrows raised in surprise, too.

Her mother stood and turned to face Sean, not saying a word.

"That's why you wanted to meet me," he continued. "They'd learned a secret you wanted kept. You had to beat them to the punch."

Tara had never heard Sean Ryland speak so gently. "Tell me now, Rachel. What were you afraid I might learn?"

Her mother's body softened, her gaze, too, looking at Sean. It was as if they were the only two people in the room. They clearly had a relationship that Tara knew nothing about.

"It's about Faye, isn't it?" Sean said. "She's mine."

Her mother dropped her head and her shoulders sagged before she spoke, her voice low and rough. "There was no use in telling you."

Tara's brain stalled. What? Sean was Faye's *father?* Her mother had been *with* Sean? She saw that Dylan was stunned, too.

"How did Faye find out?" Sean asked. "Did you tell her?"

Her mother raised her head, pulled herself together, taking a shuddering breath. "She had tests. Because of Joseph's genes. She sneaked out hair from Abbott's brush, replaced his toothbrush with a new one. The results showed that Abbott was not her biological father. She came to me and demanded I tell her who it was."

"And did you?" Sean asked. "Did you tell her?" Tara could tell he was holding back anger, making a supreme effort for her mother's sake.

Her mother shook her head, her eyes downcast. "Not at first. I told her those companies are scams, they mix up the tests all the time, but she kept at me and kept at me." She lifted her anguished gaze to Sean. "I gave in."

"You cheated on Dad?" Tara blurted.

"We weren't together at the time. We'd broken up."

"But Faye was born months after you were married...." Her words trailed off, the answer obvious. Her mother had been pregnant when they married. Another jolt.

"We told everyone she was premature," her mother said. "We had to say that. Your father's family...their status...we had no choice."

"So you and Dad broke up...then you dated Sean?" The words sounded strange to Tara's ears, felt like hard marbles on her tongue.

"I thought it was over with your father. I was devastated and Sean was kind."

"Kind?" The word held Sean's usual bitterness. "I was in

love with you, Rachel. And you loved me, too. When Abbott called, you ran to him. You chose money over love."

"That's not fair," she said sharply, head up, her shame diminished for a moment. "You wanted me because he wanted me. You always envied him."

"That's not true." Sean jutted his jaw.

"I chose a life I could count on. You were restless and moody. Abbott knew what he wanted for himself and in a wife. I needed that. I needed a safe place. I grew up in chaos. I wanted security."

"You didn't give me a chance," he said gruffly.

"It was too late, Sean."

Everything about this moment was surreal to Tara. Revealing this terrible secret, her mother's voice was more natural and her demeanor more open than Tara had ever seen or heard. But she still didn't know what had caused that night's events.

"So Faye told Dad?" Tara guessed.

"No. I made her swear she wouldn't. Abbott accidentally found the results. The envelope from the genetics company got stuck between two folders Faye gave him at work."

With a jolt, Tara pictured the address on the envelope in her father's bloody shirt pocket. *CGC Gen* was all she'd been able to see. She'd assumed it was some technology firm— *Gen* part of *Generator*. Instead it had been *Genetics*. She remembered the books on his desk on the subject, too.

"Abbott was furious," Tara's mother said, her eyes going distant. "*On principle*. Abbott and his principles. Forget people when there were rules to be followed, a high moral ground to march on. He wanted a divorce. He wanted to destroy everything we'd built, all we'd achieved. Faye tried to calm him down, reassure him that he was still her father, that knowing didn't change anything."

Tara remembered the text on her father's phone.

Nothing changes. Let it go.

"What happened that night, Mom? Before the accident?" Tara asked, dreading what she would hear. Her heart thudded so hard she could hardly hear her mother over the beat.

As if he'd read her mind, Dylan moved beside her and put a warm hand to her back, grounding her. He'd been with her through every trauma in her life, she realized. Even the one he'd caused.

"Abbott wouldn't let it go. He decided you had to know." She looked at Sean, who stood still as stone, as if he expected a firing squad to take aim any second. "What was the point? Why cause you pain, too?"

Sean didn't move or speak, but Tara could feel his anger, his hurt. Her mother must have, too, because her voice went high and desperate. "It was one night forty years ago, Sean. You never asked. We hardly spoke in all those years. You didn't want to know. Abbott was Faye's father in all the ways that mattered."

She turned her gaze back to Tara. "Faye wanted me to go with Abbott to talk to Sean, to make sure they didn't lose their tempers, destroy the peace they'd come to." Her mother stopped and took harsh breaths, clearly fighting her emotions.

"I should have gone. I know that now. But I was angry at Faye, hurt that she'd turned against me, that she'd torn us apart at the seams, put my marriage at risk. I told her that she had caused this mess, she would have to live with the consequences."

Her mother's eyes flicked from person to person, as if seeking asylum in some face, begging someone to take her side. No one spoke.

"Faye exploded at me. I'd never seen her so angry. She

called me selfish and cruel. She said I lied to myself and everyone else, and the lies had ruined my marriage, ruined our family. Such terrible things." Her mother shook her head. "Then she said she was going with her father to talk to Sean. I told her if she did that, she was no longer my daughter. She'd hurt me so deeply. Don't you see? She'd betrayed me. She chose her father over me, Sean over me, blamed me for everything."

Her mother began to cry again. "But she was right. I *was* selfish and cruel. And I was punished. I killed my husband and almost killed her."

Tara, Dylan and Joseph stood in shocked silence, while Tara's mother sobbed quietly in the chair beside a sleeping Faye. Dylan rubbed Tara's back in slow circles, reminding her that he'd promised to be whatever she needed.

He'd kept that promise from the moment they'd first talked.

He'd helped her investigate the accident and now she knew the truth—all the truth. The accident happened because of confused ideas about love and loyalty—both in her mother and in Matt Sutherland.

There was one final mystery. "Did you empty Dad's desk of files?" Tara asked.

"I couldn't find the genetics report. There were papers about the divorce, I knew. I didn't know what other terrible item was there, so I shredded it all. It had to be gone. It was all a mistake." Her mother made a wiping gesture with her hands.

Her mother's behavior horrified Tara. All her decisions had been aimed at hiding, lying, keeping secrets she shouldn't have, shredding the truth right and left, culminating in running away from the accident she'd caused.

"Wha... Is... Where...am...?"

Faye's words were a whispered rasp in the silence. They all turned to stare at her. She blinked, looking startled.

"You're in the hospital. You were in an accident," Tara said.

Faye touched her throat.

"You're thirsty! Right." Tara grabbed the plastic cup of water Rita had placed there for when Faye awoke.

Faye nodded against the pillow, still blinking, still confused.

With shaking fingers, Tara put the straw between her sister's lips. When she'd finished, Tara set down the cup. "Welcome back. We missed you. All of us." Tara nodded toward the people now crowded around the bed—Joseph, their mother, Dylan and Sean, the father Faye had barely learned about.

Would she remember the accident? Did she know her father was dead? Would she remember them?

"Baby." Joseph dropped to his knees beside the bed and grabbed Faye's hands, pressing them to his mouth. "Do you know me?"

She nodded slowly, as if just awakened from anesthesia. "Jo...seph."

"And me?" Tara had to ask. "You recognize me?"

"My...sis...ter." Her eyes moved over all of them. "Mom...?"

Her mother sucked in a breath, then turned and left the room.

"You...here...all..." Faye said, then her eyelids dropped.

"The neurologist said she would sleep a lot at first," Tara explained. "It's hard work to stay awake. We should let Joseph have some time." She motioned for Sean and Dylan to step out with her.

She didn't know what she would say to her mother. Her feelings were in turmoil. They found her in the hall, pale as a ghost, frozen outside the room the way she'd been when she'd first arrived. "I can't face her," she said to Tara. "Not after what I did. I killed her father and left her to die. She'll never forgive me. She shouldn't."

As angry as she was at her mother, Tara thought of Faye's words. *When you love someone, you forgive them.* That's how Faye lived her life. "Faye loves you, Mom," she said. "She will forgive you. I know that."

Her mother's gaze locked on, digging at Tara, testing the truth of her words. Finally she said, "You don't lie, do you?"

"No."

"Thank you," she said.

"You can face her, Rachel," Sean said. "You have to."

Tara's mother's gaze shifted to meet Sean's. Something passed between them, something from the past, something they'd shared, and her mother seemed to gather her composure, stand taller, look certain. Turning her gaze to Tara, her mother spoke solemnly, as if the moment with Sean had given her new strength. "Will you take me to the police station, Tara? I have to turn myself in. I should be punished for what I did. It was unforgivable."

Tara didn't know what to say to her mother. Her thoughts were jumbled, her feelings confused, most of them harsh. Then she looked at Dylan. His eyes held compassion and tenderness for Tara.

You know how to love, he'd told her. He said he'd admired her efforts to make peace with her mother. He believed in her. It was time she believed in herself. Tara let her own compassion rise to the surface and override her hurt and anger. Her mother had done a terrible thing, but she was willing to answer for it. Tara was proud of her. And, more than that, she loved her. "Faye will forgive you, Mom. And I forgive you, too." The words rang in Tara's ears, truer every second that passed.

She forgave her mother for the childhood hurts, the constant criticism, the indifference and for the terrible accident that had devastated their family.

"You do?" Her mother's eyes filled with tears. "You forgive me?"

"Yes. That's what people who love each other do," she said, glancing at Dylan, her voice about to crack. "They focus on the good. They work around flaws. They don't walk away."

"Tara," Dylan said, so much feeling in his voice her heart seemed to lock in her chest.

"You're more like your sister than I realized," her mother said, tears actually sliding down her cheeks. She touched Tara's hair with shaking fingers. "I'm getting used to this style." She gave a hesitant smile.

"You're not turning yourself in to Bill Fallon," Tara said. "He broke the law urging you to leave the scene. That doesn't excuse what you did, but it was a factor." Would her mother go to prison? The thought made Tara's stomach drop.

"You need to get your attorney on this," Sean said gruffly. "Make sure you protect your rights. For now, we'll take you home."

"Thank you," Rachel said, looking at him. "About Faye. I'm sorry, Sean. I did what I thought was best."

"It's not right what you did. I need time to think it through."

"Of course," she said humbly, then turned with Sean toward the elevator. He placed a hand on her back.

"I'll be there in a bit," Dylan said, staying with Tara. After the elevator closed on their parents, Dylan turned to her. "I'm so glad Faye's awake."

"Me, too. I don't know if she'll remember the accident or how it came about, or about her father. She might not know that Dad was killed."

"What she doesn't remember, you'll tell her. You and your mother."

"There's a lot to tell. Are you as shocked by all this as I am?" Her head was still spinning.

"I am. I can't believe your mom and my dad…"

"I know. It explains why they were so frosty to each other when we were growing up. My mom kept that secret all these years. And look what she did to protect it. It's hard to accept." She swallowed over a dry throat.

"What you said to her was beautiful," Dylan said, his eyes warm on her face, almost glowing. "That you forgave her and why."

"I remembered what you said about me—that I *did* know how to love. When I looked at you, I felt this rush of love for her, for you. So I said what I said and I believe it."

"You're a better person than you were, Tara."

"And so are you." Staring into his eyes, she got a start. "You have Faye's eyes. Yours are smoky, but they're the same gray-green."

Dylan smiled. "It makes sense, since she's my sister. Half sister anyway."

"How do you feel about that?"

"I'm honored. Faye's a great person. Though it's still a shock."

"No kidding. Your father surprised me. He seemed calmer, less angry somehow."

"Exactly. The way he looked at your mom… His whole demeanor changed. It was like a deep wound had suddenly started to heal."

"He resented my father for a lot more than buying his company at a rock-bottom price," Tara said.

"And let that fester inside him all these years." Dylan shook his head in sad wonder.

"He got trapped in the past," Tara said, recognizing the experience.

"It happens," he said with a smile.

"It does," she said.

"But it doesn't have to limit us. We can learn from the past, from who we were then and become better. Hell, we can reinterpret the past."

"Turn *suffocating* into *cozy* and *nosy* to *friendly?*" She smiled, feeling a lightness she hadn't felt in a long, long time. Dylan was right. They'd let themselves get trapped in how they'd been, in the old hurt.

Their eyes met for a long, silent moment. "I sure as hell don't want to end up like my father."

"Or me like my mother."

"We won't," he said firmly. He put his hands on her cheeks. "I've got to go now, and you've got a lot to handle. In a day or two, I want us to talk."

"I'd like that, too." Could they possibly try again? Could they forgive each other, trust each other? Could she stay the independent woman she'd worked so hard to become while being with Dylan in Wharton?

Dylan watched her face. "I don't suppose there's any point in me telling you not to think this to death, is there?"

She laughed. "It's scary how well you know me."

"Scary good, I hope."

"Very good." And she hoped he'd know her even better in the future.

"Maybe we should wait," Dylan's father said to him, stopping short at the entrance to the hospital. "Maybe tomorrow would be better."

"It was your idea to come. To support Rachel, remember?"

Faye had been awake for three days. She'd been asking

about the accident and Rachel was going to tell her what had happened today.

His father had changed since the revelation that Faye was his daughter. He seemed kinder, more open-hearted than Dylan remembered him, even when he was young.

As a result, the talk about changing Ryland Engineering had gone more smoothly than Dylan had even hoped. It was as if his father's old resentments, his bitterness, had melted away.

"She's not going to tell Faye who I am yet," Sean said. "But if it slips out, I want to be there to back her up."

Faye hadn't remembered anything about the accident or the events that had preceded it. Tara had told him the plan was to reveal things gradually, letting Faye adjust in between.

"You think she'll be ashamed to have me as blood?" Sean turned to Dylan and frowned. "I'm no Wharton. I came up from nothing."

"Faye doesn't think like that. She wanted you and Abbott to talk, remember? She wanted her mother to tell the truth."

"That's right. Faye's a good egg. Solid. The best of the bunch over there, I always said." His father's face just plain lit up. Dylan felt a tightness in his chest. Seeing his father's heart expand these past days had restored so much of their old closeness. He would always be grateful to Tara for bringing this about.

His father stopped walking and turned to him. "You're still my son. That doesn't change. So don't you go feeling left out."

"I don't, Dad," he said, hiding his smile.

"And you know I loved your mother...."

"I know that, Dad."

"Rachel was from a different time in my life. I know I made mistakes. With Rachel. And with your mother."

This new humility was like a fresh breeze blowing

through their relationship. Dylan couldn't get enough of the positive changes his father was showing. He would always be obstinate, opinionated and moody, but the burden of resentment and regret was lighter every day. "Do you still have feelings for Rachel?" he asked.

His father shot him a look, his face bright pink. "Too much time has passed. We both moved on."

"Don't give up before you've even tried, Dad."

Sean seemed to ponder that, his lips twitching with a smile he was fighting.

Dylan intended to take his own advice with Tara. They could shake off the old hurts and start fresh. He planned to tell her so today. Sweat made his hands clammy. He was as nervous as his father.

There were obstacles—geography and career demands topping the list—but that wouldn't stop them. They were two smart, stubborn people. Why couldn't they be smart and stubborn when it came to each other?

"You ready?" Dylan said, hitting the elevator button.

"As I'll ever be." Determination showed in his face. *Same here.*

"Maybe it's too soon," Tara's mother said, stopping just past the nurses' station, making the foil crackle on the plate of Ruthie's empanadas Judith had insisted her mother bring to Faye *to put some meat on her bones*. Judith had told Tara her praise of Ruthie's cooking at Ruby's had helped convince Ruthie to take the job with the food truck in Tucson, after all.

"Maybe this will set back her healing," her mother finished.

"She's asking. She deserves the truth." Faye had surprised the doctors with the speed of her recovery. Even Rita was impressed.

Her mother turned to her. "I don't think I can handle it today. She's been so sweet so far. After this, I don't know."

"Trust Faye, Mom. You know the kind of person she is."

"And now she'll know the kind of person I am." Her mother's face sagged. "So will everyone in town. I'll never survive the scandal. All my good works will come to nothing because of what I did."

"That's not true. Your real friends will stick. Your charity work speaks for you. Your past doesn't have to define you." That was her lesson, too.

Since the revelation, her mother had been more open around Tara. She would never smother her with affection or be her best friend, but they were on good terms. They were talking. *You take one step, then the next.*

"If she doesn't remember about the divorce lawyer, we don't need to tell her," her mother said. "Your father would never have gone through with that once he calmed down."

"Do you really think so?"

"Of course I do. We loved each other, your father and I, no matter what you think. We built a life that worked. We were content."

"I believe you." It made Tara sad that her mother had settled for less. Tara would not do that. She wanted to be content, but she also wanted joy and passion, even if it got scary, even if she had to lean back and trust she would be caught.

That *Dylan* would catch her. The thought of him made her stomach jump and her heart turn over. They were going to talk today. He'd texted her that if his father didn't lose his nerve, they'd be coming to the hospital to be moral support for her mother.

"We should tell her, Mom. She would want to know. She'll understand. She knew Dad well. She worked with him every day. Secrets have only hurt this family." Faye had cried when Tara told her that their father had been killed in the accident, but she'd accepted it bravely, ready to go forward—exactly as she'd handled the difficulties of her therapy.

"I suppose you're right," her mother said, giving Tara a new look of respect. "I hope I can be half as brave as Faye when I hear what I'll be charged with."

Her mother's lawyer expected to hear soon from the county prosecutor on what charges he intended to file against her. With the police chief's behavior mitigating the situation, her mother was likely to get probation and community service. Everyone involved was asking for leniency.

Rachel's conscience would punish her plenty, along with the good citizens of Wharton. *She has friends,* Tara reminded herself. Not all the minds in town were small. More and more, Tara was opening her eyes to the good things about Wharton, and the people who lived here. She was letting the imprint fade.

As far as the rest of those involved in the accident, Chief Fallon maintained that he'd removed Tara's mother from the scene so the investigation could continue. Though he would likely not be charged with anything, Dylan had offered him early retirement, which he was expected to take.

Because everyone wanted leniency, Matt would likely be charged with assault or reckless endangerment, a misdemeanor for which he would likely receive probation.

Jeb had fired him, but Miriam Zeller had made sure his family would be kept on the insurance roster through the baby's birth. Employees from both Wharton and Ryland had started collections to help the family. Their generosity had made Tara feel even better about the town.

Faye's survival far outweighed Tara's anger toward either her mother or Matt for what they'd done.

The meeting with Ryland the day before had gone well. Dylan and Sean had accepted Wharton's offer of compensation for financial losses due to the false tests, and hadn't pushed for punitive damages. The feud between the two families seemed to be over for good.

Inside Faye's room, bouquets and houseplants covered every surface, and bunches of Mylar balloons caught the light in bright flashes. As soon as word had gotten out that Faye was awake, gifts, flowers and cards had flooded in.

Faye was crossing the room using her walker. She stopped and formed a smile, slower than usual, but a Faye smile nonetheless.

"M-Mom...Tara." She let go of the walker to open her arms for hugs. Their mother went first, holding on tight, eyes squeezed shut.

Then Tara wrapped her arms around Faye, still rail thin. Her fragility set off a pang in Tara's heart. "You get better every day," she said, which was true.

Faye made a face and pulled at the hair on one side of her head. It was frizzy. "Not...my hair."

"I'll fix it for you. I did your hair while you were sleeping. Did Rita tell you?"

Faye lifted one hand from the walker and wiggled her fingers. The neon polish flashed in the light. "You...do...this?"

"I did."

"Not...my color."

"Orange sherbet? Come on. It's all the rage."

This time, Faye's smile filled her face.

"Could you sit down, Faye?" her mother said. She sat in a chair, back straight, hands in her lap. "I need to tell you something."

Faye considered her mother's face. "It's...bad?"

Her mother nodded. "It's about the accident."

Faye's features assumed a resigned look. She'd had to hear plenty of bad news the past few days. She made her way to the recliner, which faced her mother's chair, and lowered herself onto the seat. "Tell...me."

"The accident was my fault," her mother said. "You and I argued that night. You went with your father in his car. I chased after you. I tried to pass, to make you stop, but I bumped the car."

"You hit…us." Faye seemed to take a bit to grasp that.

"Yes. That's right. I hit you."

"A broken part made the car speed up after Mom bumped you," Tara added. "That's why you went over the barrier."

"I'm so sorry, Faye," her mother said. "I never meant to hurt you or your father. I was stupid and a coward and selfish like you said, and I wouldn't blame you if you never forgave me."

"I'm…alive…. It was…an ac…cident. Don't talk like that." She waved her hand in their mother's direction, her voice firm.

"It's worse," her mother said miserably. "I didn't help you. I didn't stay with you. I didn't check on you. And I didn't tell anyone what I did."

Faye pondered her mother's words for a minute, her eyes moving back and forth, sorting it out, making sense of it. Finally she exhaled. "It. Was. An. Accident." She took care to enunciate each word. "It. Is. Over."

Tara's heart bloomed with pride in her sister. Faye was good, kind and forgiving, with a big, big heart. Tara was so grateful she'd always felt her sister's love.

Their mother stared at Faye. "But it's not," her mother said. "It was a hit-and-run. The police might arrest me. I could go to jail."

Faye's eyes widened. "No. I'll…tell them no."

"She won't be arrested," Tara said. "It will likely be probation. Don't scare her, Mom. You told her what happened. That's enough."

"We go from here," Faye said. "We are…a f-fam'ly." Faye

held out her arms, but her mother shook her head, clearly not feeling worthy of an embrace.

"Go to her, Mom," Tara said.

Her mother dropped to her knees beside Faye's chair. Faye put her thin arms around her mother's narrow shape. Tara looked away to give them some privacy, her throat tight.

After that, Faye sampled the food Judith had sent, and they talked about Faye's therapy, her upcoming release, and Tara told her about what her father had given them—the bottled ships, the library and the shotgun.

"He thought of us," Faye said. "In...his...way."

"I wish I'd talked to him," Tara said. "Straightened things out."

"He knew." Faye tapped the side of her head. "He has your...in...stincts."

"You think so?"

"Of course," her mother said with her usual archness. "You're your father's daughter. Smart and bullheaded."

Tara smiled, touched by the comparison.

"So...glad...you're...here," Faye said to Tara, reaching to pat her hand. "For me...and for Wharton."

"I'm glad, too," Tara said. She would consult as long as she was needed, then visit often. Depending on what she and Dylan decided to do, maybe every weekend. "You think Dad would want me working at Wharton?" Tara asked.

Before Faye could answer, her mother said. "Certainly. He waved around your business card at his Kiwanis meeting."

Tara felt the sting of tears, but fought them back. *He was proud of her.*

She wished Dylan were here to hear that.

At that moment, he walked through the door, as if conjured by her heart, his father behind him.

Tara stood. So did her mother.

Sean stepped forward and held out a wilted-looking bouquet wrapped in plastic.

"Oh. There's no place to put them," her mother said looking around at the clusters of baskets and bouquets.

"They're for you, Rachel," Sean said. "Water's in the bag so they'll last until you get them home."

Tara's mother flushed. "Why, thank you." She took the flowers, which quivered in her hands, the paper crackling.

"I came in case you wanted me to speak up or explain or whatnot," he said gravely, watching her closely. "Dylan said you were telling the tale today."

"Thank you, but we…talked. That's all for now. Later on…?"

"You tell me where and when and I'll be there."

"I will," her mother said.

Sean stared at Faye, who was watching the exchange with a puzzled expression on her face. "You're doing better, I can see," he said. "All of us at Ryland are glad. I always said you were the best of the bunch over there."

"Thank you," Faye said.

"It's good to see you, Faye," Dylan said, squeezing the hand Faye held out in both of his. "Your sister's been pretty anxious for you to wake up and give her hell."

"I will…if you will." Faye smiled up at him.

Dylan laughed. "It's a deal."

"Just what I need—you two ganging up on me," Tara said, hoping they'd both give her hell until the day she died.

"If it's all right with you, I'd like to talk to Tara for a bit," Dylan said to Rachel. "I'll drive her home, if you could give my dad a lift."

"Certainly," Tara's mother said, startled by the idea. She glanced at Sean, who ducked his head. Tara had never seen him so subdued. Before the settlement meeting, she'd gone into his office and apologized for accusing him of putting the faulty device on her father's car.

He'd lectured her, as she'd expected, about rudeness and temper tantrums, but when he told her that he missed her father like a brother, tears in his eyes, she was moved.

He'd also told her not to judge her mother too harshly. *Not unless you walk a mile in her moccasins.*

"Okay with you?" Dylan said to Tara, giving her a look that sent electricity pouring through her.

"Sounds great." She grinned, not caring how goofy she looked.

He grinned back just as goofily.

Before long they were flying down the highway toward home, neither of them saying much. Dylan had a plan, so she would let it unfold. She felt good beside him. She felt safe, she felt content, she felt right. And when she glanced at him and their eyes met, she felt wanted. So wanted it made her breathless.

When he turned off the highway toward the river, she peered at him. "Don't tell me your plan includes paintball?"

"Not this time, no." He parked below the caves and they walked up to the ridge. Dylan sat on top of a picnic table near a wall draped in bougainvillea, the blossoms bright magenta. The fall sun warmed her shoulders; the breeze lifted her hair and sent the earthy smell of the river to her nose. "What's up?" she asked him.

"I have a business proposition for you," he said, his smile wide, though he was trying to sound serious.

"Business? Really?" She'd assumed they'd be talking about their relationship. She felt a twinge of disappointment, but she knew better than to assume the worst. She would wait and see, trust the man she loved with all her heart.

"Yes. Ryland Engineering will be restructuring soon. The plan is to break off a research and development division my father will run. That's where his heart is. He's happiest behind a drafting table. Victor Lansing will take over for me with full authority over manufacturing."

"Wow. That *is* big."

"I'll serve as an adviser, but intend to focus on my work with Wharton. So, we could use some help with the transition. Are you interested?"

"It's intriguing," she said. "I have to admit. I'll be working at Wharton Electronics for a while, too. I'd have to do some juggling, but…"

"So, you'll do it? I should warn you I won't take no for an answer."

She loved the look on his face, like he wanted her and her alone. She felt the same about him.

"Just to seal the deal," he continued, "I'd like to take you on a little Chamber of Commerce tour, give you a fresh look at the town."

"Okay."

"Here you can see the natural beauty of this area. It's a bird sanctuary, a protected river region, popular for paintball wars, rock hopping or making love, depending on your mood."

"And whether you've got vinegar chips and German chocolate cake?"

"Exactly." He explained that he wanted to add new hiking trails, camping spots and guided tours with an ecological bent.

They returned to Dylan's car, then drove toward town. He described where new business might be located, possible housing developments, an amphitheater for concerts, more shopping and office parks. Along the way, he pointed out places they'd spent time together—the Egyptian theater, Ruby's, the bowling alley, the park, the high school.

When he reached the intersection where he would turn

toward her house, he said, "That's it then. I could take you home…unless there's anything else you'd like to see?" He looked at her, eyes twinkling.

"Actually I heard there's a golden retriever who does tricks. And a computer-guided telescope for stargazing and a kitchen full of gourmet cookware."

"I know exactly where you mean. There might even be clean sheets on the bed."

"Sounds perfect," she said.

He hadn't said a word, but she knew that Dylan wanted what she wanted—to be together, to make it work. Her whole body was alive to him, and her heart sang. New confidence filled her. This was right.

She wasn't walking away. She would work at it and so would he.

They drove to Dylan's place and went inside. "Golden retriever," Dylan announced. Tara crouched for European greeting.

"The telescope's out back, so you'll have to stick around until the stars come out."

"I think I can handle that. As long as the sheets are as advertised?"

"If they're not, I'll make them so."

"Then I'm in," she said, sexy and teasing, but serious, too.

"Me, too. All in." He pulled her close. "What do you think of the new Wharton?"

"New or old, if you're in it, it's fine by me."

"I love you. I can't lose you." He touched her cheek, the contact warming her to her toes. "You're first in my heart. Whatever I have to do to prove it to you, I'll do."

"You already have. You've been there for me from the beginning, with a hand at my back, a listening ear, a shoulder to cry on. You've been there for me in all the ways that count."

"I always wanted to be, Tara."

"I was afraid if I let myself love you, I'd go back to how I was—lost and insecure and a failure. But I'm not like that anymore. I *am* better. And I do know how to love. You helped me to see that."

"Good. Because it's true."

"I'm not an easy person. I know that."

"Easy's overrated. I need you to keep me on my toes, keep me thinking, challenge me."

"Tickle your brain?"

"And other parts." He gave her that look.

She shivered.

"You helped me see that it was time to leave Ryland Engineering. Hell, you practically saved the company." He paused. "You saved me." The look in his eyes and the rough emotion in his voice told her how much he loved her. "I was so lonely and I didn't even know it."

"Me, too. Until I saw you again and felt like I fit, like I was known…and loved." Tara swallowed over the lump in her throat. "Let's face it, I'm never going to love Wharton, but you're here and my family's here, and that's enough for me."

"Don't forget the empanadas."

"How could I? We'll have to go to Tucson for those, though. Turns out Ruthie's taking that food truck opportunity."

"I'll convince her to leave us the recipe. I'm town manager, after all."

She laughed, then she got serious. "I'll be away a lot, you know. Travel can hurt relationships."

"But you'll always come home to me. If our love can last ten years, it can last a few hundred miles…or a few thousand."

"Sometimes the first love *is* the best love."

"Who knew?" He leaned in and kissed her, and her entire being rose to meet him. Tara breathed him in. *Dylan. Home.*

In the background, Duster lumbered toward the bedroom. He knew where they were headed before they did.

* * * * *

COMING NEXT MONTH FROM

◆ H HARLEQUIN®

super romance®

Available April 2, 2013

#1842 TALK OF THE TOWN • *In Shady Grove*
by Beth Andrews

Neil Pettit and Maddie Montesano share a history and a daughter. But that's it. Their relationship has been, well, *tense* for years. That wasn't a problem when Neil lived out of state. But now that he's in town, sparks are flying and everyone's talking about where they'll end up!

#1843 RIGHT FROM THE START by Jeanie London

A divorce mediator, Kenzie James has seen it all when it comes to commitment. And she can tell Will Russell is *not* a good bet. So why does she look forward to their encounters at work? Luckily she knows better than to fall for this single dad...or does she?

#1844 THE FIRST MOVE by Jennifer Lohmann

Seeing Renia Milek again is a clear sign to Miles Brislenn. Back in high school he might not have had the courage to approach her, but this chance meeting...? He's not letting it pass him by. The attraction is clearly mutual, until Renia's past threatens to come between them.

#1845 A BETTER FATHER by Kris Fletcher

Sam Catalano needs to prove he's a good father to his young son. And to do that he needs stability, which is why he's bought the summer camp he used to attend. But buying it puts him in conflict with Libby Kovak—his old flame and the rightful owner.

#1846 YOU ARE INVITED... • *A Valley Ridge Wedding*
by Holly Jacobs

The best man? Mattie Keith—maid of honor—thinks Finn Wallace is anything but. She's the legal guardian for his nieces and nephew, but he's suing for custody! They've vowed not to let their conflict spoil their friends' wedding, but when temperatures and attraction rise, promises may be broken....

#1847 THE SUMMER PLACE by Pamela Hearon

When it comes to fun and games, Rick Warren and Summer Delaney are definitely on opposite sides. Summer has a lot at stake in making this camp program work and proving she's right. Too bad the working rivalry is sparking a big attraction!

HSRCNM0313

Maddie Montesano swung her crowbar at the wall, focused on finishing this demolition. The back of her neck prickled with a warning of being watched...and let her know who stood there.

When it came to Neil Pettit, it was like some sort of homing device was imbedded inside of her. *There he is! The man of your adolescent dreams!*

It was annoying and as powerful as it had been when she'd been young and stupid with love for him.

Well, she'd gotten over Neil a long time ago.

Neil leaned against the doorjamb, his broad shoulders filling the space as he lazily slid his gaze from her head to the toes of her work boots.

There should be a law that when a woman saw her ex, she looked hot. Sexy hot…not sweaty, I've-been-working-and-am-a-total-mess hot.

"Hey, babe. Looking good." His greeting was the same as in high school when he'd wait by her locker. Oh, how her heart had raced with so many wonderful, conflicting emotions.

"It's the tool belt," she said, not bothering to keep the flatness from her voice.

He grinned at her tone, one of his slow, panty-melting smiles. It was more potent now than it'd been twelve years ago. "It's not the tool belt." He came closer until the toes of his sneakers bumped against her boots. "It's the whole package."

She rolled her eyes. "Please."

Golden stubble covered his cheeks and she noticed the dark circles under his eyes. He looked tired and that hint of vulnerability had her weakening. Not allowed.

"Something I can do for you, Neil?"

His expression changed. "Is Bree here? I'd like to see my daughter."

**What are Neil's intentions?
Find out in TALK OF THE TOWN
by Beth Andrews, available April 2013
from Harlequin® Superromance®.
And be sure to look for the other
three books about the Montesano siblings
in Beth's IN SHADY GROVE series
available later in 2013.**

REQUEST YOUR FREE BOOKS!
2 FREE NOVELS PLUS 2 FREE GIFTS!

H HARLEQUIN®

super romance®

Exciting, emotional, unexpected!

YES! Please send me 2 FREE Harlequin® Superromance® novels and my 2 FREE gifts (gifts are worth about $10). After receiving them, if I don't wish to receive any more books, I can return the shipping statement marked "cancel." If I don't cancel, I will receive 6 brand-new novels every month and be billed just $4.69 per book in the U.S. or $5.24 per book in Canada. That's a savings of at least 15% off the cover price! It's quite a bargain! Shipping and handling is just 50¢ per book in the U.S. and 75¢ per book in Canada.* I understand that accepting the 2 free books and gifts places me under no obligation to buy anything. I can always return a shipment and cancel at any time. Even if I never buy another book, the two free books and gifts are mine to keep forever.

135/336 HDN FVS7

Name _____ (PLEASE PRINT) _____

Address _____ Apt. # _____

City _____ State/Prov. _____ Zip/Postal Code _____

Signature (if under 18, a parent or guardian must sign)

Mail to the **Harlequin® Reader Service:**
IN U.S.A.: P.O. Box 1867, Buffalo, NY 14240-1867
IN CANADA: P.O. Box 609, Fort Erie, Ontario L2A 5X3

**Are you a current subscriber to Harlequin Superromance books
and want to receive the larger-print edition?
Call 1-800-873-8635 or visit www.ReaderService.com.**

* Terms and prices subject to change without notice. Prices do not include applicable taxes. Sales tax applicable in N.Y. Canadian residents will be charged applicable taxes. Offer not valid in Quebec. This offer is limited to one order per household. Not valid for current subscribers to Harlequin Superromance books. All orders subject to credit approval. Credit or debit balances in a customer's account(s) may be offset by any other outstanding balance owed by or to the customer. Please allow 4 to 6 weeks for delivery. Offer available while quantities last.

Your Privacy—The Harlequin® Reader Service is committed to protecting your privacy. Our Privacy Policy is available online at www.ReaderService.com or upon request from the Harlequin Reader Service.

We make a portion of our mailing list available to reputable third parties that offer products we believe may interest you. If you prefer that we not exchange your name with third parties, or if you wish to clarify or modify your communication preferences, please visit us at www.ReaderService.com/consumerschoice or write to us at Harlequin Reader Service Preference Service, P.O. Box 9062, Buffalo, NY 14269. Include your complete name and address.

HSR13

Get ready for the event of the year!

The best man? Mattie Keith—maid of honor—thinks Finn Wallace is anything but. She's the legal guardian for his nieces and nephew, but he's suing for custody! They've vowed not to let their conflict spoil their friends' wedding, but when temperatures and attractions rise, promises may be broken....

**Pick up a copy of the first book in
A Valley Ridge Wedding trilogy!**

You Are Invited...
by Holly Jacobs

AVAILABLE IN APRIL

Plus, look for books 2 & 3, **April Showers** (May) and **A Walk Down the Aisle** (June).

H HARLEQUIN®

super romance®

More Story...More Romance

www.Harlequin.com